Two Can Keep a Secret

BOOKS BY KAREN M. MCMANUS

One of Us Is Lying

Two Can Keep a Secret

Two Can Keep a Secret

Karen M. McManus

DELACORTE PRESS

Text copyright © 2019 by Karen M. McManus
Front cover photographs © 2019 by Johner Images/Getty Images
and Jamie Grill/Getty Images

Visit us on the Web! GetUnderlined.com

Educators and librarians, for a variety of teaching tools,
visit us at RHTeachersLibrarians.com

Library of Congress Cataloging-in-Publication Data
Names: McManus, Karen M., author.
Title: Two can keep a secret / Karen McManus.
Description: First edition. | New York : Delacorte Press, [2019] | Summary:
While true-crime aficionado Ellery and her twin brother are staying with their
grandmother in a Vermont community known for murder, a new friend goes
missing and Ellery may be next.
Identifiers: LCCN 2018022931 (print) | LCCN 2018029202 (ebook) |
ISBN 978-1-5247-1474-1 (el) | ISBN 978-1-5247-1472-7 (hc) |
ISBN 978-1-5247-1473-4 (glb) | ISBN 978-1-9848-5190-1 (intl. tr. pbk.)
Subjects: | CYAC: Murder—Fiction. | Missing persons—Fiction. | Community
life—Vermont—Fiction. | Brothers and sisters—Fiction. | Twins—Fiction. |
Moving, Household—Fiction. | Grandmothers—Fiction. | Mystery and
detective stories.
Classification: LCC PZ7.1.M4637 (ebook) | LCC PZ7.1.M4637 Two 2019 (print) |
DDC [Fic]—dc23

The text of this book is set in 11.75-point Adobe Garamond Pro.
Interior design by Ken Crossland

For Gabriela, Carolina, and Erik

CHAPTER ONE

ELLERY
FRIDAY, AUGUST 30

If I believed in omens, this would be a bad one.

There's only one suitcase left on the baggage carousel. It's bright pink, covered with Hello Kitty stickers, and definitely not mine.

My brother, Ezra, watches it pass us for the fourth time, leaning on the handle of his own oversized suitcase. The crowd around the carousel is nearly gone, except for a couple arguing about who was supposed to keep track of their rental car reservation. "Maybe you should take it," Ezra suggests. "Seems like whoever owns it wasn't on our flight, and I bet they have an interesting wardrobe. A lot of polka dots, probably. And glitter." His phone chimes, and he pulls it out of his pocket. "Nana's outside."

"I can't believe this," I mutter, kicking the toe of my sneaker against the carousel's metal side. "My entire life was in that suitcase."

It's a slight exaggeration. My *actual* entire life was in La Puente, California, until about eight hours ago. Other than a few boxes shipped to Vermont last week, the suitcase contains what's left.

"I guess we should report it." Ezra scans the baggage claim area, running a hand over his close-cropped hair. He used to have thick dark curls like mine, hanging in his eyes, and I still can't get used to the cut he got over the summer. He tilts his suitcase and pivots toward the information desk. "Over here, probably."

The skinny guy behind the desk looks like he could still be in high school, with a rash of red pimples dotting his cheeks and jawline. A gold name tag pinned crookedly to his blue vest reads "Andy." Andy's thin lips twist when I tell him about my suitcase, and he cranes his neck toward the Hello Kitty bag still making carousel laps. "Flight 5624 from Los Angeles? With a layover in Charlotte?" I nod. "You sure that's not yours?"

"Positive."

"Bummer. It'll turn up, though. You just gotta fill this out." He yanks open a drawer and pulls out a form, sliding it toward me. "There's a pen around here somewhere," he mutters, pawing half-heartedly through a stack of papers.

"I have one." I unzip the front of my backpack, pulling out a book that I place on the counter while I feel around for a pen. Ezra raises his brows when he sees the battered hardcover.

"Really, Ellery?" he asks. "You brought *In Cold Blood* on the plane? Why didn't you just ship it with the rest of your books?"

"It's valuable," I say defensively.

Ezra rolls his eyes. "You *know* that's not Truman Capote's actual signature. Sadie got fleeced."

"Whatever. It's the thought that counts," I mutter. Our mother bought me the "signed" first edition off eBay after she landed a role as Dead Body #2 on *Law & Order* four years ago. She gave Ezra a Sex Pistols album cover with a Sid Vicious autograph that was probably just as forged. We should've gotten a car with reliable brakes instead, but Sadie's never been great at long-term planning. "Anyway, you know what they say. When in Murderland . . ." I finally extract a pen and start scratching my name across the form.

"You headed for Echo Ridge, then?" Andy asks. I pause on the second *c* of my last name and he adds, "They don't call it that anymore, you know. And you're early. It doesn't open for another week."

"I know. I didn't mean the theme park. I meant the . . ." I trail off before saying *town* and shove *In Cold Blood* into my bag. "Never mind," I say, returning my attention to the form. "How long does it usually take to get your stuff back?"

"Shouldn't be more than a day." Andy's eyes drift between Ezra and me. "You guys look a lot alike. You twins?"

I nod and keep writing. Ezra, ever polite, answers, "We are."

"I was supposed to be a twin," Andy says. "The other one got absorbed in the womb, though." Ezra lets out a surprised little snort, and I bite back a laugh. This happens to my brother all the time; people overshare the strangest things with him. We might have almost the same face, but his is the one everyone trusts. "I always thought it would've been cool to have a twin.

You could pretend to be one another and mess with people." I look up, and Andy is squinting at us again. "Well. I guess you guys can't do that. You aren't the right kind of twins."

"Definitely not," Ezra says with a fixed smile.

I write faster and hand the completed form to Andy, who tears off the top sheets and gives me the yellow carbon. "So somebody will get in touch, right?" I ask.

"Yep," Andy says. "You don't hear from them tomorrow, call the number at the bottom. Have fun in Echo Ridge."

Ezra exhales loudly as we head for the revolving door, and I grin at him over my shoulder. "You make the nicest friends."

He shudders. "Now I can't stop thinking about it. *Absorbed.* How does that even happen? Did he . . . No. I'm not going to speculate. I don't want to know. What a weird thing to grow up with, though, huh? Knowing how easily you could've been the wrong twin."

We push through the door into a blast of stifling, exhaust-filled air that takes me by surprise. Even on the last day of August, I'd expected Vermont to be a lot cooler than California. I pull my hair off my neck while Ezra scrolls through his phone. "Nana says she's circling because she didn't want to park in a lot," he reports.

I raise my brows at him. "Nana's texting and driving?"

"Apparently."

I haven't seen my grandmother since she visited us in California ten years ago, but from what I can remember, that seems out of character.

We wait a few minutes, wilting in the heat, until a forest-green Subaru station wagon pulls up beside us. The passenger-side window rolls down, and Nana sticks her head out. She doesn't look much different than she does over Skype, although her thick gray bangs appear freshly cut. "Go on, get in," she calls, side-eyeing the traffic cop a few feet from us. "They won't let you idle for more than a minute." She pulls her head back in as Ezra wheels his solitary suitcase toward the trunk.

When we slide into the backseat Nana turns to face us, and so does a younger woman behind the steering wheel. "Ellery, Ezra, this is Melanie Kilduff. Her family lives down the street from us. I have terrible night vision, so Melanie was kind enough to drive. She used to babysit your mother when she was young. You've probably heard the name."

Ezra and I exchange wide-eyed glances. *Yes.* Yes, we have.

Sadie left Echo Ridge when she was eighteen, and she's only been back twice. The first time was the year before we were born, when our grandfather died from a heart attack. And the second time was five years ago, for Melanie's teenage daughter's funeral.

Ezra and I watched the *Dateline* special—"Mystery at Murderland"—at home while our neighbor stayed with us. I was transfixed by the story of Lacey Kilduff, the beautiful blond homecoming queen from my mother's hometown, found strangled in a Halloween theme park. Airport Andy was right; the park's owner changed its name from Murderland to Fright Farm a few months later. I'm not sure the case would have gotten as much national attention if the park hadn't had such an on-the-nose name.

Or if Lacey hadn't been the second pretty teenager from Echo Ridge—and from the same exact street, even—to make tragic headlines.

Sadie wouldn't answer any of our questions when she got back from Lacey's funeral. "I just want to forget about it," she said whenever we asked. Which is what she's been saying about Echo Ridge our entire lives.

Ironic, I guess, that we ended up here anyway.

"Nice to meet you," Ezra says to Melanie, while I somehow manage to choke on my own saliva. He pounds me on the back, harder than necessary.

Melanie is pretty in a faded sort of way, with pale blond hair pulled into a French braid, light blue eyes, and a sprinkling of freckles. She flashes a disarming, gap-toothed smile. "You as well. Sorry we're late, but we hit a surprising amount of traffic. How was your flight?"

Before Ezra can answer, a loud rap sounds on the roof of the Subaru, making Nana jump. "You need to keep moving," the traffic cop calls.

"Burlington is the *rudest* city," Nana huffs. She presses a button on the door to close her window as Melanie eases the car behind a taxi.

I fumble with my seat belt as I stare at the back of Melanie's head. I wasn't expecting to meet her like this. I figured I would eventually, since she and Nana are neighbors, but I thought it would be more of a wave while taking out the trash, not an hour-long drive as soon as I landed in Vermont.

"I was so sorry to hear about your mother," Melanie says as she exits the airport and pulls onto a narrow highway dotted with green signs. It's almost ten o'clock at night, and a small cluster of buildings in front of us glows with lit windows. "But I'm glad she's getting the help she needs. Sadie is such a strong

6

woman. I'm sure you'll be back with her soon, but I hope you enjoy your time in Echo Ridge. It's a lovely little town. I know Nora is looking forward to showing you around."

There. *That's* how you navigate an awkward conversation. No need to lead with *Sorry your mom drove her car into a jewelry store while she was high on opioids and had to go to rehab for four months.* Just acknowledge the elephant in the room, sidestep, and segue into smoother conversational waters.

Welcome to Echo Ridge.

I fall asleep shortly after we hit the highway and don't stir until a loud noise jolts me awake. It sounds as though the car is being pelted from every direction with dozens of rocks. I turn toward Ezra, disoriented, but he looks equally confused. Nana twists in her seat, shouting to be heard over the roar. "Hail. Not uncommon this time of year. Although these are rather large."

"I'm going to pull over and let this pass," Melanie calls. She eases the car to the side of the road and shifts into park. The hail is hitting harder than ever, and I can't help but think that she's going to have hundreds of tiny dents in her car by the time it stops. One particularly large hailstone smacks right into the middle of the windshield, startling us all.

"How is it *hailing*?" I ask. "It was hot in Burlington."

"Hail forms in the cloud layer," Nana explains, gesturing toward the sky. "Temperatures are freezing there. The stones will melt quickly on the ground, though."

Her voice isn't warm, exactly—I'm not sure warmth is possible for her—but it's more animated than it's been all night.

Nana used to be a teacher, and she's obviously a lot more comfortable in that role than that of Custodial Grandparent. Not that I blame her. She's stuck with us during Sadie's sixteen weeks of court-ordered rehab, and vice versa. The judge insisted we live with family, which severely limited our options. Our father was a one-night stand—a stuntman, or so he claimed during the whopping two hours he and Sadie spent together after meeting at an LA club. We don't have aunts, uncles, or cousins. Not a single person, except for Nana, to take us in.

We sit in silence for a few minutes, watching hailstones bounce off the car hood, until the frequency tapers and finally stops altogether. Melanie pulls back onto the road, and I glance at the clock on the dashboard. It's nearly eleven; I slept for almost an hour. I nudge Ezra and ask, "We must almost be there, right?"

"Almost," Ezra says. He lowers his voice. "Place is hopping on a Friday night. We haven't passed a building for miles."

It's pitch black outside, and even after rubbing my eyes a few times I can't see much out the window except the shadowy blur of trees. I try, though, because I want to see the place Sadie couldn't wait to leave. "It's like living in a postcard," she used to say. "Pretty, shiny, and closed in. Everyone who lives in Echo Ridge acts like you'll vanish if you venture outside the border."

The car goes over a bump, and my seat belt digs into my neck as the impact jolts me to one side. Ezra yawns so hard that his jaw cracks. I'm sure that once I crashed he felt obligated to stay awake and make conversation, even though neither of us has slept properly for days.

"We're less than a mile from home." Nana's voice from the front seat startles us both. "We just passed the 'Welcome to Echo Ridge' sign, although it's so poorly lit that I don't suppose you even noticed."

She's right. I didn't, though I'd made a mental note to look for it. The sign was one of the few things Sadie ever talked about related to Echo Ridge, usually after a few glasses of wine. "'Population 4,935.' Never changed the entire eighteen years I lived there," she'd say with a smirk. "Apparently if you're going to bring someone in, you have to take someone out first."

"Here comes the overpass, Melanie." Nana's voice has a warning edge.

"I know," Melanie says. The road curves sharply as we pass beneath an arch of gray stone, and Melanie slows to a crawl. There are no streetlights along this stretch, and Melanie switches on the high beams.

"Nana is the worst backseat driver ever," Ezra whispers.

"Really?" I whisper back. "But Melanie's so careful."

"Unless we're at a red light, we're going too fast."

I snicker, just as my grandmother hollers, "Stop!" in such a commanding voice that both Ezra and I jump. For a split second, I think she has supersonic hearing and is annoyed at our snarking. Then Melanie slams on the brakes, stopping the car so abruptly that I'm pitched forward against my seat belt.

"What the—?" Ezra and I both ask at the same time, but Melanie and Nana have already unbuckled and scrambled out of the car. We exchange confused glances and follow suit. The ground is covered with puddles of half-melted hail, and I pick my way around them toward my grandmother. Nana is standing in front of Melanie's car, her gaze fixed on the patch of road bathed in bright headlights.

And on the still figure lying right in the middle of it. Covered in blood, with his neck bent at a horribly wrong angle and his eyes wide open, staring at nothing.

CHAPTER TWO

ELLERY

SATURDAY, AUGUST 31

The sun wakes me up, burning through blinds that clearly weren't purchased for their room-darkening properties. But I stay immobile under the covers—a thin crocheted bedspread and petal-soft sheets—until a low knock sounds on the door.

"Yeah?" I sit up, futilely trying to push hair out of my eyes, as Ezra enters. The silver-plated clock on the nightstand reads 9:50, but since I'm still on West Coast time I don't feel as though I've slept nearly enough.

"Hey," Ezra says. "Nana said to wake you up. A police officer is on his way over. He wants to talk to us about last night."

Last night. We stayed with the man in the road, crouching next to him between dark pools of blood, until an ambulance came. I couldn't bring myself to look at his face at first, but once I did I couldn't look away. He was so *young.* No older than thirty, dressed in athletic clothes and sneakers. Melanie, who's a nurse, performed CPR until the EMTs arrived, but more like she was praying for a miracle than because she thought it would do any good. She told us when we got back into Nana's car that he was dead before we arrived.

"Jason Bowman," she'd said in a shaking voice. "He's—he *was*—one of the science teachers at Echo Ridge High. Helped out with marching band, too. Really popular with the kids. You would have . . . you *should* have . . . met him next week."

Ezra, who's fully dressed, hair damp from a recent shower, tosses a small plastic pack onto the bed, bringing me back to the present. "Also, she said to give you these."

The unopened package has the Hanes logo on the front, along with a picture of a smiling blond woman wearing a sports bra and underpants that come halfway up her waist. "Oh no."

"Oh yes. Those are *literally* granny panties. Nana says she bought a couple sizes too small by mistake and forgot to return them. Now they're yours."

"Fantastic," I mutter, swinging my legs out of bed. I'm wearing the T-shirt I had layered under my sweater yesterday, plus a rolled-up pair of Ezra's sweatpants. When I learned I'd be moving to Echo Ridge, I went through my entire closet and ruthlessly donated anything I hadn't worn in the past few months. I pared my wardrobe down so much that everything, except for a few coats and shoes that I shipped last week, fit into a single suitcase. At the time, it felt like I was bringing order and control to at least one small part of my life.

Now, of course, all it means is that I have nothing to wear.

I pick my phone up from the nightstand, checking for a

luggage-related text or voice mail. But there's nothing. "Why are you up so early?" I ask Ezra.

He shrugs. "It's not *that* early. I've been walking around the neighborhood. It's pretty. Very leafy. I posted a couple of Insta stories. And made a playlist."

I fold my arms. "Not another Michael playlist."

"No," Ezra says defensively. "It's a musical tribute to the Northeast. You'd be surprised how many songs have a New England state in the title."

"Mm-hmm." Ezra's boyfriend, Michael, broke up with him preemptively the week before we left because, he said, "long-distance relationships don't ever work." Ezra tries to act like he doesn't care, but he's created some seriously emo playlists since it happened.

"Don't judge." Ezra's eyes drift toward the bookcase, where *In Cold Blood* is lined up neatly next to my Ann Rule collection, *Fatal Vision, Midnight in the Garden of Good and Evil,* and the rest of my true-crime books. They're the only things I unpacked last night from the boxes stacked in one corner of the room. "We all have our coping mechanisms."

He retreats to his room, and I gaze around the unfamiliar space I'll be living in for the next four months. When we arrived last night, Nana told me that I'd be sleeping in Sadie's old room. I was both eager and nervous opening the door, wondering what echoes of my mother I'd find inside. But I walked into a standard guest bedroom without a scrap of personality. The furniture is dark wood, the walls a pale eggshell. There's not much in the way of decor except for lacy curtains, a plaid area rug, and a framed print of a lighthouse. Everything smells faintly of lemon

Pledge and cedar. When I try to imagine Sadie here—fixing her hair in the cloudy mirror over the dresser or doing her homework at the old-fashioned desk—the images won't come.

Ezra's room is the same. There's no hint that a teenage girl ever lived in either of them.

I drop to the floor beside my moving boxes and root around in the nearest one until I come across plastic-wrapped picture frames. The first one I unwrap is a photo of Ezra and me standing on Santa Monica Pier last year, a perfect sunset behind us. The setting is gorgeous, but it's not a flattering picture of me. I wasn't ready for the shot, and my tense expression doesn't match Ezra's wide grin. I kept it, though, because it reminded me of another photo.

That's the second one I pull out—grainy and much older, of two identical teenage girls with long, curly hair like mine, dressed in '90s grungewear. One of them is smiling brightly, the other looks annoyed. My mother and her twin sister, Sarah. They were seventeen then, seniors at Echo Ridge High like Ezra and I are about to be. A few weeks after the photo was taken, Sarah disappeared.

It's been twenty-three years and no one knows what happened to her. Or maybe it'd be more accurate to say that if anybody does know, they're not telling.

I place the photos side by side on top of the bookcase, and think about Ezra's words in the airport last night, after Andy overshared his origin story. *What a weird thing to grow up with, though, huh? Knowing how easily you could've been the wrong twin.*

Sadie never liked talking about Sarah, no matter how hungry I was for information. There weren't any pictures of her around our apartment; I had to steal this one off the Internet. My true-crime kick started in earnest with Lacey's death, but ever since I was old enough to understand what happened to Sarah, I was obsessed with her disappearance. It was the worst thing I could imagine, to have your twin go missing and never come back.

Sadie's smile in the photo is as blinding as Ezra's. She was a star back then—the popular homecoming queen, just like Lacey. And she's been trying to be a star ever since. I don't know if Sadie would have done better than a handful of walk-on roles if she'd had her twin cheering her on. I *do* know there's no possible way she can feel complete. When you come into the world with another person, they're as much a part of you as your heartbeat.

There are lots of reasons my mother got addicted to painkillers—a strained shoulder, a bad breakup, another lost role, moving to our crappiest apartment yet on her fortieth birthday—but I can't help but think it all started with the loss of that serious-faced girl in the photo.

The doorbell rings, and I almost drop the picture. I completely forgot I was supposed to be getting ready to meet a police officer. I glance at the mirror over the dresser, wincing at my reflection. My hair looks like a wig, and all my anti-frizz products are in my missing suitcase. I pull my curls into a ponytail, then twist and turn the thick strands until I can knot the ends together into a low bun without needing an elastic. It's one of the first hair tricks Sadie ever taught me. When I was little we'd stand at the double sink in our bathroom, me watching her in the mirror so I could copy the quick, deft motion of her hands.

My eyes prick as Nana calls up the stairs. "Ellery? Ezra? Officer Rodriguez is here."

Ezra's already in the hall when I leave my room, and we head downstairs to Nana's kitchen. A dark-haired man in a blue uniform, his back to us, takes the cup of coffee Nana holds toward him. She looks like she just stepped out of an L. L. Bean catalog in khakis, clogs and a boxy oxford shirt with horizontal stripes.

"Maybe the town will finally do something about that overpass," Nana says, then catches my eye over the officer's shoulder. "There you are. Ryan, this is my granddaughter and grandson. Ellery and Ezra, meet Officer Ryan Rodriguez. He lives down the street and came by to ask us a few questions about last night."

The officer turns with a half smile that freezes as the coffee mug slips out of his hand and goes crashing to the floor. None of us react for a second, and then everybody leaps into action at once, grabbing at paper towels and picking thick pieces of ceramic mug off Nana's black-and-white tiled floor.

"I'm so sorry," Officer Rodriguez keeps repeating. He can't be more than five years older than me and Ezra, and he looks as though even he's not sure whether he's an actual adult yet. "I have no idea how that happened. I'll replace the mug."

"Oh, for goodness' sake," Nana says crisply. "Those cost two dollars at Dalton's. Sit down and I'll get you another one. You too, kids. There's juice on the table if you want some."

We all settle around the kitchen table, which is neatly set with three place mats, silverware, and glasses. Officer Rodriguez pulls a notepad from his front pocket and flips through it with a knitted brow. He has one of those hangdog faces that looks worried even now, when he's not breaking my grandmother's stuff. "Thanks for making time this morning. I just came from the Kilduffs' house, and Melanie filled me in on what happened at

16

the Fulkerson Street overpass last night. Which, I'm sorry to say, looks like it was a hit-and-run." Nana hands him another cup of coffee before sitting down next to Ezra, and Officer Rodriguez takes a careful sip. "Thank you, Mrs. Corcoran. So it would be helpful if all of you could tell me everything you observed, even if it doesn't seem important."

I straighten in my chair, and Ezra rolls his eyes. He knows exactly what's going through my head. Even though last night was awful, I can't *not* feel a slight thrill at being part of an actual police investigation. I've been waiting for this moment half my life.

Unfortunately I'm no help, because I hardly remember anything except Melanie trying to help Mr. Bowman. Ezra's not much better. Nana is the only one who noticed little details, like the fact that there was an umbrella and a Tupperware container scattered on the street next to Mr. Bowman. And as far as investigating officers go, Ryan Rodriguez is disappointing. He keeps repeating the same questions, almost knocks over his fresh cup of coffee, and stumbles constantly over Melanie's name. By the time he thanks us and Nana walks him to the front door, I'm convinced he needs a few more years of training before they let him out on his own again.

"That was kind of disorganized," I say when Nana returns to the kitchen. "Do people take him seriously as a police officer around here?"

She takes a pan out from a cabinet next to the stove and places it on a front burner. "Ryan is perfectly capable," she says matter-of-factly, crossing to the refrigerator and pulling out the butter dish. She sets it on the counter and slices off a huge

17

chunk, dropping it into the pan. "He may be a little out of sorts. His father died a few months ago. Cancer. They were very close. And his mother passed the year before, so it's been one thing after another for that family. Ryan is the youngest and the only one still at home. I imagine it's been lonely."

"He lived with his parents?" Ezra asks. "How old is he?" My brother is kind of judgy about adults who still live at home. He'll be one of those people, like Sadie, who moves out as soon as the ink is dry on his diploma. He has a ten-year plan that involves taking a grunt job at a radio station while deejaying on the side, until he has enough experience to host his own show. I try not to panic whenever I imagine him leaving me behind to do . . . who even knows what.

"Twenty-two, I think? Or twenty-three," Nana says. "All the Rodriguez kids lived at home during college. Ryan stayed once his father got sick." Ezra hunches his shoulders guiltily as my ears prick up.

"Twenty-three?" I repeat. "Was he in Lacey Kilduff's class?"

"I believe so," Nana says as she cracks an egg into the now-sizzling pan.

I hesitate. I barely know my grandmother. We've never talked about my missing aunt on our awkward, infrequent Skype calls, and I have no idea if Lacey's death is extra-painful for her because of what happened to Sarah. I should probably keep my mouth shut, but . . .

"Were they friends?" I blurt out. Ezra's face settles into a *here we go* expression.

"I couldn't say. They knew one another, certainly. Ryan grew up in the neighborhood and they both worked at . . . Fright

Farm." Her hesitation before the new name is so slight that I almost miss it. "Most kids in town did. Still do."

"When does it open?" Ezra asks. He glances at me like he's doing me a favor, but he didn't have to bother. I looked up the schedule as soon as I learned we were moving to Echo Ridge.

"Next weekend. Right before you two start school," Nana says. Echo Ridge has the latest start date of any school we've ever attended, which is one point in its favor. At La Puente, we'd already been in school two weeks by Labor Day. Nana gestures with her spatula toward the kitchen window over the sink, which looks out into the woods behind her house. "You'll hear it once it does. It's a ten-minute walk through the woods."

"It is?" Ezra looks baffled. I am too, but mostly by his utter lack of research. "So the Kilduffs still live right behind the place where their daughter . . . where somebody, um . . ." He trails off as Nana turns toward us with two plates, each holding an enormous fluffy omelet, and deposits them in front of us. Ezra and I exchange surprised glances. I can't remember the last time either of us had anything for breakfast other than coffee. But my mouth waters at the savory scent, and my stomach rumbles. I haven't eaten anything since the three Kind bars I had for dinner on last night's flight.

"Well." Nana sits down between us and pours herself a glass of orange juice from the ceramic pitcher on the table. *Pitcher.* Not a carton. I spend a few seconds trying to figure out why you'd bother emptying a carton into a pitcher before taking a sip of mine and realizing it's freshly squeezed. How are she and Sadie even related? "It's their home. The two younger girls have lots of friends in the neighborhood."

19

"How old are they?" I ask. Melanie wasn't just Sadie's favorite babysitter; she was almost a mentor to her in high school—and pretty much the only person from Echo Ridge my mother ever talked about. But I still know hardly anything about her except that her daughter was murdered.

"Caroline is twelve and Julia is six," Nana says. "There's quite a gap between the two of them, and between Lacey and Caroline. Melanie's always had trouble conceiving. But there's a silver lining, I suppose. The girls were so young when Lacey died, looking after them might be the only thing that kept Melanie and Dan going during such a terrible time."

Ezra cuts into the corner of his omelet and releases a small cloud of steam. "The police never had any suspects in Lacey's murder, huh?" he asks.

"No," Nana says at the same time as I say, "The boyfriend."

Nana takes a long sip of juice. "Plenty of people thought that. *Think* that," she says. "But Declan Kelly wasn't an official suspect. Questioned, yes. Multiple times. But never held."

"Does he still live in Echo Ridge?" I ask.

She shakes her head. "He left town right after graduation. Best for all involved, I'm sure. The situation took an enormous toll on his family. Declan's father moved away shortly after he did. I thought the mother and brother would be next, but . . . things worked out differently for them."

I pause with my fork in midair. "Brother?" I hadn't known Lacey's boyfriend had a brother; the news never reported much about his family.

"Declan has a younger brother, Malcolm. Around your age," Nana says. "I don't know him well, but he seems a quieter sort.

Doesn't strut around town as if he owns it, at any rate, the way his brother did."

I watch her take a careful bite of omelet, wishing I could read her better so I'd know whether Lacey and Sarah are as intertwined in her mind as they are in mine. It's been so long since Sarah disappeared; almost a quarter century with no answers. Lacey's parents lack a different kind of closure—they know *what, when,* and *how,* but not *who* or *why.* "Do you think Declan Kelly is guilty?" I ask.

Nana's brow wrinkles, as though she suddenly finds the entire conversation distasteful. "I didn't say that. There was never any hard evidence against him."

I reach for the saltshaker without responding. That might be true, but if years of reading true-crime books and watching *Dateline* have taught me anything, it's this: it's *always* the boyfriend.

CHAPTER THREE

MALCOLM
WEDNESDAY, SEPTEMBER 4

My shirt's stiff with too much starch. It practically crackles when I bend my arms to drape a tie around my neck. I watch my hands in the mirror, trying and failing to get the knot straight, and give up when it's at least the right size. The mirror looks old and expensive, like everything in the Nilssons' house. It reflects a bedroom that could fit three of my old one. And at least half of Declan's apartment.

What's it like living in that house? my brother asked last night, scraping the last of his birthday cake off a plate while Mom was in the bathroom. She'd brought a bunch of balloons that looked tiny in the Nilssons' foyer, but kept batting Declan in the head in the cramped alcove he calls a kitchen.

Fucked up, I said. Which is true. But no more fucked up than the past five years have been. Declan's spent most of them living four hours away in New Hampshire, renting a basement apartment from our aunt.

A sharp knock sounds at my bedroom door, and hinges squeak as my stepsister pokes her head in without waiting for an answer. "You ready?" she asks.

"Yep," I say, picking up a blue suit coat from my bed and shrugging it on. Katrin tilts her head and frowns, ice-blond hair spilling over one shoulder. I know that look: *There's something wrong with you, and I'm about to tell you exactly what it is and how to fix it.* I've been seeing it for months now.

"Your tie's crooked," she says, heels clicking on the floor as she walks toward me, hands outstretched. A crease appears between her eyes as she tugs at the knot, then disappears when she steps back to view her work. "There," she says, patting my shoulder with a satisfied expression. "Much better." Her hand skims down to my chest and she plucks a piece of lint from my suit coat with two pale-pink fingernails and lets it drop to the floor. "You clean up all right, Mal. Who would've thought?"

Not her. Katrin Nilsson barely spoke to me until her father started dating my mother last winter. She's the queen of Echo Ridge High, and I'm the band nerd with the disreputable family. But now that we live under the same roof, Katrin has to acknowledge my existence. She copes by treating me like either a project or a nuisance, depending on her mood.

"Let's go," she says, tugging lightly at my arm. Her black dress hugs her curves but stops right above her knees. She'd almost be conservative if she weren't wearing tall, spiky heels that basically force you to look at her legs. So I do. My new stepsister might be a pain in the ass, but she's undeniably hot.

23

I follow Katrin into the hallway to the balcony staircase overlooking the massive foyer downstairs. My mother and Peter are at the bottom waiting for us, and I drop my eyes because whenever they're standing that close, his hands are usually someplace I don't want to see. Katrin and her superjock boyfriend commit less PDA than those two.

But Mom's happy, and I guess that's good.

Peter looks up and takes a break from manhandling my mom. "Don't you two look nice!" he calls out. He's in a suit too, same dark blue as mine, except he gets his tailored so they fit him perfectly. Peter's like one of those suave *GQ* watch ads come to life—square jaw, penetrating gaze, wavy blond hair with just enough gray to be distinguished. Nobody could believe he was interested in my mother when they first started dating. People were even more shocked when he married her.

He saved them. That's what the entire town thinks. Peter Nilsson, the rich and charming owner of the only law firm in town, took us from town pariahs to town royalty with one tasteful justice of the peace ceremony at Echo Ridge Lake. And maybe he did. People don't avoid my mother anymore, or whisper behind her back. She gets invited to the garden club, school committees, tonight's fund-raiser, and all that other crap.

Doesn't mean I have to like him, though.

"Nice having you back, Malcolm," he adds, almost sounding like he means it. Mom and I have been gone a week, visiting family across a few towns in New Hampshire and then finishing up at Declan's place. Peter and Katrin didn't come. Partly because he had to work, and partly because neither of them leave Echo Ridge for anyplace without room service and a spa.

24

"Did you have dinner with Mr. Coates while we were gone?" I ask abruptly.

Peter's nostrils flare slightly, which is the only sign of annoyance he ever shows. "I did, on Friday. He's still getting his business up and running, but when the time is right he'd be happy to talk with Declan. I'll keep checking in with him."

Ben Coates used to be mayor of Echo Ridge. After that, he left to run a political consulting business in Burlington. Declan is a few—okay, a *lot*—of credits short from finishing his poli-sci degree at community college, but he's still hoping for a recommendation. It's the only thing he's ever asked of Peter. Or of Mom, I guess, since Declan and Peter don't really talk.

Mom beams at Peter, and I let it drop. Katrin steps forward, reaching out a hand to touch the twisted beaded necklace Mom's wearing. "This is so pretty!" she exclaims. "Very bohemian. Such a nice change from all the pearls we'll see tonight."

Mom's smile fades. "I have pearls," she says nervously, looking at Peter. "Should I—"

"You're fine," he says quickly. "You look beautiful."

I could kill Katrin. Not literally. I feel like I have to add that disclaimer even in my own thoughts, given our family history. But I don't understand her constant need to make digs at Mom's expense. It's not like Mom broke up Katrin's parents; she's Peter's *third* wife. Katrin's mother was long gone to Paris with a new husband before Mom and Peter even went on their first date.

And Katrin has to know that Mom is nervous about tonight. We've never been to the Lacey Kilduff Memorial Scholarship fund-raiser before. Mostly because we've never been invited.

Or welcome.

Peter's nostrils flare again. "Let's head out, shall we? It's getting late."

He opens the front door, stepping aside to let us through while pressing a button on his key chain. His black Range Rover starts idling in the driveway, and Katrin and I climb into the back. My mother settles herself in the passenger seat and flips the radio from the Top 40 station that Katrin likes to blast to NPR. Peter gets in last, buckling his seat belt before shifting the car into gear.

The Nilssons' winding driveway is the longest part of the trip. After that, it's a few quick turns and we're in downtown Echo Ridge. So to speak. There's not much to it—a row of white-trimmed redbrick buildings on either side of Manchester Street, lined with old-fashioned, wrought iron streetlights. It's never crowded here, but it's especially dead on a Wednesday night before school's back in session. Half the town is still on vacation, and the other half is attending the fund-raiser in the Echo Ridge Cultural Center. That's where anything notable at Echo Ridge happens, unless it happens at the Nilssons' house.

Our house. Can't get used to that.

Peter parallel parks on Manchester Street and we spill out of the car and onto the sidewalk. We're right across the street from O'Neill's Funeral Home, and Katrin heaves a sigh as we pass the pale-blue Victorian. "It's too bad you were out of town for Mr. Bowman's service," she says. "It was really nice. The show choir sang 'To Sir with Love' and everybody lost it."

My gut twists. Mr. Bowman was my favorite teacher at Echo Ridge High, by a lot. He had this quiet way of noticing what you were good at, and encouraging you to get better. After Declan moved away and my dad took off, when I had a lot of pissed-off

26

energy and nowhere to put it, he was the one who suggested I take up the drums. It makes me sick that somebody mowed him down and left him to die in the middle of the road.

"Why was he even out in a hailstorm?" I ask, because it's easier to fixate on that than to keep feeling like shit.

"They found a Tupperware container near him," Peter says. "One of the teachers at the funeral thought he might have been collecting hail for a lesson he was planning on climate change. But I guess we'll never know for sure."

And now I feel worse, because I can picture it: Mr. Bowman leaving his house late at night with his umbrella and his plastic container, all enthusiastic because he was going to *make science real.* He said that kind of thing a lot.

After a couple of blocks, a gold-rimmed wooden sign welcomes us to the cultural center. It's the most impressive of all the redbrick buildings, with a clock tower on top and wide steps leading to a carved wooden door. I reach for the door, but Peter's faster. Always. You can't out-gentleman that guy. Mom smiles gratefully at him as she steps through the entrance.

When we get inside, a woman directs us down a hallway to an open room that contains dozens of round tables. Some people are sitting down, but most of the crowd is still milling around and talking. A few turn toward us, and then, like human dominoes, they all do.

It's the moment everyone in Echo Ridge has been waiting for: for the first time in five years, the Kellys have shown up at a night honoring Lacey Kilduff.

The girl who most people in town still believe my brother killed.

"Oh, there's Theo," Katrin murmurs, slipping away into the crowd toward her boyfriend. So much for solidarity. My mother licks her lips nervously. Peter folds her arm under his and pastes on a big, bright smile. For a second, I almost like the guy.

Declan and Lacey had been fighting for weeks before she died. Which wasn't like them; Declan could be an arrogant ass a lot of the time, but not with his girlfriend. Then all of a sudden they were slamming doors, canceling dates, and sniping at each other over social media. Declan's last, angry message on Lacey's Instagram feed was the one that news stations showed over and over in the weeks after her body was found.

I'm so fucking done with you. DONE. You have no idea.

The crowd at the Echo Ridge Cultural Center is too quiet. Even Peter's smile is getting a little fixed. The Nilsson armor is supposed to be more impenetrable than this. I'm about to say or do something desperate to cut the tension when a warm voice floats our way. "Hello, Peter. And Alicia! Malcolm! It's good to see you both."

It's Lacey's mom, Melanie Kilduff, coming toward us with a big smile. She hugs my mother first, then me, and when she pulls back nobody's staring anymore.

"Thanks," I mutter. I don't know what Melanie thinks about Declan; she's never said. But after Lacey died, when it felt like the entire world hated my family, Melanie always made a point to be nice to us. *Thanks* doesn't feel like enough, but Melanie brushes my arm like it's too much before turning toward Mom and Peter.

"Please, have a seat wherever you'd like," she says, gesturing toward the dining area. "They're about to start serving dinner."

She leaves us, heading for a table with her family, her neighbor, and a couple of kids my age I've never seen before. Which is unusual enough in this town that I crane my neck for a better look. I can't get a good glimpse of the guy, but the girl is hard to miss. She's got wild curly hair that seems almost alive, and she's wearing a weird flowered dress that looks like it came out of her grandmother's closet. Maybe it's retro, I don't know. Katrin wouldn't be caught dead in it. The girl meets my eyes, and I immediately look away. One thing I've learned from being Declan's brother over the past five years: nobody likes it when a Kelly boy stares.

Peter starts toward the front of the room, but Katrin returns just then and tugs on his arm. "Can we sit at Theo's table, Dad? There's plenty of space." He hesitates—Peter likes to lead, not follow—and Katrin puts on her most wheedling voice. "Please? I haven't seen him all week, and his parents want to talk to you about that stoplight ordinance thing."

She's good. There's nothing Peter likes better than in-depth discussions about town council crap that would bore anybody else to tears. He smiles indulgently and changes course.

Katrin's boyfriend, Theo, and his parents are the only people sitting at the ten-person table when we approach. I've gone to school with Theo since kindergarten, but as usual he looks right through me as he waves to someone over my shoulder. "Yo, Kyle! Over here."

Oh hell.

Theo's best friend, Kyle, takes a seat between him and my mother, and the chair next to me scrapes as a big man with a graying blond buzz cut settles down beside me. Chad McNulty,

Kyle's father and the Echo Ridge police officer who investigated Lacey's murder. Because this night wasn't awkward enough already. My mother's got that deer-in-the-headlights look she always gets around the McNultys, and Peter flares his nostrils at an oblivious Theo.

"Hello, Malcolm." Officer McNulty unfolds his napkin onto his lap without looking at me. "How's your summer been?"

"Great," I manage, taking a long sip of water.

Officer McNulty never liked my brother. Declan dated his daughter, Liz, for three months and dumped her for Lacey, which got Liz so upset that she dropped out of school for a while. In return, Kyle's always been a dick to me. Standard small-town crap that got a lot worse once Declan became an unofficial murder suspect.

Waiters start moving around the room, putting plates of salad in front of everyone. Melanie steps behind a podium on the stage in front, and Officer McNulty's jaw tenses. "That woman is a tower of strength," he says, like he's daring me to disagree.

"Thank you so much for coming," Melanie says, leaning toward the microphone. "It means the world to Dan, Caroline, Julia, and me to see how much the Lacey Kilduff Memorial Scholarship fund has grown."

I tune the rest out. Not because I don't care, but because it's too hard to hear. Years of not being invited to these things means I haven't built up much resistance. After Melanie finishes her speech, she introduces a University of Vermont junior who was the first scholarship recipient. The girl talks about her medical school plans as empty salad plates are replaced with the main course. When she's done, everyone applauds and turns their attention to the food. I poke half-heartedly at my dry chicken while Peter holds court about stoplights. Is it too soon for a bathroom break?

"The thing is, it's a delicate balance between maintaining town aesthetics and accommodating changing traffic patterns," Peter says earnestly.

Nope. Not too soon. I stand, drop my napkin onto my chair, and take off.

When I've washed my hands as many times as I can stand, I exit the men's room and hesitate in the corridor between the banquet hall and the front door. The thought of returning to that table makes my head pound. Nobody's going to miss me for another few minutes.

I tug at my collar and push open the door, stepping outside into the darkness. It's still muggy, but less stifling than inside. Nights like this make me feel like I can't breathe, like every-thing my brother did, actual and alleged, settled over me when I was twelve years old and still weighs me down. I became *Declan Kelly's brother* before I got a chance to be anything else, and sometimes it feels like that's all I'll ever be.

I inhale deeply, and pause when a faint chemical smell hits me. It gets stronger as I descend the stairs and head toward the lawn. With my back to the lights I can't see much, and almost trip over something lying in the grass. I bend down and pick it up. It's a can of spray paint that's missing its top.

That's what I'm smelling: fresh paint. But where is it coming from? I turn back toward the cultural center. Its well-lit exte-rior looks the same as ever. There isn't anything else nearby that might have been recently painted, except . . .

31

The cultural center sign is halfway across the lawn between the building and the street. I'm practically on top of it before I can see clearly in the dim glow thrown from the nearest street-light. Red letters cover the back of the sign from top to bottom, stark against the pale wood:

MURDERLAND
THE SEQUEL
COMING SOON

I'm not sure how long I stand there, staring, before I realize I'm not alone anymore. The girl from Melanie's table with the curly hair and the weird dress is standing a few feet away. Her eyes dart between the words on the sign and the can in my hand, which rattles when I drop my arm.

"This isn't what it looks like," I say.

CHAPTER FOUR

ELLERY
SATURDAY, SEPTEMBER 7

How's everything going?

I consider the text from my friend Lourdes. She's in California, but not La Puente. I met her in sixth grade, which was three towns before we moved there. Or maybe four. Unlike Ezra, who jumps easily into the social scene every time we switch schools, I hang on to my virtual best friend and keep the in-person stuff surface level. It's easier to move on that way. It requires fewer emo playlists, anyway.

Let's see. We've been here a week and so far the highlight is yard work.

Lourdes sends a few sad-face emojis, then adds, *It'll pick up when school starts. Have you met any cute preppy New England guys yet?*

Just one. But not preppy. And possibly a vandal.

Do tell.

I pause, not sure how to explain my run-in with the boy at Lacey Kilduff's fund-raiser, when my phone buzzes with a call from a number with a California area code. I don't recognize it, but my heart leaps and I fire off a quick text to Lourdes: *Hang on, getting a call about my luggage I hope.* I've been in Vermont a full week, and my suitcase is still missing. If it doesn't show up within the next two days, I'm going to have to start school in the clothes my grandmother bought at Echo Ridge's one and only clothing store. It's called Dalton's Emporium and also sells kitchen goods and hardware, which should tell you everything you need to know about its fashion cred. No one who's older than six or younger than sixty should shop there, ever.

"Hello?"

"Ellery, hi!" I almost drop my phone, and when I don't answer the voice doubles down on its cheerful urgency. "It's me!"

"Yeah, I know." I lower myself stiffly onto my bed, gripping the phone in my suddenly sweaty palm. "How are you calling me?"

Sadie's tone turns reproachful. "You don't sound very happy to hear from me."

"It's just— I thought we were supposed to start talking next Thursday." Those were the rules of rehab, according to Nana: Fifteen-minute Skype sessions once a week after two full weeks of treatment had been completed. Not random calls from an unknown number.

"The rules here are ridiculous," Sadie says. I can practically hear the eye roll in her voice. "One of the aides is letting me use her phone. She's a *Defender* fan." The only speaking role Sadie ever had was in the first installment of what turned out to be a huge action series in the '90s, *The Defender*, about a down-on-his-luck soldier turned avenging cyborg. She played a sexy robot named Zeta Voltes, and even though she had only one line—*That does not compute*—there are still fan websites dedicated to the character. "I'm dying to see you, love. Let's switch to FaceTime."

I pause before hitting Accept, because I'm not ready for this. At all. But what am I going to do, hang up on my mother? Within seconds Sadie's face fills the screen, bright with anticipation. She looks the same as ever—nothing like me except for the hair. Sadie's eyes are bright blue, while mine are so dark they almost look black. She's sweet-faced with soft, open features, and I'm all angles and straight lines. There's only one other trait we share, and when I see the dimple in her right cheek flash with a smile, I force myself to mirror it back. "There you are!" she crows. Then a frown creases her forehead. "What's going on with your hair?"

My chest constricts. "Is that seriously the first thing you have to say to me?"

I haven't talked to Sadie since she checked into Hamilton House, the pricey rehab center Nana's paying for. Considering she demolished an entire storefront, Sadie lucked out: she didn't hurt herself or anyone else, and she wound up in front of a judge who believes in treatment instead of jail time. But she's never been particularly grateful. Everyone and everything else is at fault: the doctor who gave her too strong a prescription, bad lighting on the street, our car's ancient brakes. It didn't fully hit me until just now—sitting in a bedroom that belongs to a grandmother I barely know, listening to Sadie criticize my hair through a phone that someone could probably get fired for giving her—how *infuriating* it all is.

"Oh, El, of course not. I'm just teasing. You look beautiful. How are you?"

How am I supposed to answer that? "I'm fine."

"What's happened in your first week? Tell me everything."

I could refuse to play along, I guess. But as my eye catches the photo of Sadie and her sister on my bookcase, I already feel myself wanting to please her. To smooth things over and make her smile. I've been doing it my entire life; it's impossible to stop now. "Things are just as weird as you've always said. I've already been questioned twice by the police."

Her eyes pop. "What?"

I tell her about the hit-and-run, and the graffiti at Lacey's fund-raiser three days ago. "Declan Kelly's *brother* wrote that?" Sadie asks, looking outraged.

"He said he just found the paint canister."

She snorts. "Likely story."

"I don't know. He looked pretty shocked when I saw him."

"God, poor Melanie and Dan. That's the last thing they need."

"The police officer I talked to at the fund-raiser said he knew you. Officer McNulty? I forget his first name."

Sadie grins. "Chad McNulty! Yeah, we dated sophomore year. God, you're going to meet all my exes, aren't you? Was Vance Puckett there, by any chance? He used to be *gorgeous*." I shake my head. "Ben Coates? Peter Nilsson?"

None of those names are familiar except the last one. I met

him at the fund-raiser, right after his stepson and I reported the sign vandalism. "You dated that guy?" I ask. "Doesn't he own, like, half the town?"

"I guess so. Cute, but kind of a tight-ass. We went out twice when I was a senior, but he was in college then and we didn't really click."

"He's Malcolm's stepfather now," I tell her.

Sadie's face scrunches in confusion. "Who?"

"Malcolm Kelly. Declan Kelly's brother? The one with the spray paint?"

"Good Lord," Sadie mutters. "I cannot keep up with that place."

Some of the tenseness that's been keeping me rigid ebbs away, and I laugh as I settle back against my pillow. Sadie's superpower is making you feel as though everything's going to be fine, even when it's mostly disastrous. "Officer McNulty said his son's in our class," I tell her. "I guess he was at the fund-raiser, but I didn't meet him."

"Ugh, we're all so *old* now. Did you talk to him about the hit-and-run, too?"

"No, that officer was really young. Ryan Rodriguez?" I don't expect Sadie to recognize the name, but an odd expression flits across her face. "What? Do you know him?" I ask.

"No. How would I?" Sadie asks, a little too quickly. When she catches my dubious squint, she adds. "Well. It's just . . . now, don't go making too much of this, Ellery, because I *know* the way you think. But he fell apart at Lacey's funeral. Way more than her boyfriend did. It caught my attention, so I remembered it. That's all."

"Fell apart how?"

Sadie heaves a theatrical sigh. "I knew you'd ask that."

"You brought it up!"

"Oh, just . . . you know. He cried a lot. Almost collapsed. His friends had to carry him out of the church. And I said to Melanie, 'Wow, they must have been really close.' But she said they barely knew one another." Sadie lifts a shoulder in a half shrug. "He probably had a crush, that's all. Lacey was a beauty. What's that?" She glances off to one side, and I hear the murmur of another voice. "Oh, okay. Sorry, El, but I have to go. Tell Ezra I'll call him soon, okay? I love you, and . . ." She pauses, something like regret crossing her face for the first time. "And . . . I'm glad you're meeting people."

No apology. Saying she's sorry would mean acknowledging that something's wrong, and even when she's calling me cross-country from rehab on a contraband phone, Sadie can't do it. I don't answer, and she adds, "I hope you're doing something fun for your Saturday afternoon!"

I'm not sure if *fun* is the right word, but it's something I've been planning since I learned I was going to Echo Ridge. "Fright Farm opens for the season today, and I'm going."

Sadie shakes her head with exasperated fondness. "Of course you are," she says, and blows me a kiss before she disconnects.

Hours later, Ezra and I are walking through the woods behind Nana's house toward Fright Farm, leaves crunching beneath our feet. I'm wearing some of my new Dalton's clothes, which Ezra has been snickering at since we left the house.

"I mean," he says as we step over a fallen branch, "what would you even call those? Leisure pants?"

"Shut up," I grumble. The pants, which are some kind of synthetic stretchy material, were the most inoffensive piece of clothing I could find. At least they're black, and sort of fitted. My gray-and-white checked T-shirt is short and boxy, and has such a high neck that it's almost choking me. I'm pretty sure I've never looked worse. "First Sadie with the hair, now you with the clothes."

Ezra's smile is bright and hopeful. "She looked good, though?" he asks. He and Sadie are so similar sometimes, so blissfully optimistic, that it's impossible to say what you really think around them. When I used to try, Sadie would sigh and say, *Don't be such an Eeyore, Ellery.* Once—only once—she'd added under her breath, *You're just like Sarah.* Then pretended not to hear me when I asked her to repeat what she'd said.

"She looked great," I tell Ezra.

We hear noise from the park before we see it. Once we emerge from the woods it's impossible to miss: the entrance looms across the road in the shape of a huge, monstrous head with glowing green eyes and a mouth, wide open in a scream, that serves as the door. It looks exactly like it did in pictures from the news coverage about Lacey's murder, except for the arched sign that reads FRIGHT FARM in spiky red letters.

Ezra shades his eyes against the sun. "I'm just gonna say it: Fright Farm is a crap name. Murderland was better."

"Agreed," I say.

There's a road running between the woods and the Fright Farm entrance, and we wait for a few cars to pass before crossing it. A tall, black spire fence circles the park, enclosing clusters of tents and rides. Fright Farm opened less than an hour ago, but it's already packed. Screams fill the air as a salt-and-pepper-shaker ride flips back and forth. When we get closer to the entrance, I see that the face is covered with mottled and red-specked grayish paint so it looks like a decaying corpse. There's a row of four booths directly inside, with one cashier to a booth, and at least two dozen people waiting. Ezra and I get in line, but I break away after a few minutes to check out the information board and grab a bunch of papers stacked up beneath it.

"Maps," I tell Ezra. I hand him one, plus another sheet of paper. "And job applications."

His brow furrows. "You want to *work* here?"

"We're broke, remember? And where else would we work? I don't think there's anyplace in walking distance." Neither of us have our driver's license, and I can tell already Nana's not the chauffeuring type.

Ezra shrugs. "All right. Hand it over."

I fish a couple of pens out of my messenger bag, and we almost complete the applications before it's our turn to buy tickets. I fold Ezra's and mine together and stuff them both in the front pocket of my bag as we leave the booths. "We can drop them off before we go home."

"Where should we go first?" Ezra asks.

I unfold my map and study it. "It looks like we're in the kids' section right now," I report. "Dark Matters is to the left. That's an evil science laboratory. Bloody Big Top to the right. Probably self-explanatory. And the House of Horrors is straight ahead. That doesn't open till seven, though."

Ezra leans over my shoulder and lowers his voice. "Where did Lacey die?"

I point to a tiny picture of a Ferris wheel. "Under there. Well, that's where they found her body, anyway. Police thought she was probably meeting someone. Echo Ridge kids used to sneak into the park after hours all the time, I guess. It didn't have any security cameras back then." We both glance up at the nearest building, where a red light blinks from one corner. "Does now, obviously."

"Do you want to start there?" Ezra asks.

My throat gets dry. A group of masked kids dressed in black swoops past us, one of them knocking into my shoulder so hard that I stumble. "Maybe we should check out the games," I say, refolding the map. It was a lot easier to take ghoulish pleasure at visiting a crime scene before I met the victim's family.

We walk past snack stands and carnival games, pausing to watch a boy our age sink enough baskets in a row to win a stuffed black cat for his girlfriend. The next station has the kind of shooting gallery game where two players each try to knock over twelve targets in a box. A guy wearing a ratty hunting jacket who looks like he's forty or so pumps his fist in the air and lets out a loud guffaw. "Beat ya!" he says, punching the shoulder of the kid next to him. The man stumbles a little with the movement, and the boy recoils and backs away.

"Maybe you should give someone else a turn." The girl behind the counter is about my age and pretty, with a long brown ponytail that she winds anxiously around her fingers.

The man in the hunting jacket waves the toy gun he's holding. "Plenty of room next to me. Anybody can play if they're not too chicken." His voice is loud and he's slurring his words.

The girl crosses her arms, as if she's steeling herself to sound tough. "There are lots of other games you could play."

"You're just mad 'cause nobody can beat me. Tell you what, if any of these losers can knock down more than me I'll bow out. Who wants to try?" He turns toward the small crowd gathering around the stand, revealing a lean, scruffy face.

Ezra nudges me. "How can you resist?" he asks under his breath.

I hesitate, waiting to see if someone older or bigger might help out, but when nobody does I step forward. "I will." I meet the girl's eyes, which are hazel, heavily mascaraed, and shadowed with dark circles. She looks like she hasn't slept in a week.

The guy blinks at me a few times, then bends at the waist in an exaggerated bow. The movement almost topples him, but he rights himself. "Well, hello, madam. Challenge accepted. I'll even pay for you." He fishes two crumpled dollars out of his pocket and hands them to the girl. She takes them gingerly and drops them into a box in front of her as if they were on fire. "Never let it be said that Vance Puckett isn't a gentleman."

"Vance Puckett?" I burst out before I can stop myself. *This* is Sadie's ex? The "gorgeous" one? Either her standards were a lot lower in Echo Ridge, or he peaked in high school.

His bloodshot eyes narrow, but without a spark of recognition. Not surprising; with my hair pulled back, there's nothing Sadie-like about me. "Do I know you?"

"Ah. No. It's just . . . that's a good name," I say limply.

The ponytailed girl presses a button to reset the targets.

I move to the second station as Vance raises the gun and sets his sights. "Champions first," he says loudly, and starts firing off shots in quick succession. Even though he's clearly drunk, he manages to knock over ten of the twelve targets. He raises the gun when he's finished and kisses the barrel, causing the girl to grimace. "Still got it," Vance says, making a sweeping gesture toward me. "Your move, milady."

I raise the gun in front of me. I happen to possess what Ezra calls freakishly good aim, despite having zero athletic talent in any other capacity. My hands are slick with sweat as I close one eye. *Don't overthink it,* I remind myself. *Just point and shoot.*

I press the trigger and miss the first target, but not by much. Vance snickers beside me. I adjust my aim, and hit the second. The crowd behind me starts murmuring when I've lowered the rest of the targets in the top row, and by the time I've hit nine they're clapping. The applause spikes at number ten, and turns into whoops and cheers when I knock over the last one and finish with eleven down. Ezra raises both arms in the air like I just scored a touchdown.

Vance stares at me, slack-jawed. "You're a goddamn ringer."

"Move along, Vance," someone calls. "There's a new sheriff in town." The crowd laughs, and Vance scowls. For a few beats I think he won't budge. Then he flings his gun on the counter with a snort.

"Game's fixed, anyway," he mutters, stepping back and shoving his way through the crowd.

The girl turns toward me with a tired but grateful smile. "Thanks. He's been here for almost half an hour, freaking everyone out. I thought he was going to start firing into the crowd any minute now. They're only pellets, but still." She reaches under the counter and pulls out a Handi Wipe, swiping it thoroughly across Vance's gun. "I owe you one. Do you guys want free wristbands to the House of Horrors?"

I almost say yes, but pull out my and Ezra's job applications instead. "Actually, would you mind putting a good word in for us with your boss? Or whoever does the hiring around here?"

The girl tugs on her ponytail instead of taking the papers from me. "Thing is, they only hire kids from Echo Ridge."

"We are," I say, brightly. "We just moved here."

She blinks at us. "You did? Are you— *Ohhh.*" I can almost see the puzzle pieces lock together in her mind as she glances between Ezra and me. "You must be the Corcoran twins."

It's the same reaction we've been getting all week—like all of a sudden, she knows everything about us. After spending our lives in the orbit of a city where everyone's fighting for recognition, it's weird to be so effortlessly visible. I'm not sure I like it, but I can't argue with the results when she extends her hand toward the applications with a beckoning motion. "I'm Brooke Bennett. We'll be in the same class next week. Let me see what I can do."

CHAPTER FIVE

MALCOLM
SUNDAY, SEPTEMBER 8

"You have four kinds of sparkling water," Mia reports from the depths of our refrigerator. "Not flavors. *Brands.* Perrier, San Pellegrino, LaCroix, and Polar. The last one's a little down-market, so I'm guessing it's a nod to your humble roots. Want one?"

"I want a Coke," I say without much hope. The Nilssons' housekeeper, who does all the grocery shopping, isn't a fan of refined sugar.

It's the Sunday before school starts, and Mia and I are the only ones here. Mom and Peter left for a drive after lunch, and Katrin and her friends are out back-to-school shopping. "I'm afraid that's not an option," Mia says, pulling out two bottles of lemon Polar seltzer and handing one to me. "This refrigerator contains only clear beverages."

"At least it's consistent." I set my bottle down on the kitchen island next to a stack of the college brochures that have started to arrive for Katrin on a daily basis: Brown, Amherst, Georgetown, Cornell. They seem like a stretch for her GPA, but Peter likes people to aim high.

Mia unscrews the cap from her bottle and takes a long swig, making a face. "Ew. This tastes like cleaning solution."

"We could go to your house, you know."

Mia shakes her head so violently that her red-tipped dark hair flies in her face. "No thank you. Tensions are high in the Kwon household, my friend. The Return of Daisy has everyone shook."

"I thought Daisy's coming home was temporary."

"So did we all," Mia says in her narrator voice. "And yet, she remains."

Mia and I are friends partly because, a long time ago, Declan and her sister, Daisy, were. Lacey Kilduff and Daisy Kwon had been best friends since kindergarten, so once Declan and Lacey started dating, I saw almost as much of Daisy as I did of Lacey. Daisy was my first crush; the most beautiful girl I'd ever seen in real life. I could never figure out what Declan saw in Lacey when Daisy was *right there*. Meanwhile, Mia was in love with both Lacey and Declan. We were a couple of awkward preteens trailing around after our golden siblings and their friends, lapping up whatever scraps of attention they'd throw our way.

And then it all imploded.

Lacey died. Declan left, suspected and disgraced. Daisy went to Princeton just like she was supposed to, graduated with honors, and got a great job at a consulting firm in Boston. Then, barely a month after she started, she abruptly quit and moved back home with her parents.

46

Nobody knows why. Not even Mia.

A key jingles in the lock, and loud giggles erupt in the foyer. Katrin comes sweeping into the kitchen with her friends Brooke and Viv, all three of them weighed down by brightly colored shopping bags.

"Hey," she says. She swings her bags onto the kitchen island, almost knocking over Mia's bottle. "Do *not* go to the Bellevue Mall today. It's a zoo. Everybody's buying their homecoming dresses already." She sighs heavily, like she wasn't doing the exact same thing. We all got a "welcome back" email from the principal last night, including a link to a new school app that lets you view your schedule and sign up for stuff online. The homecoming ballot was already posted, where theoretically you can vote anyone from our class onto the court. But in reality, everybody knows four of the six spots are already taken by Katrin, Theo, Brooke, and Kyle.

"Wasn't planning on it," Mia says drily.

Viv smirks at her. "Well, they don't have a Hot Topic, so." Katrin and Brooke giggle, although Brooke looks a little guilty while she does it.

There's a lot about my and Katrin's lives that don't blend well, and our friends top the list. Brooke's all right, I guess, but Viv's the third wheel in their friend trio, and the insecurity makes her bitchy. Or maybe that's just how she is.

Mia leans forward and rests her middle finger on her chin, but before she can speak I grab a bouquet of cellophane-wrapped flowers from the island. "We should go before it starts raining," I say. "Or hailing."

Katrin waggles her brows at the flowers. "Who are *those* for?"

"Mr. Bowman," I say, and her teasing grin drops. Brooke makes a strangled sound, her eyes filling with tears. Even Viv shuts up. Katrin sighs and leans against the counter.

"School's not going to be the same without him," she says.

Mia hops off her stool. "Sucks how people in this town keep getting away with murder, doesn't it?"

Viv snorts, pushing a strand of red hair behind one ear. "A hit-and-run is an *accident.*"

"Not in my book," Mia says. "The hitting part, maybe. Not the running. Mr. Bowman might still be alive if whoever did it stopped to call for help."

Katrin puts an arm around Brooke, who's started to cry, silently. It's been like that all week whenever I run into people from school; they're fine one minute and sobbing the next. Which does kind of bring back memories of Lacey's death. Minus all the news cameras. "How are you getting to the cemetery?" Katrin asks me.

"Mom's car," I say.

"I blocked her in. Just take mine," she says, reaching into her bag for the keys.

Fine by me. Katrin has a BMW X6, which is fun to drive. She doesn't offer it up often, but I jump at the chance when she does. I grab the keys and make a hasty exit before she can change her mind.

"How can you stand living with her?" Mia grumbles as we walk out the front door. Then she turns and walks backward, gazing up at the Nilssons' enormous house. "Well, I guess the perks aren't bad, are they?"

I open the X6's door and slide into the car's buttery leather interior. Sometimes, I still can't believe this is my life. "Could be worse," I say.

It's a quick trip to Echo Ridge Cemetery, and Mia spends most of it flipping rapidly through all of Katrin's preprogrammed radio stations. "Nope. Nope. Nope. Nope," she keeps muttering, right up until we pull through the wrought iron gates.

Echo Ridge has one of those historic cemeteries with graves that date back to the 1600s. The trees surrounding it are ancient, and so huge that their branches act like a canopy above us. Tall, twisting bushes line gravel paths, and the whole space is enclosed within stone walls. The gravestones are all shapes and sizes: tiny stumps barely visible in the grass; tall slabs with names carved across the front in block letters; a few statues of angels or children.

Mr. Bowman's grave is in the newer section. We spot it right away; the grass in front is covered with flowers, stuffed animals, and notes. The simple gray stone is carved with his name, the years of his life, and an inscription:

Tell me and I forget
Teach me and I may remember
Involve me and I learn

I unwrap our bouquet and silently add it to the pile. I thought there'd be something I'd want to say when I got here, but my throat closes as a wave of nausea hits me.

Mom and I were still visiting family in New Hampshire when Mr. Bowman died, so we missed his funeral. Part of me was sorry, but another part was relieved. I haven't been to a funeral since I went to Lacey's five years ago. She was buried in her homecoming dress, and all her friends wore theirs to her funeral, splashes of bright colors in the sea of black. It was hot for October, and I remember sweating in my itchy suit beside my father. The stares and whispers about Declan had already started. My brother stood apart from us, still as a statue, while my father pulled at the collar of his shirt like the scrutiny was choking him.

My parents lasted about six months after Lacey was killed. Things weren't great before then. On the surface their arguments were always about money—utility bills and car repairs and the second job Mom thought Dad should get when they cut his hours at the warehouse. But really, it was about the fact that at some point over the years, they'd stopped liking one another. They never yelled, just walked around with so much simmering resentment that it spread through the entire house like poisonous gas.

At first I was glad when he left. Then, when he moved in with a woman half his age and kept forgetting to send support checks, I got angry. But I couldn't show it, because *angry* had become something people said about Declan in hushed, accusing tones.

Mia's wobbly voice brings me back into the present. "It sucks that you're gone, Mr. Bowman. Thanks for always being so nice and never comparing me to Daisy, unlike every other teacher in the history of the world. Thanks for making science almost interesting. I hope karma smacks whoever did this in the ass and they get exactly what they deserve."

My eyes sting. I blink and look away, catching an unexpected glimpse of red in the distance. I blink again, then squint. "What's that?"

Mia shades her eyes and follows my gaze. "What's what?"

It's impossible to tell from where we're standing. We start picking our way across the grass, through a section of squat, Colonial-era graves carved with winged skulls. *Here lyeth the Body of Mrs. Samuel White* reads the last one we pass. Mia, momentarily distracted, aims a pretend kick at the stone. "She had her own name, asshole," she says. Then we're finally close enough to make out what caught our eye back at Mr. Bowman's grave, and stop in our tracks.

This time, it's not just graffiti. Three dolls hang from the top of a mausoleum, nooses around their necks. They're all wearing crowns and long, glittering dresses drenched in red paint. And just like at the cultural center, red letters drip like blood across the white stone beneath them:

I'M BACK
PICK YOUR QUEEN, ECHO RIDGE
HAPPY HOMECOMING

A garish, red-spattered corsage decorates a grave next to the mausoleum, and my stomach twists when I recognize this section of the cemetery. I stood almost exactly where I'm standing now when Lacey was buried. Mia chokes out a furious gasp as she makes the same connection, and lunges forward like she's about to sweep the bloody-looking corsage off the top of Lacey's grave. I catch her arm before she can.

"Don't. We shouldn't touch anything." And then my disgust takes a brief backseat to another unwelcome thought. "Shit. I have to be the one to report this *again*."

I got lucky last week, sort of. The new girl, Ellery, believed me enough that when we went inside to tell an adult, she didn't mention she'd found me holding the can. But the whispers started buzzing through the cultural center anyway, and they've been following me around ever since. Twice in one week isn't great. Not in line with the *Keep Your Head Down Till You Can Get Out* strategy I've been working on ever since Declan left town.

"Maybe somebody else already has and the police just haven't gotten here yet?" Mia says, looking around. "It's the middle of the day. People are in and out of here all the time."

"You'd think we'd have heard, though." Echo Ridge gossip channels are fast and foolproof. Even Mia and I are in the loop now that Katrin has my cell number.

Mia bites her lip. "We could take off and let somebody else make the call. Except . . . we told Katrin we were coming here, didn't we? So that won't work. It'd actually look worse if you *didn't* say something. Plus it's just . . . mega creepy." She digs the toe of her Doc Marten into the thick, bright-green grass. "I mean, do you think this is a *warning* or something? Like what happened to Lacey is going to happen again?"

"Seems like the impression they're going for." I keep my voice casual while my brain spins, trying to make sense of what's in front of us. Mia pulls out her phone and starts taking pictures, circling the mausoleum so she can capture every angle. She's nearly done when a loud, rustling noise makes us both jump. My heart thuds against my chest until a familiar figure bursts through a pair of bushes near the back of the cemetery. It's Vance Puckett. He lives behind the cemetery and probably cuts through here every day on his way to . . . wherever he goes. I'd say the liquor store, but it's not open on Sunday.

Vance starts weaving down the path toward the main entrance. He's only a few feet away when he finally notices us, flicking a bored glance our way that turns into a startled double take when he sees the mausoleum. He stops so short that he almost falls over. "What the hell?"

Vance Puckett is the only person in Echo Ridge who's had a worse post–high school descent than my brother. He used to run a contracting business until he got sued over faulty wiring in a house that burned down in Solsbury. It's been one long slide into the bottom of a whiskey bottle ever since. There were a rash of petty break-ins in the Nilssons' neighborhood right around the same time that Vance installed a satellite dish on Peter's roof, so everyone assumes he's found a new strategy for paying his bills. He's never been caught at anything, though.

"We just found this," I say. I don't know why I feel the need to explain myself to Vance Puckett, but here we are.

He shuffles closer, his hands jammed into the pockets of his olive-green hunting jacket, and circles the mausoleum, letting out a low whistle when he finishes his examination. He smells faintly of booze like always. "Pretty girls make graves," he says finally. "You know that song?"

"Huh?" I ask, but Mia replies, "The Smiths." You can't stump her on anything music-related.

Vance nods. "Fits this town, doesn't it? Echo Ridge keeps losing its homecoming queens. Or their sisters." His eyes roam across the three dolls. "Somebody got creative."

"It's not *creative,*" Mia says coldly. "It's horrible."

"Never said it wasn't." Vance sniffs loudly and makes a shooing motion with one hand. "Why are you still here? Run along and tell the powers that be."

I don't like getting ordered around by Vance Puckett, but I don't want to stay here, either. "We were just about to."

I start toward Katrin's car with Mia at my side, but Vance's sharp "Hey!" makes us turn. He points toward me with an unsteady finger. "You might want to tell that sister of yours to lie low for a change. Doesn't seem like a great year to be homecoming queen, does it?"

CHAPTER SIX

ELLERY
MONDAY, SEPTEMBER 9

"It's like *Children of the Corn* around here," Ezra mutters, scanning the hallway.

He's not wrong. We've been here only fifteen minutes, but there are already more blond-haired, blue-eyed people than I've ever seen gathered in one place. Even the building Echo Ridge High is housed in has a certain Puritan charm—it's old, with wide pine floors, high arched windows, and dramatic sloped ceilings. We're heading from the guidance counselor's office to our new homeroom, and we might as well be leading a parade for all the stares we're getting. At least I'm in my airplane wardrobe, washed last night in preparation for the first day of school, instead of a Dalton's special.

We pass a bulletin board covered with colorful flyers, and Ezra pauses. "It's not too late to join the 4-H Club," he tells me.

"What's that?"

He peers closer. "Agriculture, I think? There seem to be cows involved."

"No thanks."

He sighs, running his eyes over the rest of the board. "Something tells me they don't have a particularly active LGBTQ-Straight Alliance here. I wonder if there's even another out kid."

Normally I'd say there must be, but Echo Ridge is pretty small. There are less than a hundred kids in our grade, and only a few hundred total in the school.

We turn from the board as a cute Asian girl in a Strokes T-shirt and stack-heeled Doc Martens passes by, her hair buzzed short on one side and streaked red on the other. "Hey, Mia, you forgot to cut the other half!" a boy calls out, making the two football-jacketed boys on either side of him snicker. The girl lifts her middle finger and shoves it in their faces without breaking stride.

Ezra gazes after her with rapt attention. "Hello, new friend."

The crowd in front of us parts suddenly, as three girls stride down the hallway in almost perfect lockstep—one blonde, one brunette, and one redhead. They're so obviously Somebodies at Echo Ridge High that it takes me a second to realize that one of them is Brooke Bennett from the Fright Farm shooting range. She stops short when she sees us and offers a tentative smile.

"Oh, hi. Did Murph ever call you?"

"Yeah, he did," I say. "We have interviews this weekend. Thanks a lot."

The blond girl steps forward with the air of someone who's used to taking charge. She's wearing a sexy-preppy outfit: collared shirt under a tight sweater, plaid miniskirt, and high-heeled booties. "Hi. You're the Corcoran twins, aren't you?"

Ezra and I nod. We've gotten used to our sudden notoriety. Yesterday, while I was grocery shopping with Nana, a cashier I'd never seen before said, "Hello, Nora . . . and Ellery," as we were checking out. Then she asked me questions about California the entire time she was bagging our groceries.

Now, the blond girl tilts her head at us. "We've heard all about you." She stops there, but the tone of her voice says: *And when I say* all, *I mean the one-night-stand father, the failed acting career, the jewelry store accident, the rehab. All of it.* It's kind of impressive, how much subtext she manages to pack into one tiny word. "I'm Katrin Nilsson. I guess you've met Brooke, and this is Viv." She points to the red-haired girl on her left.

I should have known. I've heard the Nilsson name constantly since I got to Echo Ridge, and this girl has *town royalty* written all over her. She's not as pretty as Brooke, but somehow she's much more striking, with crystal-blue eyes that remind me of a Siamese cat's.

We all murmur hellos, and it feels like some sort of uncomfortable audition. Probably because of the assessing look Katrin keeps giving Ezra and me, as though she's weighing whether we're worth her continued time and attention. Most of the hallway is only pretending to be busy with their lockers while they wait for her verdict. Then the bell rings, and she smiles.

"Come find us at lunch. We sit at the back table next to the biggest window." She turns away without waiting for an answer, blond hair sweeping across her shoulders.

Ezra watches them leave with a bemused expression, then

turns to me. "I have a really strong feeling that on Wednesdays, they wear pink."

Ezra and I have most of the same classes that morning, except for right before lunch, when I head to AP calculus and Ezra goes to geometry. Math isn't his strong suit. So I end up going to the cafeteria on my own. I make my way through the food line assuming that he'll join me at any minute, but when I exit with a full tray, he's still nowhere in sight.

I hesitate in front of the rows of rectangular tables, searching the sea of unfamiliar faces, when my name rings out in a clear, commanding voice. "Ellery!" I look up, and spot Katrin with her arm in the air. Her hand makes a beckoning motion.

I'm being summoned.

It feels as though the entire room is watching me make my way to the back of the cafeteria. Probably because they are. There's a giant poster on the wall beside Katrin's window table, which I can read when I'm less than halfway there:

SAVE THE DATE

Homecoming is October 5!!!

Vote now for your King and Queen!

When I reach Katrin and her friends, the redheaded girl, Viv, shifts to make room on the bench. I put my tray down and slide in next to her, across from Katrin.

"Hi," Katrin says, her blue cat's eyes scanning me up and down. If I have to dress in clothes from Dalton's tomorrow, she's definitely going to notice. "Where's your brother?"

"I seem to have misplaced him," I say. "But he always turns up eventually."

"I'll keep an eye out for him," Katrin says. She digs one pale-pink nail into an orange and tears off a chunk of the peel, adding, "So, we're all *super* curious about you guys. We haven't had a new kid since . . ." She scrunches her face. "I don't know. Seventh grade, maybe?"

Viv straightens her shoulders. She's small and sharp-featured, wearing bright-red lipstick that goes surprisingly well with her hair. "Yes. That was me."

"Was it? Oh, right. Such a happy day." Katrin smiles distractedly, still focused on me. "But moving in middle school is one thing. Senior year is rough. Especially when everything is so . . . new. How do you like living with your grandmother?"

At least she didn't ask, like the grocery store cashier yesterday, if I'd left a "Hollywood hottie" behind. The answer to that is no, by the way. I haven't had a date in eight months. Not that I'm counting. "It's all right," I tell Katrin, sliding my eyes toward Brooke. Other than a muted hello when I sat down, she's been totally silent. "A little quiet, though. What do you guys do around here for fun?"

I'm hoping to draw Brooke into the conversation, but it's Katrin who answers. "Well, we're cheerleaders," she says, waving a hand between her and Brooke. "That takes up a lot of time in the fall. And our boyfriends play football." Her eyes drift a few tables away, where a blond boy is setting down his tray. The entire table is a sea of purple-and-white athletic jackets. The boy catches her eye and winks, and Katrin blows him a kiss. "That's my boyfriend, Theo. He and Brooke's boyfriend, Kyle, are co-captains of the team."

Of course they are. She doesn't mention a boyfriend for Viv. I feel a small surge of solidarity—*single girls unite!*—but when

I flash a smile at Viv she meets it with a cool stare. I get the feeling, suddenly, that I've stumbled onto territory she'd rather not share. "That sounds fun," I say limply. I've never been part of the football-and-cheerleading crowd, although I appreciate the athleticism of both.

Viv narrows her eyes. "Echo Ridge might not be Hollywood, but it's not *boring*."

I don't bother correcting Viv that La Puente is twenty-five miles outside Hollywood. Everyone in Echo Ridge just assumes we lived in the middle of a movie set, and nothing I say will convince them otherwise. Besides, that's not our main issue right now. "I didn't say it was," I protest. "I mean, I can tell already there's a lot going on around here."

Viv looks unconvinced, but it's Brooke who finally speaks up. "None of it good," she says flatly. Her eyes are shiny as she turns toward me, and she looks like she's in desperate need of a full night's sleep. "You—your grandmother found Mr. Bowman, didn't she?" I nod, and tears begin to spill down her pale cheeks.

Katrin swallows a piece of orange and pats Brooke's arm. "You have to stop talking about it, Brooke. You keep getting worked up."

Viv heaves a dramatic sigh. "It's been an awful week. First Mr. Bowman, then all that vandalism cropping up around town." Her tone is concerned, but her eyes are almost eager as she adds, "It's going to be our first feature of the year for the school paper. A summary of what's been going on all week, juxtaposed with this year's seniors talking about where they were five years ago. It's the kind of story that might even get picked up by the local news." She looks at me with slightly more warmth. "I should

60

interview you. You found the graffiti at the cultural center, didn't you? You and Malcolm."

"Yeah," I say. "It was awful, but not nearly as awful as the cemetery." That made me sick when I heard about it, especially when I tried to imagine how the Kilduffs must feel.

"The whole thing is *horrible*," Viv agrees, turning toward Katrin and Brooke. "I hope nothing bad happens when you guys are announced next Thursday."

"Announced?" I ask.

"They're going to announce the homecoming court at assembly next Thursday morning," Viv explains, gesturing toward the homecoming poster over Brooke's shoulder. "Everyone's voting between now and then. Did you download the Echo Ridge High app? Homecoming votes are on the main menu."

I shake my head. "No, not yet."

Viv makes a tsking noise. "Better hurry. Voting closes next Wednesday. Although most of the court is already a done deal. Katrin and Brooke are total shoo-ins."

"You might get nominated too, Viv," Katrin says graciously. Even though I just met her, I can tell she doesn't actually believe there's a chance in hell of that happening.

Viv shudders delicately. "No thank you. I don't want to be on the radar of some murderous creep who's decided to strike again."

"Do you really think that's what this is about?" I ask, curious. Viv nods, and I lean forward eagerly. I've been thinking about the vandalism almost nonstop for the past couple of days, and I'm dying to share theories. Even with Viv. "Interesting. Maybe. I mean, it's definitely what the person who's doing it *wants* us to think. And that's disturbing on its own. But I keep wondering—even if you were brazen enough to get away with murder and then brag about doing it again five years later, the MO's are completely different."

Katrin's face is a total blank. "MO?" she asks.

"Modus operandi," I say, warming to the topic. It's one where I'm perfectly confident. "You know, the method somebody uses to commit a crime? Lacey was strangled. That's a very personal and violent way to kill someone, and not likely to be premeditated. But these threats are public, and they require planning. Plus they're much less, well, *direct.* To me, it feels more like a copycat. Which isn't to say that person isn't dangerous. But maybe they're dangerous in a different way."

There's a moment of silence at the table, until Katrin says, "Huh," and bites into an orange slice. She chews carefully, her eyes fixed on a spot somewhere over my shoulder. *There it is,* I think. She just mentally dismissed me from the popular crowd. That didn't take long.

If Ezra's told me once, he's told me a hundred times. *Nobody wants to hear your murder theories, Ellery.* Too bad he bailed on me for lunch.

Then a new expression crosses Katrin's face, one that's sort of irritated and indulgent at the same time. "You're going to get kicked out of school one day for wearing that shirt," she calls to someone.

I turn to see Malcolm Kelly in a faded gray T-shirt with "KCUF" written across the front in block letters. "Hasn't happened yet," he replies. In the bright fluorescent lights of the Echo Ridge High cafeteria, I get a much better look at him than

I did at the cultural center. He's wearing a backward baseball cap over unruly brown hair, framing an angular face and wide-set eyes. They meet mine and flicker with recognition. He waves, and the movement jars his tray enough that he almost drops the whole thing. It's totally awkward and also, weirdly, kind of cute.

"I'm sorry," Viv says as Malcolm turns away, in the least apologetic tone I've ever heard. "But I find it *super sketch* that the first person to see both threats is Declan Kelly's weirdo brother." She shakes her head emphatically. "Uh-uh. Something's off there."

"Oh, Viv," Katrin sighs, like they've had some variation on this conversation at least a dozen times before. "Malcolm's all right. Kind of nerdy, but all right."

"I don't think he's a nerd." Brooke's been quiet for so long that her sudden pronouncement startles everyone. "Maybe he used to be, but he's gotten cute lately. Not as cute as Declan, but still." Then she drops her head again and starts playing listlessly with her spoon, as if contributing to the conversation sapped whatever small reserves of energy she had.

Katrin gives her a speculative look. "Didn't realize you'd noticed, Brooke."

My head swivels, looking for Malcolm, and I spot him sitting with that girl Mia from the hallway, and my brother. I'm not surprised; Ezra has a knack for inserting himself into whatever social group he's decided to join. At least I'll have another lunch option when I don't get invited back to Katrin's table.

Viv snorts. "Cute, my ass," she says flatly. "Declan should be in jail."

"You think he killed Lacey Kilduff?" I ask, and she nods.

Katrin cocks her head, confused. "But weren't you just saying that whoever killed Lacey is leaving those threats around town?" she asks. "Declan lives in another state."

Viv leans an elbow on the table, staring at her friend, eyes wide. "You live with the Kellys and you seriously don't know?"

Katrin frowns. "Know what?"

Viv waits a few beats for maximum impact, then smirks. "Declan Kelly is back in town."

CHAPTER SEVEN

MALCOLM
MONDAY, SEPTEMBER 9

Echo Ridge has one bar, which technically is only half in town because it sits right on the border of neighboring Solsbury. Unlike most Echo Ridge businesses, Bukowski's Tavern has a reputation for leaving people alone. They won't serve minors, but they don't card at the door. So that's where I meet Declan on Monday afternoon, after spending the first day back at school pretending that *yeah, sure, I knew my brother was around.*

Bukowski's doesn't look like it belongs in Echo Ridge. It's small and dark, with a long bar at the front, a few scarred tables scattered around the room, and a dartboard and pool table in the back. The only thing on the walls is a neon Budweiser sign with a flickering *w.* There's nothing cute or quaint about it.

"You couldn't give me a heads-up you were in town?" I ask when I slide into a seat across from Declan. I mean to say it like a joke, but it doesn't come out that way.

"Hello to you too, little brother," Declan says. I saw him less than a week ago, but he looks bigger here than he did in Aunt Lynne's basement apartment. Maybe because Declan was always larger than life in Echo Ridge. Not that the two of us ever hung out at Bukowski's before. Or anywhere, really. Back in grade school, when my dad was trying to make me and football happen, Declan would occasionally deign to play with me. He'd get bored fast, though, and the more I missed, the harder he'd throw. After a while I'd give up trying to catch the ball and just put my hands up to protect my head. *What's your problem?* he'd complain. *I'm not trying to hit you. Trust me, would you?*

He'd say that as if he'd ever done anything to earn it.

"You want something to drink?" Declan asks.

"Coke, I guess."

Declan raises his hand to an elderly waitress in a faded red T-shirt cleaning beer taps behind the bar. "Two Cokes, please," he says when she arrives at our table. She nods without much interest.

I wait until she leaves to ask, "What are you doing here?"

A muscle twitches in Declan's jaw. "You say it like I'm violating some kind of restraining order. It's a free country."

"Yeah, but . . ." I trail off as the waitress returns, placing cocktail napkins and tall glasses of Coke with ice in front of us. My phone exploded during lunch once word got out that Declan was in Echo Ridge. And he *knows* that. He knows exactly the kind of reaction this would get.

Declan leans forward, resting his forearms on the table. They're almost twice the size of mine. He works construction jobs when he's not taking classes, and it keeps him in better shape than football did in high school. He lowers his voice, even though the only other people in Bukowski's are two old guys wearing baseball caps at the end of the bar. "I'm sick of being treated like a criminal, Mal. *I didn't do anything.* Remember?" He rubs a hand over his face. "Or do you not believe that anymore? Did you ever?"

"Of course I did. Do." I stab at the ice in my drink with my straw. "But why now? First Daisy's back and now you. What's going on?"

The ghost of a frown flits across Declan's face when I mention Daisy, so quick I almost miss it. "I'm not *back,* Mal. I still live in New Hampshire. I'm here to see someone, that's all."

"Who? Daisy?"

Declan heaves an exasperated sigh. "Why are you so hung up on Daisy? Do you still have a thing for her?"

"No. I'm just trying to figure this out. I saw you *last week,* and you never said you were coming." Declan shrugs and takes a sip of Coke, avoiding my eyes. "And it's kind of shitty timing, you know. With all the crap going on around town."

"What does that have to do with me?" He breaks into a scowl when I don't respond right away. "Wait. Are you kidding me? People think I had something to do with that? What's next? Am I responsible for global warming now, too? Fucking hell, Mal." One of the old guys at the bar looks over his shoulder, and Declan slumps back against the chair, glowering. "For the record. Just so we're clear. I didn't come here to write creepy-ass slogans on signs and walls or whatever."

"Graves," I correct.

"Whatever," Declan grits out, low and dangerous.

I believe him. There's no possible universe in which my hot-headed, testosterone-fueled brother dresses a trio of dolls up like homecoming queens and ties them to a mausoleum. It's easier to imagine him placing his hands around Lacey's throat and squeezing the life out of her.

Jesus. My hand shakes as I pick up my glass, rattling the ice in it. I can't believe I just thought that. I take a sip and swallow hard. "Then why *did* you come? And how long are you staying?"

Declan drains his Coke and signals for the waitress. "Jack and Coke this time," he says when she arrives.

Her lips thin as she glances between us. "ID first."

Declan reaches for his wallet, then hesitates. "You know what? Forget it. Just another Coke." She shrugs and walks away. Declan shakes his head like he's disgusted with himself. "See what I did there? Decided not to get a drink, even though I wanted one, because I don't feel like showing my name to some woman I don't even know. That's my fucking life."

"Even in New Hampshire?" I ask. One of the old guys at the bar keeps glancing our way. I can't tell whether it's because I'm so obviously underage or . . . because.

"Everywhere," Declan says. He goes silent again as the wait-ress brings a Coke, then raises the glass to me in a toast. "You know, you and Mom have a good thing going here, Mal. Peter likes to pretend I don't exist, but he's solid with you guys. You might even get college out of the deal."

He's right. I might. Which makes me feel guilty, so I say, "Peter says he's talking to Mr. Coates about a job for you." Since Ben Coates was the mayor of Echo Ridge when Lacey died, he got interviewed a few times about what he thought might have happened. *A tragic, random act of violence,* he always said. *Some depraved individual passing through.*

Declan laughs darkly. "I guarantee you that's bullshit."

"No, they got together Labor Day weekend, and—"

"I'm sure they did. And they might even have mentioned me. Probably along the lines of how it'd be career suicide to hire me. It is what it is, Mal, and I won't be a pain in Peter's ass about it. I'm not trying to drive a wedge between him and Mom. Or you. I'll stay out of your way."

"I don't want you to stay out of my way. I just want to know why you're here."

Declan doesn't answer right away. When he does, he sounds less angry and more tired. "You know what happened with me and Lacey, before she died? We outgrew each other. But we didn't know that, because we were a couple of dumb kids who'd been together forever and thought we were supposed to stay that way. If we were regular people, we would've eventually figured out how to break up and that would have been that. We'd have moved on. Wound up with someone else." His voice dips lower. "That's how things should've ended."

The guy at the bar who's been staring at us gets up and starts moving our way. When he's crossed half the room I realize he's not as old as I thought he was: early fifties, maybe, with thick arms and a barrel chest. Declan doesn't turn around, but gets up abruptly and pulls out his wallet. "I gotta go," he says, dropping a ten on the table. "Don't worry, all right? Everything's fine."

He brushes past the guy, who half turns to call after him, "Hey. You Declan Kelly?" Declan continues toward the door, and the guy raises his voice. "*Hey.* I'm talking to you."

Declan grasps the doorknob and leans against the door, shouldering it open. "I'm nobody," he says, and disappears outside.

I'm not sure what the guy's going to do—keep coming toward me, maybe, or follow Declan outside—but he just shrugs and heads for the bar, settling himself back onto his stool. His friend leans toward him, muttering something, and they both laugh.

It hits me, as I finish my Coke in silence, that Declan's life is a lot shittier up close than it seems from a state away.

Half an hour later I'm dragging my ass home, because it didn't occur to my brother before making his dramatic exit to ask if I might need a ride. I'm rounding the bend toward Lacey's old house when I spot someone a few feet ahead of me on the road, wheeling an oversized suitcase behind her.

"Hey," I call when I get close enough to tell who it is. "Leaving town already?"

Ellery Corcoran turns just as her suitcase wheels hit a rock on the ground, almost jerking the luggage out of her hand. She pauses and balances it carefully next to her. While she's waiting for me to catch up, she pulls her hair back and knots it into some kind of twist, so quickly I barely see her hands move. It's kind of mesmerizing. "The airline lost my luggage more than a week ago, and they just delivered it." She rolls her eyes. "To our *neighbors.*"

"That sucks. At least it showed up, though." I gesture to the suitcase. "You need help with that?"

"No thanks. It's easy to roll. And my grandmother's house is right there."

A breeze stirs, sending stray tendrils of hair across Ellery's face. She's so pale, with sharp cheekbones and a stubborn chin, that she'd look severe if it weren't for her eyes. They're inky black, huge and a little bit tilted at the edges, with eyelashes so long they look fake. I don't realize I'm staring until she says, "What?"

I shove my hands into my pockets. "I'm glad I ran into you. I've been meaning to thank you for the other night. At the fundraiser? For not, you know, assuming I was the . . . perpetrator."

A smile tugs at the corners of her mouth. "I don't know a lot of vandals, but I have to imagine most of them don't look quite so horrified by their own handiwork."

"Yeah. Well. It would be easy to assume. Most people here do. And that would've been . . . not great for me."

"Because your brother was a suspect in Lacey's murder," she says. Matter-of-factly, like we're talking about the weather.

"Right." We start walking again, and I have this weird impulse to tell her about my meeting with Declan. I've been out of sorts about it since I left Bukowski's Tavern. But that would be oversharing, to say the least. Instead, I clear my throat and say, "I, um, met your mother. When she came back for Lacey's funeral. She was . . . really nice."

Nice isn't the right word. Sadie Corcoran was like this bolt of energy that swept through town and electrified everybody, even in the middle of mourning. I got the sense that she considered Echo Ridge one big stage, but I didn't mind watching the performance. We all needed the distraction.

Ellery squints into the distance. "It's funny how everyone

71

remembers Sadie here. I'm pretty sure I could visit every town I've ever lived in and nobody would notice."

"I doubt that." I shoot her a sideways glance. "You call your mom by her first name?"

"Yeah. She used to have us pretend she was our older sister when she went on auditions, and it stuck," Ellery says in that same matter-of-fact tone. She shrugs when I raise my brows. "Mothers of preschoolers aren't considered particularly sexy in Hollywood."

An engine roars behind us—faintly at first, then so loud that we both turn. Headlights flash, coming way too fast, and I grab Ellery's arm to yank her out of the road. She loses her grip on the suitcase and yelps as it topples into the path of the oncoming car. Brakes squeal, and the bright-red BMW's wheels stop inches in front of the handle.

The driver's side window lowers, and Katrin pokes her head out. She's in her purple Echo Ridge cheerleading jacket; Brooke is in the passenger seat. Katrin's eyes drop to the suitcase as I grab it off the ground and haul it back to safety. "Are you going somewhere?" she asks.

"Christ, Katrin. You almost ran us over!"

"I did not," she scoffs. She arches a brow as Ellery takes the suitcase handle from me. "Is that yours, Ellery? You're not moving again, are you?"

"No. Long story." Ellery starts rolling the oversized suitcase toward the grassy knoll in front of her grandmother's house. "I'm almost home, so . . . I'll catch you guys later."

"See you tomorrow," I say, as Katrin waves and utters a lazy "Byeeeee." Then she raps her palm against the car door and narrows her eyes at me. "You've been keeping secrets. You didn't tell me Declan was back in town."

"I had no idea until today," I say.

Katrin shoots me a look of pure skepticism. Brooke leans forward in her seat, pulling the sleeves of her purple cheerleading jacket over her hands as if she's cold. Her eyes dart between Katrin and me as Katrin asks, "You expect me to believe that?"

I feel my temper flare. "I don't care if you believe it or not. It's the truth."

My stepsister and my brother have nothing to do with one another. Declan didn't come to our mom's wedding to Peter and doesn't visit. Katrin hasn't mentioned his name once in the entire four months we've been living together.

She looks unconvinced, but jerks her head toward the backseat. "Come on, we'll give you a ride." She turns toward Brooke and adds, just loud enough for me to hear, "You're welcome."

Brooke lets out an irritated little huff. I don't know what that's about, and I'm not tempted to ask. Katrin's in peak pain-in-the-ass mode right now, but I'm tired of walking. I climb into the backseat, and barely have a chance to close the door before Katrin floors the gas again. "So what's Declan doing here, anyway?" she asks.

"I don't know," I say, and then I realize what's been bothering me about my half-hour conversation with Declan ever since I left Bukowski's. It's not just that I didn't know he was here.

It's that he avoided every single one of my questions.

CHAPTER EIGHT

ELLERY

MONDAY, SEPTEMBER 9

As soon as I close the door behind me in Nana's hallway, I drop to my knees beside my suitcase and reach for the zipper. Inside is a jumbled mess of clothes and toiletries, but it's all so beautifully familiar that I gather as much as I can hold in my arms and hug it to my chest for a few seconds.

Nana appears in the doorway between the kitchen and the hall. "I take it everything's there?" she asks.

"Looks like it," I say, holding up my favorite sweater like a trophy.

Nana heads upstairs without another word, and I spy a flash of red against my dark clothes: the small velvet pouch that holds my jewelry. I scatter its contents on the floor, picking a necklace out of the pile. The thin chain holds an intricate silver charm that looks like a flower until you examine it closely enough to realize it's a dagger. "For my favorite murder addict," Sadie said when she gave it to me for my birthday two years ago.

I used to wish she'd ask me why I was so drawn to stuff like that, and then maybe we could have a real conversation about Sarah. But I guess it was easier to just accessorize.

I'm fastening the dagger around my neck when Nana comes down the stairs with a shopping tote dangling from one arm. "You can bring your things upstairs later. I want to make a trip to Dalton's before dinnertime." At my questioning look, she lifts the bag on her arm. "We may as well return the clothes I bought you last week. It hasn't escaped my notice that you've been borrowing from your brother instead of wearing them."

My cheeks heat as I scramble to my feet. "Oh. Well. I just hadn't gotten around to—"

"It's fine," Nana says drily, plucking her keys from a board on the wall. "I harbor no illusions about my familiarity with teen fashion. But there's no reason to let these go to waste when someone else can use them."

I peer hopefully behind her. "Is Ezra coming with us?"

"He's out for a walk. Hurry up, I need to get back and make dinner."

After ten days with my grandmother, there are a few things I know. She'll drive fifteen miles under the speed limit the entire way to Dalton's. We'll get home at least forty minutes before six o'clock, because that's when we eat and Nana doesn't like to rush when she cooks. We'll have a protein, a starch, and a vegetable. And Nana expects us to be in our rooms by ten o'clock. Which we don't protest, since we have nothing better to do.

It's weird. I thought I'd chafe under the structure, but there's something almost soothing about Nana's routine. Especially in contrast to the past six months with Sadie, after she found a doctor who'd keep refilling her Vicodin prescription and went from distracted and disorganized to full-on erratic. I used to wander around our apartment when she stayed out late, eating microwave mac and cheese and wondering what would happen to us if she didn't come home.

And then finally one night, she didn't.

The Subaru crawls to Dalton's, giving me plenty of time to stare out the window at the slender trees lining the road, gold leaves starting to mix with the green. "I didn't know leaves changed color this early," I say. It's September ninth, a week after Labor Day, and the temperature is still warm and almost summery.

"Those are green ash trees," Nana says in her teacher voice. "They change early. We're having good weather for peak foliage this year: warm days and cool nights. You'll see reds and oranges popping up in a few weeks."

Echo Ridge is by far the prettiest place I've ever lived. Nearly every house is spacious and well maintained, with interesting architecture: stately Victorians, gray-shingled Capes, historic Colonials. The lawns are freshly mowed, the flower beds neat and orderly. All the buildings in the town center are red brick and white-windowed, with tasteful signs. There's not a chain-link fence, a dumpster, or a 7-Eleven in sight. Even the gas station is cute and almost retro-looking.

I can see why Sadie felt hemmed in here, though, and why Mia stalks through school like she's searching for an escape hatch. Anything different stands out a mile.

My phone buzzes with a text from Lourdes, checking on the luggage situation. When I update her about my newly recovered suitcase, she texts back so many celebratory GIFs that I almost miss my grandmother's next words. "Your guidance counselor called."

I stiffen in my seat, trying to imagine what I could've done wrong on the first day of school when Nana adds, "She's been reviewing your transcript and says your grades are excellent, but that there's no record of you taking the SATs."

"Oh. Well. That's because I didn't."

"You'll need to take them this fall, then. Have you prepped?"

"No. I didn't think . . . I mean . . ." I trail off. Sadie doesn't have a college degree. She's gotten by on a small inheritance from our grandfather, plus temp work and the occasional acting job. While she's never discouraged Ezra and me from applying to college, she's always made it clear that we'd be on our own if we did. Last year I took one look at tuition for the school closest to home, and immediately bounced off their website. I might as well plan a trip to Mars. "I'm not sure I'm going to college."

Nana brakes well in advance of a stop sign, then inches toward the white line. "No? And here I thought you were a future lawyer."

Her eyes are fixed firmly on the road, so she doesn't catch my startled look. Somehow, she managed to land on my one and only career interest—the one I stopped mentioning at home because Sadie would groan *ugh, lawyers* every time I did. "Why would you think that?"

"Well, you're interested in criminal justice, aren't you? You're analytical and well spoken. Seems like a good fit." Something light and warm starts spreading through my chest, then stops when I glance down at the wallet sticking out of my messenger bag. Empty, just like my bank account. When I don't answer right away, Nana adds, "I'll help you and your brother out, of course. With tuition. As long as you keep your grades up."

"You *will*?" I turn and stare at her, the spark of warmth returning and zipping through my veins.

"Yes. I mentioned it to your mother a few months ago, but—well, she wasn't in the best frame of mind at the time."

"No. She wasn't." My mood deflates, but only for a second. "You'd really do that? You can, um, afford it?" Nana's house is nice and all, but it's not exactly a mansion. And she clips coupons, although I have the feeling it's more of a game with her than a necessity. She was really pleased with herself over the weekend when she scored six free rolls of paper towels.

"State school," she says crisply. "But you have to take the SATs first. And you need time to prepare, so you should probably sign up for the December session."

"All right." My head's in a whirl, and it takes a minute for me to finish the sentence properly. "Thank you, Nana. That's seriously awesome of you."

"Well. It would be nice to have another college graduate in the family."

I tug at the silver dagger around my neck. I feel . . . not *close* to my grandmother, exactly, but like maybe she won't shoot me down if I ask the question I've been holding in since I arrived in Echo Ridge. "Nana," I say abruptly, before I lose my nerve. "What was Sarah like?"

I can feel my aunt's absence in this town, even more than

my mother's. When Ezra and I are out running errands with Nana, people have no problem talking to us as though they've known us their entire lives. Everyone skirts around Sadie's rehab, but they have plenty of other things to say; they'll quote her *Defender* line, joke about how Sadie must not miss Vermont winters, or marvel at how similar my hair is to hers. But they never mention Sarah—not a memory, an anecdote, or even an acknowledgment. Every once in a while I think I see the flicker of an impulse, but they always pause or look away before changing the subject.

Nana is silent for so long that I wish I'd kept my mouth shut. Maybe we can both spend the next four months pretending I did. But when she finally speaks, her tone is calm and even. "Why do you ask?"

"Sa—my mom doesn't talk about her." Nana's never said anything when we call our mother by her first name, but I can tell she doesn't like it. Now isn't the time to annoy her. "I've always wondered."

A light rain starts to fall, and Nana switches on windshield wipers that squeak with every pass. "Sarah was my thinker," she says finally. "She read constantly, and questioned everything. People thought she was quiet, but she had the sort of dry humor that snuck up on you. She loved Rob Reiner movies—you know, *Spinal Tap, The Princess Bride*?" I nod, even though I've never seen the first one. I make a mental note to look it up on Netflix when we get home. "Sarah could quote them all by heart. Very smart girl, especially in math and science. She liked astronomy and used to talk about working for NASA when she grew up."

I absorb the words like a thirsty sponge, amazed that Nana

told me so much in one fell swoop. And all I had to do was *ask*. What a concept. "Did she and my mom get along?" I ask. They sound so different, even more so than I'd imagined.

"Oh yes. Thick as thieves. Finished each other's sentences, like you and your brother do. They were very distinct personalities, but could mimic one another like you wouldn't believe. Used to fool people all the time."

"Airport Andy would be jealous," I say, before forgetting that I never told Nana the absorbed-twin story.

Nana frowns. "What?"

"Nothing. Just a joke." I swallow the small lump that's formed in my throat. "Sarah sounds great."

"She was marvelous." There's a warmth to Nana's voice I've never heard before, not even when she talks about her former students. *Definitely* not when she talks about my mother. Maybe that was another thing about Echo Ridge that Sadie couldn't stand.

"Do you think— Could she still . . . be somewhere?" I fumble over the words, my fingers twisting the chain at my neck. "I mean, like she ran away or something?" I regret it as soon as I say it, like I'm accusing Nana of something, but she just shakes her head decisively.

"Sarah would never." Her voice drops a little, like the words hold too much weight.

"I wish I could have met her."

Nana pulls into a parking spot in front of Dalton's and shifts the Subaru into park. "So do I." I sneak a glance at her, afraid I'll see tears, but her eyes are dry and her face relaxed. She doesn't seem to mind talking about Sarah at all. Maybe she's been waiting for someone to ask. "Could you grab the bag from the backseat please, Ellery?"

"Okay," I say. My thoughts are a tangled whirl, and I nearly drop the plastic bag into the rain-soaked gutter next to the sidewalk when I get out of the car. I wrap the bag's handles around my wrist to keep it secure, and follow Nana inside Dalton's Emporium.

The cashier greets Nana like an old friend, and graciously takes the pile of clothes without asking the reason for the return. She's scanning tags I never removed when a high, sweet voice floats through the store. "I want to see myself in the big window, Mommy!" Seconds later a girl in a gauzy blue dress appears, and I recognize Melanie Kilduff's daughter. It's the little one, about six years old, and she stops short when she sees us.

"Hello, Julia," Nana says. "You look very nice."

Julia catches the hem of her dress in one hand and fans it out. She's like a tiny version of Melanie, right down to the gap between her front teeth. "It's for my dance recital."

Melanie appears behind her, trailed by a pretty preteen with crossed arms and a sulky expression. "Oh, hi," Melanie says with a rueful smile as Julia runs for a raised dais surrounded by mirrors near the front of the store. "Julia wants to see herself *onstage,* as she calls it."

"Well, of course she does," the clerk says indulgently. "That dress was made to be seen." A phone rings behind her, and she disappears into a back room to answer it. Nana lifts her purse off the counter as Julia hops onto the dais and spins, the dress's skirt floating around her.

"I look like a princess!" she crows. "Come look, Caroline!"

Melanie follows and fusses with the bow on the back of the dress, but the older daughter hangs behind, her mouth pulling downward.

"A princess," she mutters under her breath, staring at the rack of homecoming dresses to our right. "What a stupid thing to want to be."

Maybe Caroline isn't thinking about Lacey, or the dolls at the cemetery with their red-spattered gowns. Maybe she's just being a moody almost teenager, annoyed at getting dragged along for her little sister's shopping expedition. Or maybe it's more than that.

As Julia twirls again, a bolt of hot, white anger pulses through me. It's not a normal reaction to such an innocent moment—but the common thread running through this store isn't normal, either. We've all lost our version of a princess, and none of us know why. I'm sick of being tangled up in Echo Ridge's secrets, and of the questions that never end. I want answers. I want to help this little girl and her sister, and Melanie, and Nana. And my mother.

I want to do *something*. For the missing girls, and the ones left behind.

CHAPTER NINE

MALCOLM
THURSDAY, SEPTEMBER 19

"What's up, loser?" I tense a split second before Kyle McNulty's shoulder rams into mine, so I stumble but don't crash against the locker bay. "Your dickhead brother still in town?"

"Fuck you, McNulty." It's my standard response to Kyle, no matter the situation, and it's never not applicable.

Kyle's jaw twitches as Theo smirks beside him. I used to play football with both of them in elementary school, back when my father was still hoping I'd turn into Declan 2.0. We weren't friends then, but we didn't actively hate one another. That started in middle school. "He'd better stay the hell away from my sister," Kyle spits.

"Declan couldn't care less about your sister," I say. It's true, and ninety percent of the reason Kyle can't stand me. He scowls, edging closer, and I curl my right hand into a fist.

"Malcolm, hey." A voice sounds behind me as a hand tugs

at my sleeve. I turn to see Ellery leaning against a locker, her head tilted, holding one of those Echo Ridge High *Month-at-a-Glance* calendars that most people recycle instantly. Her expression is preoccupied, and I'd almost believe she didn't notice she was interrupting a near fight if her eyes didn't linger on Kyle a few seconds too long. "Do you mind showing me where the auditorium is? I know we have assembly now, but I can't remember where to go."

"I can give you a hint," Kyle sneers. "Away from this loser."

I flush with anger, but Ellery just gives him a distracted nod. "Oh, hi, Kyle. Did you know your zipper's down?"

Kyle's eyes drop automatically to his pants. "No it's not," he complains, adjusting it anyway as Theo snorts out a laugh.

"Move along, boys." Coach Gagnon comes up behind us, clapping Kyle and Theo on the shoulder. "You don't want to be late for assembly." First period is canceled today, so the entire school can be herded into the auditorium for rah-rah speeches about football season and the homecoming court announcements. In other words, it's the Kyle-and-Theo Show.

They follow Coach Gagnon down the hall. I turn toward Ellery, who's absorbed in her calendar again. I'm both impressed that she stopped Kyle in his tracks so easily and embarrassed that she thought she had to. Her eyes flick up, such a deep brown they're almost black, framed by thick lashes. When a pink tinge works its way into her cheeks, I realize I'm staring. Again. "You didn't need to do that," I say. "I can handle those guys."

God, I sound like some puffed-up little kid trying to act tough. Kyle's right. I *am* a loser.

Ellery does me the favor of acting like she didn't hear. "Every time I see Kyle, he's being an ass to someone," she says, stuffing the calendar into her bag and hoisting it higher over her shoulder. "I don't understand why he's such a big deal around here. What does Brooke even see in him?"

It's an obvious change of subject, but a fair question. "Hell if I know."

We enter the stream of students heading down the hallway toward the auditorium. "What was he saying about his sister?" Ellery asks. "Does she go here?"

"No, she's older. Liz was in Declan's class. They went out for, like, three months when they were sophomores, and she was kind of obsessed with him. He broke up with her for Lacey."

"Ah." Ellery nods. "I'm guessing she didn't take that well?"

"That's an understatement." We push through the auditorium's double doors, and I lead Ellery toward the farthest corner of the stands, where Mia and I always sit. Ellery and Ezra have been eating lunch with us since last week, and we've been doing the standard getting-to-know-you stuff: talking about music, movies, and the differences between California and Vermont. This is the first time I've been alone with Ellery since I saw her with her suitcase—and just like then, we've skipped past being polite and gone straight for the dark stuff. I'm not sure why, but I tell her, "Liz stopped going to school for a while, and ended up having to repeat. It took her two extra years to graduate."

Ellery's eyes widen. "Wow, seriously? Just because a guy broke up with her?"

I drop into a seat at the top of the bleachers. Ellery settles in beside me, lifting her bag over her head and placing it at her feet. Her hair is a lot more under control now than it was the

85

first time I met her. I kind of miss the old look. "Well, she wasn't great at school to start with," I say. "But the McNultys blamed Declan. So Kyle hates me by association."

Ellery gazes up at the rafters. They're filled with banners from Echo Ridge sports teams throughout the years: a couple dozen in football, basketball, and hockey. For such a small school, Echo Ridge brings home a lot of championships. "That's not fair. You shouldn't be blamed for whatever's going on with your brother."

I have the feeling we're not talking about Liz McNulty anymore. "Welcome to life in a small town. You're only as good as the best thing your family's done. Or the worst."

"Or the worst thing that's been done *to* them," Ellery says in a musing way.

It hits me, then, why talking to her feels so familiar sometimes: because we're two sides of the same coin. Both of us are stuck in one of Echo Ridge's unsolved mysteries, except her family lost a victim and mine has a suspect. I should say something comforting about her aunt, or at least acknowledge that I know what she's talking about. But I'm still trying to figure out the right words when a loud "Heyyyy!" rings out from our right.

Mia clomps toward us with Ezra in tow. They're both wearing black-and-white Fright Farm staff T-shirts, and when I raise my brows at them Mia crosses her arms defensively over her chest. "We didn't plan this," she says, dropping onto the bench beside me. "Purely a coincidence."

"Mind meld," Ezra says with a shrug.

I forgot the twins started working at Fright Farm this week. Half the school does; I'm one of the few kids at Echo Ridge High who's never even applied there. Even if it hadn't scared the crap out of me when I was younger, there's too much of a connection to Lacey. "How's that going?" I ask, turning toward Ellery.

"Not bad," she says. "We're checking wristbands at the House of Horrors."

"Primo job," Mia says enviously. "Brooke hooked you guys up. *So* much better than serving slushies to toddlers." Mia's not a fan of anyone under the age of twelve, but she's been stuck working in the kids' section of Fright Farm since her first season. Every time she angles for a transfer, her boss shuts her down.

Mia sighs and props her chin in her hands. "Well, here we go. At long last, the mystery of who's going to come in a distant third for homecoming queen will be answered." The bleacher rows closer to the floor start filling up, and Coach Gagnon heads toward the podium at the front of the room.

"Viv Cantrell?" Ezra guesses. "She's been posting pictures of her dress on Instagram."

Mia makes a face at him. "You follow Viv on Instagram?"

He shrugs. "You know how it is. She followed me, I followed back in a moment of weakness. She posts about homecoming a *lot*." His expression turns thoughtful. "Although, I don't think she has a date yet."

"You should unfollow," Mia advises. "That's way more information about Viv than any one person needs to have. Anyway, she doesn't have a shot at homecoming court. Maybe Kristi Kapoor, though." At Ezra's questioning glance, she adds, "She's on student council, and people like her. Plus she's one of, like, three other students of color in our class, so everybody can feel progressive when they vote for her."

"Who are the others?" Ezra asks.

"Besides me? Jen Bishop and Troy Latkins," Mia says, then glances between him and Ellery. "And maybe you guys? Are you Latinx?"

Ezra shrugs. "Could be. We don't know our dad. But Sadie did say his name was either José or Jorge, so chances are good."

"Your mom is legendary," Mia says admiringly. "She was homecoming queen too, wasn't she?"

Ezra nods as I blink at Mia. "How would you even know that?" I ask.

Mia shrugs. "Daisy. She's super into Echo Ridge homecoming history. Maybe because she was runner-up." At Ellery's curious look she adds, "My sister. Graduated five years ago. Always the bridesmaid and never the bride, if by bride you mean homecoming queen."

Ellery leans forward, looking interested. "Was she jealous?"

"If she was, you'd never know," Mia says. "Daisy is sugar and spice and everything nice. The perfect Korean daughter. Until recently."

The podium microphone screeches as Coach Gagnon taps on it. "Is this thing on?" he yells. Half the room laughs dutifully and the other half ignores him. I join the second group and tune him out, surreptitiously pulling out my phone. I haven't heard from Declan since I met him at Bukowski's Tavern. *You still around?* I text.

Delivered. Read. No response. Same story all week.

"Good morning, Echo Ridge High! Are you ready to meet your court?" I look up at the change in voice, and suppress a groan at the sight of Percy Gilpin at the podium. Percy is senior class president, and everything about him makes me tired:

his energy, his springy hair, his relentless pursuit of Echo Ridge High elective offices, and the purple blazer he's worn to every school event since we were freshmen. He's also friendly with Viv Cantrell, which is probably all that anybody needs to know about him.

"Let's kick things off with the gentlemen!" Percy rips open an envelope with a flourish, like he's about to announce an Oscar winner. "You'll be choosing your king from one of these three fine fellows. Congratulations to Theo Coolidge, Kyle McNulty, and Troy Latkins!"

Ezra watches, perplexed, as Percy raises his arms amid hoots and cheers. "What is *with* that guy? He's like one of those old-school game show hosts in a teenager's body."

"You nailed it." Mia yawns and twirls her thumb ring. "That went exactly as expected. Good for Troy, I guess. He's not a total dick. Won't win, though."

Percy lets the backslapping and high fives subside, then opens another envelope. "And now it's time for the ladies, who may be last but are definitely not least. Echo Ridge High, let's give it up for Katrin Nilsson, Brooke Bennett, and—"

He pauses, looks up, and looks down at the paper in his hand again. "Um." Another beat passes, and people start shifting in their seats. A few clap and whistle, like they think maybe he's done. Percy clears his throat too close to the microphone, and the resulting screech of feedback makes everyone wince.

Mia leans forward, her face scrunched in confusion. "Wait. Is Percy Gilpin *speechless*? That's a beautiful but unprecedented sight."

Percy turns toward Coach Gagnon, who gestures impatiently

at him to go on. "Sorry," Percy says, clearing his throat again. "Lost my place for a second. Um, so, congratulations to Ellery Corcoran!"

Ellery goes still, her eyes round with shock. "What the hell?" she says, her cheeks staining red as scattered applause ripples through the auditorium. "How did that happen? It doesn't make sense. Nobody here even knows me!"

"Sure they do," Mia says, just as somebody yells out, "Who?" to muted laughter. Mia's right, though; everybody knows who the Corcoran twins are. Not because they're high profile at school, but because Sadie Corcoran, who *almost* made it in Hollywood, is larger than life around here.

And because Sarah Corcoran is Echo Ridge's original lost girl.

"High five, princess!" Ezra says. When Ellery doesn't respond, he lifts her hand and slaps it against his own. "Don't look so glum. This is a nice thing."

"It doesn't make sense," Ellery repeats. Percy is still at the podium, talking about next week's pep rally, and the attention of the room has already started to wander. "I mean, did *you* vote for me?"

"No," Ezra says. "But don't take it personally. I didn't vote for anyone."

"Did you guys?" Ellery asks, looking at Mia and me.

"No," we both say, and I shrug apologetically. "Nonvoters over here, too."

Ellery twists her hair over one shoulder. "I've been at school less than two weeks. I've hardly talked to anybody except you three. If you guys didn't vote for me—and believe me, I'm not insulted, because I didn't vote either—then why would anyone else?"

"To welcome you to town?" I say half-heartedly.

She rolls her eyes, and I can't blame her. Even after less than two weeks here, she has to know Echo Ridge High isn't that kind of place.

Katrin's in a mood Friday morning.

Her driving is worse than ever—stop signs optional, the entire way to school. When we arrive she parks crookedly between two spots, crowding out another kid who was headed our way. He honks as she flounces out of the car, slamming her door and taking off for the entrance without a backward look.

It's one of those days when she's pretending I don't exist.

I take my time entering the building and as soon as I get to the hallway, I know something's off. There's a weird buzzing energy, and the snippets of conversation I catch don't sound like the usual gossip and insults.

"Must have broken in—"

"Somebody hates them—"

"Maybe it's not a joke after all—"

"It's not like anybody did that to Lacey, though—"

Everyone's grouped in clusters, heads bent together. The biggest crowd of people is around Katrin's locker. There's a smaller knot around Brooke's. My stomach starts to twist, and I spot Ezra and Ellery standing next to hers. Ellery's back is to me, but Ezra is turned my way, and his face stops me in my tracks. His laid-back, California-guy vibe is gone, and he looks like he wants to stab somebody.

When I get closer, I see why.

Ellery's dingy gray locker is splashed with bright-red paint.

A red-spattered, twisted doll dangles from the handle, just like the ones in the cemetery. I crane my neck to look down the hallway, and see enough to know Katrin's and Brooke's lockers got the same treatment. Thick black letters are scrawled across the red on Ellery's:

REMEMBER MURDERLAND, PRINCESS?
I DO

Ezra catches my eye. "This is messed up," he seethes as Ellery turns. Her face is composed but pale, a humorless smile at the corners of her mouth.

"So much for welcoming me to town," she says.

CHAPTER TEN

"What are we looking for?" Ezra asks.

"I don't know," I admit, placing a stack of yearbooks on the desk in front of him. We're at the Echo Ridge library on Saturday morning, armed with jumbo cups of take-out coffee from Bartley's diner. I wasn't sure we'd get them past the librarian, but she's well into her eighties and asleep in her chair. "Anything weird, I guess."

Ezra snorts. "El, we've been here three weeks. So far we've reported a dead body, gotten jobs at a murder site, and been targeted by a homecoming stalker. Although that last one was all you." He takes a sip of coffee. "You're gonna have to be more specific."

I drop into a seat across from him and slide a book from the middle of the pile. It has *Echo Ridge Eagles* on its spine, date-stamped from six years ago. Lacey's junior year, one year before she died. "I want to check out Lacey's class. It's strange, isn't it, how these people who were part of her inner circle when she died are suddenly back in town? Right when all this other stuff starts happening?"

"What, you think Malcolm's brother had something to do with that? Or Mia's sister?" Ezra raises a brow. "Maybe we should've invited them along for coffee and crime solving."

"You know what you always say, Ezra," I say, opening the yearbook. "Nobody wants to hear my murder theories. Especially when it involves their siblings. That's the kind of thing you need to ease into."

We're snarking, because that's what we do. A lifetime of living with Sadie provided a master class in pretending everything's fine. But I've barely eaten since yesterday and even Ezra—who usually inhales Nana's cooking like he's trying to make up for seventeen years of frozen dinners—refused breakfast before we left.

Now, he runs his eyes over the remaining yearbooks. "What should I do? Look at their senior year?" He sucks in his cheeks. "It's probably pretty grim. *In memoriam* for Lacey, that kind of thing."

"Sure. That or . . ." My eyes drop to the bottom of the pile. "Sadie's yearbook is in there, too. If you're curious."

Ezra stills. "About what?"

"What she was like in high school. What *they* were like. Her and Sarah."

His jaw ticks. "What does that have to do with anything?"

I lean forward and glance around the small room. Besides

the sleeping librarian, there's no one here except a mother reading quietly to her toddler. "Haven't you ever wondered why we've never been to Echo Ridge before? Like, ever? Or why Sadie never talks about her sister? I mean, if *you* suddenly . . . disappeared"—I swallow hard against the bile in my throat— "I wouldn't move across the country and act like you'd never existed."

"You don't know what you'd do," Ezra objects. "You don't know what Sadie's really thinking."

"No, I don't. And neither do you. That's my *point*." The little boy's mother turns our way, and I lower my voice. I reach up and squeeze the dagger on my necklace. "We never have. We just got jerked from one town to the next while Sadie ran away from her problems. Except she finally landed in trouble she can't make disappear, and here we are. Back where it all started."

Ezra regards me steadily, his dark eyes somber. "We can't fix her, El."

I flush and look down at the pages in front of me—rows and rows of kids our age, all smiling for the camera. Ezra and I don't have any yearbooks; we've never felt connected enough to any of our schools to bother with a keepsake. "I'm not trying to *fix* her. I just want to understand. Plus, Sarah's part of this, somehow. She has to be." I rest my chin in my hands and say what I've been thinking since yesterday. "Ezra, nobody in that school voted me onto homecoming court. You know they didn't. Someone rigged the votes, I'm sure of it. Because I'm connected to Sarah."

My locker was cleaned and repainted by lunchtime on Friday, like nothing ever happened. But I've felt exposed ever since, the back of my neck prickling when I think about the fact that someone, somewhere went to a lot of trouble to add my name to that court. I told Viv that I didn't think the vandal and Lacey's murderer are the same person, and objectively, that still makes sense. Subjectively, though, the whole thing makes me sick.

Ezra looks dubious. "How does somebody rig votes?"

"By hacking the app. It wouldn't be hard."

He cocks his head, considering. "That seems extreme."

"Oh, and bloody Barbie dolls are restrained?"

"Touché." Ezra drums his fingers on the table. "So what, then? You think Lacey and Sarah are connected, too?"

"I don't know. It seems unlikely, doesn't it? They happened almost twenty years apart. But somebody's threading all these things together, and there has to be a reason why."

Ezra doesn't say anything else, but takes Sadie's yearbook from the bottom of the pile and opens it. I pull Lacey's closer to me and flip through the junior class pictures until I reach the Ks. They're all there, the names I've been hearing since I got to Echo Ridge: Declan Kelly, Lacey Kilduff, and Daisy Kwon.

I've seen Lacey before in news stories, but not Daisy. She shares a few features with Mia, but she's much more conventionally pretty. Preppy, even, with a headband holding back her shiny, pin-straight hair. Declan Kelly reminds me of Malcolm on steroids; he's almost aggressively handsome, with piercing, dark-fringed eyes and a cleft in his chin. All three of them look like the kind of teenagers you'd find on a CW show—too beautiful to be real.

The *R* section is a lot less glam. Officer Ryan Rodriguez's high-school-junior self is an unfortunate combination of prominent Adam's apple, acne, and bad haircut. He's improved since then, though, so good for him. I turn the yearbook around to show Ezra. "Here's our neighbor."

Ezra glances at Officer Rodriguez's photo without much interest. "Nana mentioned him this morning. She's got some cardboard boxes she wants us to bring over. She says he sold the house? Or he's going to sell the house. Anyway, he's packing stuff up."

I straighten in my chair. "He's leaving town?"

He shrugs. "She didn't say that. Just that the house was too big for one person, now that his dad's dead. Maybe he's getting an apartment nearby or something."

I turn the yearbook back toward me and flip the page. The club and candid photo section comes after class pictures. Lacey was part of almost everything—soccer, tennis, student council, and choir, to name just a few. Declan mostly played football, it looks like, and was a good-enough quarterback that the team won a state championship that year. The last photo in the junior section is of the entire class, posing in front of Echo Ridge Lake during their year-end picnic.

I pick Lacey out right away—she's dead center, laughing, her hair blowing in the wind. Declan's behind her with his arms wrapped around her waist, his head tucked into her shoulder. Daisy stands beside them looking startled, as though she wasn't ready for the shot. And on the far edge of the group is gangly Ryan Rodriguez, standing stiffly apart from everyone else. It's not his awkward pose that catches my eye, though. The camera caught him staring straight at Lacey—with an expression of such intense longing that he almost looks angry.

He probably had a crush, Sadie said. *Lacey was a beauty.*

I study the three faces: Declan, Daisy, and Ryan. One who never left—until now, maybe—and two who returned. Malcolm doesn't know where Declan is staying, but Mia's mentioned more than once that her sister is back in her old room. What had Mia said about Daisy during Thursday's assembly, again? *Always a bridesmaid, never a bride.*

Ezra spins the yearbook he's been studying around so that it's facing me, and slides it across the table. "Is this what you wanted to see?"

A girl with a cloud of curly dark hair is at the top of the page, her smile so bright it's almost blinding. My mother, twenty-three years ago. Except the name under the picture reads *Sarah Corcoran.* I blink at it a couple of times; in my mind, Sarah's always been the serious, almost somber twin. I don't recognize this version. I flip to the previous page and see Sadie's picture at the bottom. It's identical, right down to the head tilt and the smile. The only difference is the color of their sweaters.

The pictures were taken their senior year, probably in September. A few weeks later, shortly after Sadie was crowned homecoming queen, Sarah was gone.

I close the book as a wave of exhaustion hits me. "I don't know," I admit, stretching and turning toward a row of tiny windows on the far wall that sends squares of sunlight across the hardwood floor. "When do we have to be at work, again?"

Ezra glances at his phone. "In about an hour."

"Should we stop by Mia's and see if she's working today?"

"She's not," Ezra says.

"Should we stop by Mia's and see if she's working today?" I repeat.

Ezra blinks in confusion, then shakes his head like he's just waking up. "Oh, sorry. Are you suggesting a reconnaissance mission?"

"I wouldn't mind meeting the mysterious Daisy," I tell him.

"Roger that," Ezra says. He gestures to the stack of yearbooks between us. "Are you gonna check any of these out?"

"No, I'm just— Hang on." I pull out my phone and snap a few photos of the yearbook pictures we've just been looking at. Ezra watches me with a bemused expression.

"What are you going to do with those?" he asks.

"Documenting our research," I say. I don't know if this morning will turn out to be worth anything, but at least it *feels* productive.

When I finish, we each take an armful of yearbooks and return them to the Reference section. I throw our empty coffee cups into a recycling bin, which makes a much louder noise than I expected. The sleeping librarian startles and blinks at us with watery, unfocused eyes as we pass her desk.

"Can I help you?" she yawns, feeling around for the glasses looped on a chain around her neck.

"No thanks, all set," I say, nudging Ezra to walk faster so we can exit before she recognizes us and we have to spend fifteen minutes making polite conversation about California. We push through the library's front door into bright sunshine, and descend wide steps to the sidewalk.

Ezra and I walked home from school with Mia a couple of days ago, and she's only a block from the library. The Kwons' house is unusual for Echo Ridge: a modern, boxy construction set on a large expanse of lawn. A stone path connects from the sidewalk to the front stairs, and we're halfway across it when a gray Nissan pulls into the driveway.

The driver's side window is half down, framing a girl with long dark hair who's gripping the steering wheel like it's a life preserver. Oversized sunglasses cover half her face, but I can see enough to tell that it's Daisy. Ezra raises his hand, about to call a greeting, then lowers it as Daisy lifts a phone to her ear.

"I don't think she sees us," I say, glancing between the car and the front door. "Maybe we should just ring the bell."

Before we can move, Daisy drops her phone, crosses her arms over the steering wheel, and lowers her head onto them. Her shoulders start to shake, and Ezra and I exchange uneasy glances. We stand there for what feels like ten minutes, although it's probably less than one, before Ezra take a tentative step forward. "Do you think we should, um . . ."

He trails off as Daisy suddenly raises her head with a strangled little scream and slams her hands, hard, on either side of the steering wheel. She whips off her sunglasses and runs her hands over her eyes like she's trying to erase any trace of tears, then shoves the glasses back on. She throws the car into reverse and starts to back up, stopping when she looks out the window and catches sight of us.

Ezra offers the sheepish half wave of someone who knows he just accidentally observed a private moment. Daisy's only indication that she sees him is to roll up her window before she backs out of the driveway and leaves in the direction she came from.

"Well, you wanted to meet the mysterious Daisy," Ezra says, watching her taillights disappear around a bend. "There she goes."

CHAPTER ELEVEN

MALCOLM
THURSDAY, SEPTEMBER 26

When I poke my head into Mia's room, she's wedged in against a small mountain of pillows on her bed, her MacBook propped on her lap. She has her earbuds in, nodding along to whatever's playing, and I have to rap on the door twice before she hears me. "Hey," she says too loudly before unplugging. "Practice over already?"

"It's past four." My one and only activity at Echo Ridge High—which is one more than Mia's ever signed up for—is band. Mr. Bowman got me into it in ninth grade when he suggested I take drum lessons, and I've been doing it ever since.

It's not the same without him. The woman who took over isn't half as funny as he was, and she's got us doing the same old crap from last year. I'm not sure I'll stick it out. But tomorrow night we're playing at a pep rally, and I have a solo that nobody else knows.

Mia stretches her arms over her head. "I didn't notice. I was just about to text you, though." She shuts her laptop and puts it aside, swinging her legs off the bed and onto the floor. "Freaking Viv's most cherished dream has come true. The *Burlington Free Press* picked up her story about the vandalism, and now they're covering it along with a five-year anniversary piece on Lacey. A reporter called a little while ago, trying to get hold of Daisy."

My stomach flops like a dying fish. "Shit."

I shouldn't be surprised. The Homecoming Stalker—so named by the *Echo Ridge Eagle* student newspaper—has been busy. He, or she, left a bloody mess of raw meat on the hood of Brooke's car Monday, which made her gag when she saw it. Ellery got off comparatively easy a day later, with a spray paint job on the side of Armstrong's Auto Repair that reads CORCO-RANS MAKE KILLER QUEENS.

Yesterday was Katrin's turn. On the street where Mr. Bowman died, in the corner that's turned into a makeshift memorial with flowers and stuffed animals, someone added an oversized print of Katrin's class picture with the eyes gouged out and an RIP date of October 5—next weekend's homecoming dance. When Peter found out about it, he got as close to losing his shit as I've ever seen him. He wanted homecoming canceled, and Katrin barely talked him out of calling Principal Slate. This morning, we got a homeroom announcement reminding us to report anything suspicious to a teacher. But so far, homecoming is still on.

Mia grabs a black studded sweatshirt from the back of her desk chair. "You didn't hear anything from Declan about it? I figured the reporter must have tried to reach him, too."

"No." Declan finally answered my texts over the weekend to tell me he was back in New Hampshire. Other than that, we haven't spoken since we met in Bukowski's Tavern. I still don't know what he was doing here, or where he was staying.

"Daisy's been holed up in her room ever since the call came in," Mia says, yanking the sweatshirt over her head. The fabric muffles her voice as she adds, "Not that there's anything unusual about *that*."

"You still want to go to Bartley's for dinner?" I ask. Dr. and Mr. Kwon both work late on Thursdays, and Peter and my mother have *date night,* so Mia and I are heading for Echo Ridge's only restaurant. "I have Mom's car, so we don't have to walk."

"Yeah, definitely. I need to get out of this house. Also, I invited the twins, so they're expecting us. I told them five, though. We can hang out and have coffee till then." She stuffs her keys into her pocket and heads for the door, hesitating as she reaches the hallway. "I'm just gonna check . . ." She backtracks a few steps to a closed door across from her bedroom, and raps on the frame. "Daisy?" No answer, so Mia knocks harder. "Daze?"

"What?" comes a quiet voice.

"Me and Malcolm are getting dinner at Bartley's. Do you want to come?"

"No thanks. I have a headache."

"You might feel better after you have some food."

Daisy's tone hardens. "I said *no,* Mia. I'm in for the night."

Mia's lip quivers a little before she scowls. "Fine," she mutters, turning away. "I don't know why I bother. Let the parents worry about her." She stalks down the stairs like she can't wait to get out of the house. Mia and I both think the other has it better, homewise: I like how the Kwons' place is bright and modern, and her parents talk to us like we actually have a clue what's going on in the world; she likes the fact that Peter and my mother barely pay attention to anything I do. The Kwons always wanted Mia to be more like Daisy—sweet, studious, and popular. The kind of person who can be counted on to say and do all the right things. Until, all of a sudden, she didn't.

"What *do* your parents think?" I ask Mia as we step outside and into the driveway.

Mia kicks a stray rock. "Who knows. In front of me they just say, *Oh, your sister was working too hard, she needed a break.* But they're having all these tense conversations in their room with the door closed."

We get into my mother's car and buckle in. "Tense how?" I ask.

"I don't know," Mia admits. "I try to listen, but I can't catch anything except tone."

I back out of the Kwons' driveway and into the road, but haven't gone far when my phone vibrates in my pocket. "Hang on," I say, pulling off to the side. "I want to make sure that's not Declan." I shift the car into park and extract my phone, grimacing when I see the name. "Never mind. It's Katrin."

"What does *she* want?"

I frown at the screen. "She says she has a favor to ask."

Mia grabs my arm in mock horror, eyes popping. "Don't answer, Mal. Whatever it is, you don't want any part of it."

I haven't replied, but Katrin's still typing. Gray dots linger for so long that I wonder if she put her phone down and forgot to finish the message. Then it finally appears. *Brooke just broke up with Kyle. I don't know why, but homecoming's next weekend and she needs a date. I was thinking you could ask her. She seems to like you. Probably just as a friend but whatever. You weren't going to go anyway, were you? Hang on, I'll send her number.*

I show the message to Mia, who snorts. "Christ, the entitlement of that girl!" She mimics Katrin's clipped, breezy tone. *"You weren't going to go anyway, were you?"*

Another text appears from Katrin, with contact information for Brooke, and I save it automatically. Then I shrug and put my phone away. "Well, she has a point. I wasn't." Mia chews her lip without responding, and I raise my brows at her. "What— were *you?*"

"Maybe. If they still have it," she says, and glares when I start to laugh. "Don't give me attitude, Mal. I can go to a dance if I want to."

"I know you can. I'm just surprised at the 'want to' part. You have the least school spirit of anyone I've ever met. I thought that was, like, a badge of honor with you."

Mia makes a face. "Ugh, I don't know. One of Daisy's old friends called to say that a bunch of them are going to be chaperones for the dance, and asked if she wanted to go too. I think she was considering it, which would be the first thing she's done besides hide in her bedroom since she came home, but then she said, *Well, Mia's not even going.* So I said, *Yeah I am,* and now I guess I have to, and you can wipe that stupid smirk off your face anytime."

I swallow my grin. "You're a good sister, you know that?"

"Whatever." She picks at the peeling black polish on her

thumbnail. "Anyway, I was thinking about asking that hot girl who works at Café Luna. If she says no, Ezra is my friend backup."

I frown. "*Ezra* is your friend backup? You've known him for two weeks!"

"We've bonded. We like all the same music. And you have no idea how nice it is to finally have a queer friend at school."

I can't fault her for that, I guess. Mia's taken shit for years from guys like Kyle and Theo who think *bisexual* equals *threesome.* "You should just go with Ezra, then," I say. "Forget the Café Luna girl. She's pretentious."

Mia tilts her head, considering. "Maybe. And *you* should go with Ellery." She shoots me a shrewd look. "You like her, don't you?"

"Of course I like her," I say, aiming for a casual tone. I fail.

"Oh my God," Mia snorts. "We're not in fourth grade, Mal. Don't make me ask if you *like* like her." She props her boots against the glove compartment. "I don't know what you're waiting for. I think she likes you, too." A lock of hair falls into her eye, and she peers into the rearview mirror to readjust the clip holding it back. Then she goes rigid, twisting in her seat to look out the back window. "What the hell?"

I'm not sure if I'm relieved or disappointed that something distracted her. "What?"

Mia's still staring out the window, scowling. "Where's she going? I thought she was *in for the night.*" I turn to see Daisy's gray Nissan backing out of the Kwons' driveway, heading in the opposite direction from us. "Follow her," Mia says abruptly. She pokes me in the arm when I don't move right away. "Come on,

Mal, please? I want to see what she's up to. She's such a freaking vault lately."

"She's probably going to buy Tylenol," I say, but execute a three-point turn to get behind Daisy's rapidly disappearing tail-lights. I'm curious, too.

We follow her through the center of town and past Echo Ridge Cemetery. Mia sits up straighter in her seat when the Nissan slows, but Daisy doesn't stop. I wonder if she thought about visiting Lacey's grave, and then couldn't bring herself to do it.

Daisy leaves Echo Ridge and winds her way through two neighboring towns. I start copying her turns like I'm on autopilot without paying much attention to where we are. It's almost four-thirty, nearly past the point when we'll be able to get to Bartley's in time to meet the twins, when she finally pulls into the driveway of a white Victorian building. I brake and ease onto the shoulder of the road, shifting into park as we wait for Daisy to get out of the car. She's wearing shades even though the sun is low on the horizon, and walks quickly toward the building's side door. When she disappears inside, I ease the car forward so Mia and I can read the sign out front.

NORTHSTAR COUNSELING
DEBORAH CREIGHTON, PSYD

"Huh," I say, feeling oddly deflated. I'd thought whatever Daisy was up to would be more surprising. "Well, I guess that's that."

Mia scrunches up her forehead. "Daisy's seeing a psychologist? Why wouldn't she just say so? What's with all the sneaking around?"

I drive past Deborah Creighton's office, looking for a good spot to turn the car around. When I reach the empty driveway of a darkened house, I pull halfway in and then reverse out so we can go back the way we came. "Maybe she wants privacy."

"All she *has* is privacy," Mia complains. "It's so weird, Mal. She always had a million friends and now she doesn't have any. Or at least, she never sees them."

"Do you think she's depressed? Because she lost her job?"

"She *quit* her job," Mia corrects. "And she doesn't seem depressed. Just . . . withdrawn. But I don't know, really. I hardly know who she is anymore." She slumps down into her seat and turns up the radio, too loud for us to keep talking.

We drive in silence until we pass the "Welcome to Echo Ridge" sign and make our way to Manchester Street, stopping at the light in front of the common. Mia snaps off the radio and looks to our left. "They're repainting Armstrong's."

"Guess they had to." There must be only one coat of paint on Armstrong Auto Repair's wall so far, because you can still see the faint outline of CORCORANS MAKE KILLER QUEENS beneath it. A ladder leans against the wall, and we watch as a man slowly makes his way to the bottom. "Is that Vance Puckett?" I ask. "Somebody actually let that guy use a ladder? And trusted him to paint in straight lines?" Echo Ridge's town drunk and alleged petty criminal isn't usually the go-to guy for odd jobs. Armstrong Auto Repair must have been desperate to get the job done fast.

"That's a worker's comp claim waiting to happen," Mia says. She cranes her neck and squints. "Hold up. Is that your future homecoming date heading his way?"

For a second I think she means Ellery, until Brooke Bennett

gets out of a car parked across the street. The light turns green, but there's no one behind me, so I stay put. Brooke slams the car door shut and walks quickly toward Vance. Almost as though she'd been waiting for him to finish. She tugs on his sleeve as he steps off the ladder, and he puts a can of paint on the ground before facing her.

"What the hell?" Mia pulls out her phone to zoom the camera in on them. "What could those two possibly be talking about?"

"Can you see anything?"

"Not really," Mia grumbles. "My zoom sucks. But her hand gestures seem sort of . . . agitated, don't you think?" She flaps one hand in a piss-poor imitation of Brooke.

The light turns red again and a car pulls up behind us. Brooke starts backing away from Vance, and I keep an eye on him in case he's about to try anything weird with her. But he doesn't move, and she doesn't seem as though she's trying to get away from him. When she turns toward the street, I glimpse her face just before the light changes. She doesn't look scared or upset, or in tears like she has been for the past couple of weeks.

She looks determined.

CHAPTER TWELVE

ELLERY
FRIDAY, SEPTEMBER 27

This time it's Ezra's phone that buzzes with the California number.

He holds it up to me. "Sadie?" he asks.

"Probably," I say, glancing instinctively at the doorway. We're in the living room killing time watching Netflix after dinner, and Nana's in the basement doing laundry. She irons everything, including our T-shirts, so she's got at least another half hour down there. Still, Ezra gets to his feet and I follow him to the staircase.

"Hello?" he answers halfway up. "Yeah, hey. We thought it was you. Hang on, we're in transit." We get ourselves settled in his room with the door closed—Ezra at his desk and me in the window seat beside it—before he props up his phone and switches to FaceTime.

"There you are!" Sadie exclaims. Her hair's pulled back into a low, loose ponytail with tendrils escaping everywhere. It makes her look younger. I search her face for clues for how she's doing, because our "official" calls over Skype don't tell me anything. And neither does Nana. But Sadie is wearing the same cheerful, determined expression she's had every time I've glimpsed her over the past few weeks. The one that says, *Everything is fine and I have nothing to explain or apologize for.* "What are you two doing at home on a Friday night?"

"Waiting for our ride," Ezra says. "We're going to a pep rally. At Fright Farm."

Sadie scratches her cheek. "A pep rally *where*?"

"Fright Farm," I say. "Apparently they do school stuff there sometimes. We get a bunch of free passes so people can hang out after."

"Oh, fun! Who are you going with?"

We both pause. "Friends," Ezra says.

It's mostly true. We're meeting Mia and Malcolm there. But our actual ride is Officer Rodriguez, because Nana wasn't going to let us leave the house until she ran into him downtown and he offered to take us. We can't tell Sadie that, though, without falling down a rabbit hole of everything we're *not* telling her.

Before we started our weekly Skype calls with Sadie, Hamilton House Rehabilitation Facility sent a three-page *Resident Interactions Guide* that opened with "Positive, uplifting communication between residents and their loved ones is a cornerstone of the recovery process." In other words: *skim the surface.* Even now, when we're having a decidedly unofficial call, we play by the rules. Needing a police escort after getting targeted by an anonymous stalker isn't on the list of rehab-approved topics.

"Anyone special?" Sadie asks, batting her eyelashes.

My temper flares, because Ezra *had* somebody special back home. She knows perfectly well he's not the type to move on a month later. "Just people from school," I say. "It's getting busy around here. We have the pep rally tonight, and homecoming next Saturday."

If Sadie notices the coolness in my voice, she doesn't react. "Oh my gosh, is it homecoming already? Are you two going to the dance?"

"I am," Ezra says. "With Mia." His glance shifts toward me, and I read in his eyes what he doesn't say: *Unless it gets canceled.*

"So fun! She sounds great. What about you, El?" Sadie asks.

I pick at a frayed seam on my jeans. When Ezra told me last night that Mia asked him to homecoming, it hit me that I'm a "princess" without a date. Even though I'm positive the votes were a setup, something about that still rankles. Maybe because, until last night, I assumed our new friends weren't the school-dance types. Now, I guess it's just Malcolm who isn't. With me, anyway.

But Sadie doesn't know about any of that. "Undecided," I say.

"You should go!" she urges. "Take the cute vandal." She winks. "I sensed a little attraction the last time we spoke, amirite?"

Ezra turns toward me with a grin. "The what, now? Is she talking about Mal?"

My skin prickles with resentment. Sadie doesn't get to do this; she doesn't get to embarrass me about something I haven't sorted out my own feelings about, when she never tells us anything that matters about herself. I straighten my shoulders and incline my head, like we're playing chess and I just figured out

113

my next move. "Homecoming is such a big deal around here, isn't it?" I say. "People are *obsessed* with the court. They even remember how you were queen, like, twenty years ago."

Sadie's smile changes into something that looks fixed, unnatural, and I lean in closer to the phone. She's uncomfortable, and I'm glad. I want her to be. I'm tired of it always being me. "You've never really talked about that," I add. "Must have been a fun night."

Her laugh is as light as spun sugar, and just as brittle. "As fun as a small-town dance can be, I guess. I hardly remember it."

"You don't remember being homecoming queen?" I press. "That's weird." Ezra tenses beside me, and even though I don't look away from Sadie, I can feel his eyes on me. We don't do this; we don't dig for information that Sadie doesn't want to give. We follow her conversational lead. Always.

Sadie licks her lips. "It wasn't that big of a deal. Probably more of an event now that kids can document the whole thing on social media." She shifts her eyes toward Ezra. "Speaking of which, I'm loving your Instagram stories, Ez. You make the town look so pretty, I almost miss living there."

Ezra opens his mouth, about to answer, but I speak first. "Who did you go to homecoming with?" I ask. My voice is challenging, daring her to try to change the subject again. I can tell she wants to, so badly that I almost backtrack and do it myself. But I can't stop thinking about what Caroline Kilduff said in Dalton's Emporium. *A princess. What a stupid thing to want to be.* Sadie was one—my extroverted, attention-loving mother hit the absolute pinnacle of high school popularity—and she never, ever talks about it.

I need her to talk about it.

At first, I don't think she'll answer. When the words spring past her lips she looks as surprised as I am. "Vance Puckett," she says. I'm not prepared for that, and my jaw drops before I can stop it. Ezra inhales sharply beside me. A crease appears between Sadie's eyes, and her voice pitches upward as she looks between us. "What? Have you met him?"

"Briefly," Ezra says, at the same time I ask, "Were you serious with him?"

"I wasn't serious about anyone back then." Sadie tugs on one of her earrings. It's her nervous tell. I twist a strand of hair around my finger, which is mine. If Sadie dislikes this line of questioning, she's going to *hate* the next one.

"Who did Sarah go with?" I ask.

It's like I took an eraser and wiped the expression right off her face. I haven't asked about Sarah in years; Sadie trained me not to bother. Ezra cracks his knuckles, which is *his* nervous tell. We're all wildly uncomfortable and I can see, all of a sudden, why Hamilton House counsels "uplifting communication."

"Excuse me?" Sadie asks.

"Who was Sarah's homecoming date? Was it someone from Echo Ridge?"

"No," Sadie says, glancing over her shoulder. "What's that? Oh, okay." She turns back to the camera with an expression of forced brightness. "Sorry, but I need to go. I wasn't supposed to use this phone for more than a couple of minutes. Love you both! Have fun tonight! Talk soon!" She makes a kissy face at us and disconnects.

Ezra stares at the newly blank screen. "There wasn't anybody behind her, was there?"

"Nope," I say as the doorbell rings.

"What was that about?" he asks quietly.

I don't answer. I can't explain it; the urge I had to make Sadie tell us something—*anything*—that was true about her time in Echo Ridge. We sit in silence until Nana's voice floats up the stairs.

"Ellery, Ezra. Your ride is here."

Ezra pockets his phone and gets to his feet, and I follow him into the hallway. I feel restless and unanchored, and have a sudden urge to grab my brother's hand the way I used to when we were little. Sadie likes to say we were born holding hands, and while I'm pretty sure that's physically impossible, she has dozens of pictures of us clutching one another's tiny fingers in our crib. I don't know if Sadie used to do that with Sarah, because—*surprise*—she's never said.

When we get downstairs, Officer Rodriguez is waiting in Nana's foyer in full uniform, his hands clasped stiffly in front of him. I can see his Adam's apple rise and fall as he swallows. "How's it going, guys?"

"Great," Ezra says. "Thanks for the ride."

"No problem. I don't blame your grandmother for being concerned, but we're working with Fright Farm staff and school administrators to make sure the pep rally is a safe environment for every student."

He sounds like he's reading from a script, and I can see the gawky teenager peeking out from beneath his new-cop veneer. I'd mentioned to Nana how Sadie had described him during our first call in Echo Ridge—broken-hearted and falling apart at Lacey's funeral—but she just made the *pshhh* noise I've come to associate with conversations about Sadie. "I don't remember that," Nana huffed. "Your mother is being dramatic."

It's her standard response to Sadie, and I guess I can't blame her. But I keep looking at the photo of Lacey's junior class picnic that I snapped on my phone. When I zoom in on sixteen-year-old Ryan Rodriguez, I can see it. I can imagine that lovesick-looking boy breaking down over losing her. What I can't tell, though, is whether he'd do it because he was sad, or because he was angry.

Nana folds her arms and glares at Officer Rodriguez as Ezra and I grab our coats. "Every student, yes. But you need to be especially vigilant about the three girls involved." Her mouth puckers. "I'd be happier if they canceled homecoming altogether. Why give whoever is behind this more ammunition?"

"Well, the opposite side of that argument is, why give them more power?" Officer Rodriguez says. I blink at him in surprise, because that actually made sense. "If anything, we feel there's safety in numbers," he continues. "Fright Farm is always packed on a Friday. Whoever we're dealing with likes to operate behind the scenes, so I'm optimistic they'll stay away entirely tonight." He pulls out his keys and almost drops them, saving them at the last second with an awkward lunge. So much for that brief flash of competence. "You guys ready?"

"As we'll ever be," Ezra says.

We follow Officer Rodriguez out the door to his squad car waiting in the driveway, and I take the front seat while Ezra slides into the back. I'm still rattled by my conversation with Sadie, but I don't want to miss the opportunity to observe Officer Rodriguez at close range. "So this will be in the Bloody Big Top area, right?" I ask as I clip my seat belt.

"Yep. Same stage where they have the Dead Man's Party show," Officer Rodriguez says.

I meet Ezra's eyes in the rearview mirror. For a town so obsessed with its own tragic past, Echo Ridge is strangely laissez-faire about holding a high school pep rally at a murder site. "Would you be going if you weren't working?" I ask.

Officer Rodriguez backs out of our driveway. "To the pep rally? No," he says, sounding amused. "These things are for you guys. Not the adults in town."

"But you didn't graduate all that long ago," I say. "I thought maybe it was the sort of thing people would meet up at when they're back in town? Like, my friend Mia might be bringing her sister." That's a total lie. As far as I know, Daisy's still shut up in her room. "She graduated a while ago. Daisy Kwon? Did you know her?"

"Sure. Everyone knows Daisy."

Her name didn't evoke a reaction; his voice is calm and he seems a little preoccupied as he turns onto the main road. So I push a different button. "And Declan Kelly's back too, huh? Malcolm wasn't sure if he'd be here tonight." Ezra kicks lightly at my seat, telegraphing a question with the movement: *What are you up to?* I ignore it and add, "Do you think he will be?"

A muscle in Officer Rodriguez's jaw twitches. "I wouldn't know."

"I'm so curious about Declan," I say. "Were you friends with him in high school?"

His lips press into a thin line. "Hardly."

"Were you friends with Lacey Kilduff?" Ezra pipes up from the backseat. He's finally gotten with the program. Better late than never.

It doesn't help, though. Officer Rodriguez reaches out an

arm and flips a knob on the dashboard, filling the car with static and low voices. "I need to check for updates from the station. Can you keep it down for a sec?"

Ezra shifts in the backseat, leaning forward so he can mutter close to my ear, "Oh-for-two."

CHAPTER THIRTEEN

ELLERY

FRIDAY, SEPTEMBER 27

Officer Rodriguez walks with us to the far end of the park, past the Demon Rollercoaster with its blood-red waterfall and the entrance to the Dark Witch Maze. Two girls giggle nervously as a masked attendant hands them each a flashlight. "You'll need these to navigate the pitch-black lair you're about to experience," he intones. "But be careful along your journey. Fear awaits the further you go."

One of the girls examines her flashlight, then shines it on the thatched wall of the maze. "These are going to shut off right when we need them, aren't they?" she asks.

"Fear awaits the further you go," the attendant repeats, stepping to one side. A clawed hand shoots out of the wall and makes a grab for the nearest girl, who shrieks and falls back against her friend.

"Gets them every time," Officer Rodriguez says, lifting the flap to one of the Bloody Big Top tents. "Here's where I leave you guys. Good luck finding seats."

The bleachers ringing a circular stage are packed, but as Ezra and I scan the crowd we spot Mia waving energetically. "About time!" she says when we reach her. "It's been hell holding these seats." She stands, picking her coat up from the bench beside her, and Ezra glances down at a small concession stand set up to the left of the stage.

"I'm going to get a drink. You guys want anything?"

"No, I'm good," I say, and Mia shakes her head. Ezra thuds down the stairs as I squeeze past Mia in the too-small space. It's not until I sit down that I notice the flash of red hair beside me.

"You certainly like to cut it close," Viv says. She's in a green corduroy jacket and jeans, a gauzy yellow scarf looped around her neck. Two other girls sit beside her, each holding steaming Styrofoam cups.

I look at her and then at the stage, where Katrin, Brooke, and the other cheerleaders are lining up. "I thought you were a cheerleader," I say, confused.

Mia fake-coughs, *"Sore point,"* as Viv stiffens.

"I don't have time for cheerleading. I run the school paper." A note of pride creeps into her voice as she gestures toward the aisle in front of the stage, where a man is setting up an oversized camera. "Channel 5 in Burlington is covering the vandalism story based on *my* article. They're getting local color."

I lean forward, intrigued despite myself. "The school's letting them?"

"You can't stop the free press," Viv says smugly. She points toward a striking, dark-haired woman standing next to the camera, microphone dangling from one hand. "That's Meli Dinglasa. She graduated from Echo Ridge ten years ago and went to Columbia's journalism school." She says it almost reverently, twisting her scarf until it's even more artfully draped. Her outfit would look incredible on TV, which I'm starting to think is the point. "I'm applying there early decision. I'm hoping she'll give me a reference."

On my other side, Mia plucks at my sleeve. "Band's about to start," she says. Ezra returns just in time, a bottled water in one hand.

I tear my eyes away from the reporter as dozens of students holding instruments file through the back entrance and array themselves across the stage. I'd been expecting traditional marching band uniforms, but they're all in black athletic pants and purple T-shirts that read "Echo Ridge High" across the front in white lettering. Malcolm's in the first row, a set of snare drums draped around his neck.

Percy Gilpin jogs onto the stage in the same purple blazer he wore to the assembly last week, and bounds up to a makeshift podium. He adjusts the microphone and raises both hands in the air as people in the stands start to clap. "Good evening, Echo Ridge! You ready for some serious fall fun? We've got a big night planned to support the Echo Ridge Eagles, who are *undefeated* heading into tomorrow's game against Solsbury High!"

More cheers from the crowd, as Mia executes a slow clap beside me. "Yay."

"Let's get this party started!" Percy yells. The cheerleaders take center stage in a V-formation, their purple-and-white pom-poms planted firmly on their hips. A small girl steps out from the band's brass section, squinting against the bright overhead lights. Percy blows a whistle and the girl brings a trombone to her lips.

When the first few notes of "Paradise City" blare out, Ezra and I lean across Mia to exchange surprised grins. Sadie is a Guns N' Roses fanatic, and we grew up with this song blasting through whatever apartment we were living in. An LED screen at the back of the stage starts flashing football game highlights, and within seconds the entire crowd is on its feet.

About halfway through, as everything's building to a crescendo, the other drummers stop and Malcolm launches into this fantastic, frenetic solo. His drumsticks move impossibly fast, the muscles in his arms tense with effort, and my hand half lifts to fan myself before I realize what I'm doing. The cheerleaders are in perfect rhythm with the beat, executing a crisp, high-energy routine that ends with Brooke being tossed into the air, ponytail flying, caught by waiting hands just as the song ends and the entire band takes a bow as one.

I'm clapping so hard my palms hurt as Mia catches my eye and grins. "I know, right?" she says. "I lose all my cynicism when the band performs. It's Echo Ridge's uniting force."

I accidentally knock into Viv when I sit back down, and she shifts away with a grimace. "There's not enough room on this bench," she says sharply, turning to her friends. "I think we might see better farther down."

"Bonus," Mia murmurs as the three of them file out of our row. "We scared Viv away."

A few minutes later, a shadow falls across Viv's vacated seat.

I glance up to see Malcolm in his purple Echo Ridge High T-shirt, minus the drums. "Hey," he says. "Room for one more?" His hair is tousled and his cheeks flushed, and he looks really, really cute.

"Yeah, of course." I shift closer to Mia. "You were great," I add, and he smiles. One of his front teeth is slightly crooked, and it softens the moody look he usually has. I gesture toward the stage, where Coach Gagnon is talking passionately about tradition and giving your all. Photos are still looping on the LED screen behind him. "Will you play an encore?"

"Nah, we're done for the night. It's football talk time."

We listen for a few minutes to the coach's speech. It's getting repetitive. "What happened six years ago?" I ask. "He keeps bringing it up."

"State championship," Malcolm says. "Echo Ridge won when Declan was a junior." And then I remember the yearbook from the library, filled with pictures of the team's huge, come-from-behind victory against a much bigger school. And Declan Kelly, being carried on his teammates' shoulders afterward.

"Oh, that's right," I say. "Your brother threw a Hail Mary touchdown with seconds left in the game, didn't he?" It's a little weird, maybe, how perfectly I remember a game I never attended, but Malcolm just nods. "That must have been amazing."

Something like reluctant pride flits across Malcolm's face. "I guess. Declan was bragging for weeks that he was going to win that game. People laughed, but he backed it up." He runs a hand through his sweat-dampened hair. It shouldn't be attractive, the way his hair spikes up afterward in uneven tufts, but it is. "He always did."

I can't tell if it's just my own nagging suspicions of Declan that make Malcolm's words sound ominous. "Were you guys close?" I ask. As soon as the words are out of my mouth, I realize I've made it sound as though Declan is dead. "*Are* you close?" I amend.

"No," Malcolm says, leaning forward with his elbows on his knees. His voice is quiet, his eyes on the stage. "Not then, and not now."

Every once in a while, it feels like Malcolm and I are having some kind of sub-conversation that we don't acknowledge. We're talking about football and his brother, supposedly, but we're also talking about *before and after*. It's how I think about Sadie—that she was one way before the kind of loss that rips your world apart, and a different version of herself afterward. Even though I didn't know her until Sarah was long gone, I'm sure it's true.

I want to ask Malcolm more, but before I can Mia reaches across me and punches him in the arm. "Hey," she says. "Did you do the thing?"

"No," Malcolm says, avoiding Mia's gaze. She glances between us and smirks, and I get the distinct feeling that I'm missing something.

"And let's not forget, after we defeat Solsbury tomorrow— and we *will*—we've got our biggest test of the season with the homecoming game next week," Coach Gagnon says. Between his perfectly bald head and the shadows cast by the Big Top's stadium lighting, he looks like an exceptionally enthusiastic alien. "We're up against Lutheran, our only defeat last year. But that's not going to happen this time around! Because *this* time—"

A loud popping noise fills my ears, making me jump. The

bright lights snap off and the LED screen goes black, then flashes to life again. Static fills the screen, followed by a photo of Lacey in her homecoming crown, smiling at the camera. The crowd gasps, and Malcolm goes rigid beside me.

Then Lacey's picture rips in two, replaced by three others: Brooke, Katrin, and me. Theirs are class photos, but mine is a candid, with my face half turned from the camera. A chill inches up my spine as I recognize the hoodie I wore yesterday when Ezra and I walked downtown to meet Malcolm and Mia at Bartley's.

Somebody was watching us. *Following* us.

Horror-movie laughter starts spilling from the speakers, literal *mua-ha-has* that echo through the tent as what looks like thick red liquid drips down the screen, followed by jagged white letters: SOON. When it fades away, the Bloody Big Top is utterly silent. Everyone is frozen, with one exception: Meli Dinglasa from Channel 5. She strides purposefully onto the stage toward Coach Gagnon, with her microphone outstretched and a cameraman at her heels.

CHAPTER FOURTEEN

MALCOLM

SATURDAY, SEPTEMBER 28

The text from Declan comes as I'm walking against the departing crowds at Fright Farm Saturday night: *In town for a few hours. Don't freak out.*

I almost text back *I'm at the scene of your alleged crime. Don't freak out,* but manage to restrain myself to a simple *What for?* Which he ignores. I stuff the phone back in my pocket. If Declan's been paying attention to the local news, he knows about last night's pep rally turned stalker sideshow. I hope he was in New Hampshire surrounded by people when all that went down, or he's only going to make the speculation worse.

Not my problem. Tonight I'm just the chauffeur, collecting Ellery and Ezra after work. There was no way their grandmother was letting them walk through the woods after what happened last night. To be honest, I'm a little surprised she agreed to let me pick them up, but Ellery says closing is two hours past Mrs. Corcoran's usual bedtime.

I expect the House of Horrors to be empty, but music and laughter spill out toward me as I approach the building. The entire park was built around this house, an old Victorian at the edge of what used to be another wooded area. I've seen pictures of it before it became a theme park attraction, and it was always stately but worn-looking—as if its turrets were about to crumble, or the steps leading up to the wide porch would collapse if you stepped on them wrong. It still looks like that, but now it's all part of the atmosphere.

I haven't been here since I was ten, when Declan and his friends brought me. They took off when we were halfway through, like the assholes they were, and I had to go through the rest of the house on my own. Every single room freaked me out. I had nightmares for weeks about a guy in a bloody bathtub with stumps for legs.

My brother laughed when I finally stumbled out of the House of Horrors, snotty-nosed and terrified. *Don't be such a wuss, Mal. None of it's real.*

The music gets louder as I climb the steps and turn the door-knob. It doesn't budge, and there's no bell. I knock a few times, which feels weird, like, who do I expect to answer the door at a haunted house, exactly? Nobody does, so I head back down the stairs and edge around to the back. When I turn the corner, I see concrete steps leading down to a door that's wedged open with a piece of wood. I descend the stairs and push the door open.

I'm in a basement room that looks like it's part dressing room, part staff room. The space is large, dimly lit, and cluttered with shelves and clothes racks. A vanity with an oversized bulb mirror is shoved to one side, its surface covered with jars and bottles. Two cracked leather couches line the walls, with a glass-topped end table between them. There's a closet-sized bathroom to the left, and a half-open door in front of me that leads into a small office.

I'm hovering a few steps inside, searching for a way upstairs, when a hand pushes open a frayed velvet curtain on the opposite end of the room. The sudden movement makes me gasp like a scared kid, and the girl who steps through the curtain laughs. She's almost as tall as I am, dressed in a tight black tank top that shows off intricate tattoos against brown skin. She looks like she could be a few years older than me. "Boo," she says, then crosses her arms and cocks her head. "Party crasher?"

I blink, confused. "What?"

She tsks. "Don't play innocent with me. I'm the makeup artist. I know everybody, and *you* are trespassing." I half open my mouth to protest, then close it as her stern look dissolves into a wide smile. "I'm just messing with you. Go upstairs, find your friends." She crosses over to a minifridge next to the vanity and pulls out a couple bottles of water, pointing one toward me like a warning. "But this is a dry party, understand? Whole thing'll get shut down if we gotta deal with a bunch of drunk teenagers. Especially after what happened last night."

"Sure. Right," I say, trying to sound like I know what she's talking about. Ellery and Ezra didn't say anything about a party. The tall girl sweeps aside the velvet curtain to let me through.

I climb a set of stairs into another hallway that opens into a dungeon-like room. I recognize the room immediately from my last visit inside, with Declan, but it looks a lot less sinister filled with party guests. A few people are still partly in costume, with masks off or pushed up on their foreheads. One guy's holding a rubber head under his arm while he talks to a girl in a witch's dress.

A hand tugs at my sleeve. I look down to see short, bright-red nails and follow them up to a face. It's Viv and she's talking, but I can't hear what she's saying over the music. I cup a hand to my ear, and she raises her voice. "I didn't know you worked at Fright Farm."

"I don't," I say back.

Viv frowns. She's drenched in some kind of strawberry perfume that doesn't smell bad, exactly, but reminds me of something a little kid would wear. "Then why did you come to the staff party?"

"I didn't know there was a party," I answer. "I'm just picking up Ellery and Ezra."

"Well, good timing. I've been wanting to talk to you." I eye her warily. I've seen Viv almost every week since I moved into the Nilssons', but we've barely exchanged a dozen words the entire time. Our whole relationship, if you can call it that, is based on *not* wanting to talk to one another. "Can I interview you for my next article?" she asks.

I don't know what she's angling for, but it can't be good. "Why?"

"I'm doing this 'Where Are They Now?' series on Lacey's murder. I thought it would be interesting to get the perspective of someone who was on the sidelines when it happened, what with your brother being a person of interest and all. We could—"

"Are you out of your mind?" I cut her off. "No."

Viv lifts her chin. "I'm going to write it anyway. Don't you want to give your side? It might make people more sympathetic to Declan, to hear from his brother."

I turn away without answering. Last night, Viv was front and center in the local news coverage of the pep rally stunt, getting interviewed like some kind of Echo Ridge crime expert. She's been in Katrin's shadow for so long, there's no way she's letting her moment in the spotlight go. But I don't have to help extend her fifteen minutes of fame.

I shoulder through the crowd and finally spot Ellery. She's hard to miss—her hair is teased into a black cloud around her head and her eyes are so heavily made up that they seem to take up half her face. She looks like some kind of goth anime character. I'm not sure what it says about me that I'm kind of into it.

She catches my eye and waves me over. She's standing with a guy a few years older than us with a man-bun, a goatee, and a tight henley shirt with the buttons undone. The whole look screams *college guy trolling for high school girls,* and I hate him instantly. "Hey," Ellery says when I reach them. "So apparently there's a party tonight."

"I noticed," I say with a glare toward Man Bun.

He's not fazed. "House of Horrors tradition," he explains. "It's always on the Saturday closest to the owner's birthday. I can't stay, though. Got a toddler at home that never sleeps. I have to give my wife a break." He swipes at his face and turns to Ellery. "Is all the blood off?"

Ellery peers at him. "Yeah, you're good."

"Thanks. See ya later," the guy says, and starts pushing his way through the crowd.

"So long," I say, watching him leave with a lot less venom now that I know he wasn't hitting on Ellery. "The blood he's referring to is makeup, right?"

Ellery laughs. "Yeah. Darren spends all night in a bloody bathtub. Some people don't bother washing their makeup off till they get home, but he tried that once and *terrified* his child. Poor kid might be scarred for life."

I shudder. "I was scarred for life going through that room, and I was ten."

Ellery's giant anime eyes get even wider. "Who brought you here when you were *ten*?"

"My brother," I say.

"Ah." Ellery looks thoughtful. Like she can see into the secret corner of my brain that I try not to visit often, because it's where my questions about what really happened between Declan and Lacey live. That corner makes me equal parts horrified and ashamed, because every once in a while, it imagines my brother losing control of his hair-trigger temper at exactly the wrong moment.

I swallow hard and push the thought aside. "I'm kind of surprised they'd have this after what happened last night."

Ellery gazes around us. "I know, right? But hey, everyone here works in a Halloween theme park. They don't scare easy."

"Do you want to stay for a while?"

She looks regretful. "Better not. Nana didn't even want us to work tonight. She's pretty freaked out."

"Are you?" I ask.

"I . . ." She hesitates, pulling on a strand of teased hair and winding it around her finger. "I want to say no, because I hate the fact that some anonymous creep can rattle me. But yeah. I am. It's just too . . . close, you know?" She shivers as someone squeezes past her in a *Scream* mask. "I keep having these conversations with my mother where she has no idea what's going on, and all I can think is—no wonder she never wanted to bring us here. Her twin sister disappears, her favorite babysitter's daughter is murdered, and now this? It's enough to make you feel like the whole town is cursed."

"Your mother doesn't know about—anything?" I ask.

"No. We're only supposed to have *uplifting communication* with her." She releases her hair. "You know she's in rehab, right? I figured the entire town knows."

"They do," I admit. She snort-laughs, but the sadness behind it tugs at my chest. "I'm sorry you're dealing with that. And I'm sorry about your aunt. I've been meaning to tell you that. I know it all happened way before we were born, but . . . that sucks. In a massively stating-the-obvious sort of way."

Ellery drops her eyes. "I'm pretty sure it's why we wound up here. I don't think Sadie's ever dealt with it. No closure, no nothing. I didn't connect the dots when Lacey died, but that's when things started going downhill. Must've brought bad memories too close to the surface. So it's sort of ironic that she's in the dark now, but—what can you do?" She raises her water bottle in a mock salute. "Three cheers to *uplifting communication.* Anyway. We should probably find Ezra, huh? He said he was going downstairs to get some water."

We make our way out of the crowded dungeon and take

the staircase down to the staff room, but there's no sign of Ezra there. It's cooler than it was upstairs, but I'm still overheated and a little thirsty. I cross over to the minifridge and take out two bottles of water, putting one on the vanity and offering the other to Ellery.

"Thanks." She reaches out a hand, but our timing's off; I let go before she's grasped it fully, and it falls to the floor between us. When we both reach for it, we almost knock heads. Ellery laughs and puts a hand on my chest.

"I have it," she says, and picks it up. She straightens, and even in the dim lighting I can see how red her cheeks are. "We're so graceful, aren't we?"

"That was my fault," I say. The whole exchange has left us standing closer than we need to be, but neither of us moves away. "Bad handoff. You can see why I never made it as a football player." She smiles and tilts her head up and, holy hell, her eyes are pretty.

"Thanks," she murmurs, getting redder.

Oh. I said that out loud.

She moves a little closer, brushing against my hip, and an electric charge runs through me. Are we . . . should I . . .

Don't be such a wuss, Mal.

God. Of all times to hear my brother's stupid voice.

I reach out a hand and trace my thumb along Ellery's jaw. Her skin is just as soft as I thought it would be. Her lips part, I swallow hard, and just then there's a loud scratching noise behind us and somebody says, "Damn it!" in a frustrated tone.

Ellery and I break apart, and she twists to face the office. She's across the room in a second, easing open the cracked door.

Brooke Bennett is slumped on the floor, wedged between the desk and some kind of giant recycling bin. Ellery goes to her and crouches down.

"Brooke? Are you okay?" she asks.

Brooke's hair hangs in her face, and when she pushes it aside she nearly stabs herself in the eye with something small and silvery. Ellery reaches over and takes it. I can see from the doorway that it's a paper clip, pulled open and unfurled so its edges are exposed. Another one just like it rests on the floor next to her. "This is harder than he said it would be," Brooke says, her voice slurring.

"Who said?" Ellery asks, setting both paper clips on the desk. "What's hard?"

Brooke snickers. "That's what *she* said."

It looks like nobody gave Brooke the heads-up about tonight being a dry party. "Do you want some water?" I ask, holding out my untouched bottle.

Brooke takes it from me and unscrews the cap. She swallows a greedy gulp, spilling some water down her front, before handing it back. "Thanks, Malcolm. You're so nice. The nicest person in your entire house. By a *lot*." She wipes her mouth on her sleeve and focuses on Ellery. "You look different. Are those your real eyes?"

Ellery and I glance at each other and we both suppress a laugh. Drunk Brooke is kind of entertaining. "What are you doing down here?" Ellery asks. "Do you want to come upstairs?"

"No." Brooke shakes her head vehemently. "I need to get it back. I shouldn't have . . . I just shouldn't have. I have to show them. It's not right, it's not okay."

"Show them what?" I ask. "What happened?"

Sudden tears spring into her eyes. "That's the million-dollar question, isn't it? *What happened?*" She puts a finger to her lips and shushes loudly. "Wouldn't you like to know?"

"Is this about the pep rally?" Ellery asks.

"No." Brooke hiccups and holds her stomach. "Ugh. I don't feel so good."

I grab a nearby wastebasket and hold it out. "Do you need this?"

Brooke takes it, but just stares listlessly at the bottom. "I want to go home."

"Do you want us to find Kyle?"

"Kyle and I are *over*," Brooke says, waving her hand as though she just made him disappear. "And he's not here anyway." She sighs. "Viv drove me, but I don't want to see her right now. She'll just lecture me."

"I can give you a ride," I offer.

"Thanks," Brooke slurs.

Ellery stands and plucks at my sleeve. "I'm going to find Ezra. Be right back."

I crouch next to Brooke after Ellery leaves. "You want some more water?" I ask. Brooke waves me away, and for the life of me I can't think of what to say next. Even after living with Katrin for four months, I'm still not comfortable around girls like Brooke. Too pretty, too popular. Too much like Lacey.

Minutes crawl by, until Brooke draws her knees up to her chest and lifts her eyes toward mine. They're unfocused and ringed with dark circles. "Have you ever made a really bad mistake?" she asks quietly.

I pause, trying to figure out what's going on with her so I can frame a good answer. "Well, yeah. Most days."

"No." She shakes her head, then burrows her face in her arms. "I don't mean regular stuff," she says, her voice muffled. "I mean something you can't take back."

I'm lost. I don't know how to be helpful. "Like what?"

Her head is still down, and I have to edge closer to hear what she's saying. "I wish I had different friends. I wish everything was different."

Footsteps approach, and I stand up as Ellery and Ezra poke their heads into the office. "Hey, Mal," Ezra says, and then his gaze drops to Brooke. "Everything okay in here?"

"I want to go home," Brooke repeats, and I offer a hand to help her to her feet.

She revives a little when we get outside, and only needs occasional steadying as we make our way toward my mother's Volvo. It's the nicest car we've ever owned, courtesy of Peter, and I really hope Brooke doesn't throw up in it. She seems to be thinking the same thing, and rolls down the window as soon as Ezra helps her into the passenger seat.

"What's your address?" I ask as I climb in behind the wheel.

"Seventeen Briar Lane," Brooke says. The far edge of town.

The twins slam the back doors and I turn to face them as they buckle themselves in. "You guys are right around the corner from here. I'll drop you off first so your grandmother doesn't worry."

"That'd be great, thanks," Ellery says.

I back the Volvo out of its spot and head for the exit. "Sorry you had to leave the party," Brooke says, scrunching down in her seat. "I shouldn't have had anything to drink. Can't hold it. That's what Katrin always says."

"Yeah, well. Katrin doesn't know everything." It seems like the thing to say, even if she was right in this particular case.

"Hope not," Brooke says in a low tone.

I glance at her before pulling onto the main road, but it's too dark to read her expression. It sounds like she and Katrin are fighting, which is weird. I've never seen them on the outs, maybe because Brooke lets Katrin take the lead in everything. "We weren't planning on staying anyway," I reassure her.

It's a quick trip to the Corcorans' house, which is dark except for a single light blazing on the front porch.

"Looks like Nana's asleep," Ezra says, pulling a set of keys from his pocket. "I was worried she'd be waiting up. Thanks for the ride, Mal."

"Any time."

Ezra opens the car door and gets out, waiting in the driveway for his sister. "Yeah, thanks Malcolm," Ellery says, slinging her bag over one shoulder. "Talk to you soon."

"Tomorrow, maybe?" I blurt out, turning to face her. She pauses, her eyes questioning, and I freeze for a second. Did I imagine that I almost kissed her in the basement, or that it seemed like she wanted me to? Then I plow ahead anyway. "I mean—I could call you, or something. If you want to, you know, talk."

God. Real smooth.

But she gives me a full smile, dimple and all. "Yeah, definitely. That sounds good. Let's talk." Brooke clears her throat, and Ellery blinks. Like she'd forgotten for a few seconds that

Brooke was in the car. I know I did. "Bye, Brooke," Ellery says, climbing out the door that Ezra just exited.

"Bye," Brooke says.

Ellery shuts the car door and turns to follow her brother up the drive. She passes Brooke's open window just as Brooke sighs deeply and rubs a listless hand across her face. Ellery pauses and asks, "Are you going to be okay?"

Brooke shifts to face her. She doesn't speak for so long that Ellery frowns, darting concerned eyes toward me. Then Brooke lifts her shoulders in a shrug.

"Why wouldn't I be?" she says.

CHAPTER FIFTEEN

ELLERY

The photo albums are more than twenty years old, dusty and brown at the edges. Even so, seventeen-year-old Sadie practically jumps off the page in her daring black homecoming dress, all wild hair and red lips. She's entirely recognizable as the younger version of her present-day self, which is more than I can say for her date.

"Wow," Ezra says, inching closer toward me on Nana's living room rug. After much trial and error with her stiff furniture, we've decided it's the most comfortable seat in the room. "Sadie wasn't kidding. Vance was hot back then."

"Yeah," I say, studying Vance's high cheekbones and lazy smirk. Then I glance at the clock over Nana's fireplace, for about the fifth time since we've been sitting here. Ezra catches the movement and laughs.

"Still only eight-thirty. Has been for an entire minute. In other words: too early for Malcolm to call you." Ezra didn't miss my moment with Malcolm in the car last night, and he wouldn't let me go to sleep until I told him about our near kiss in the Fright Farm staff room.

"Shut up," I grumble, but my stomach flutters as I fight off a smile.

Nana works her way into the living room with a can of lemon Pledge and a dustcloth. It's her usual Sunday-morning ritual: seven o'clock Mass, then housework. In about fifteen minutes she's going to send Ezra and me outside to rake the lawn. "What are you two looking at?" she asks.

"Sadie's homecoming pictures," Ezra says.

I expect her to frown, but she just aims a spray of Pledge at the mahogany table in front of the bay window. "Did you like Vance, Nana?" I ask as she wipes the surface clean. "When he and Sadie were dating?"

"Not particularly," Nana sniffs. "But I knew he wouldn't last. They never did."

I flip through the next couple of pages in the album. "Did Sarah go to homecoming?"

"No, Sarah was a late bloomer. The only boys she ever talked to were the ones Sadie went out with." Nana stops dusting and puts the can down, pushing the bay window curtain aside and peering out. "Now, what's he doing here this early on a Sunday?"

"Who?" Ezra asks.

"Ryan Rodriguez."

I close the photo album as Nana heads for the front door

and pulls it open. "Hello, Ryan," she says, but before she can say anything more he interrupts her.

"Is Ellery here?" he asks. He sounds hurried, urgent.

"Of course—"

He doesn't wait for her to finish. He pushes past her, eyes searching the room until they land on me. He's in a faded Echo Ridge High sweatshirt and jeans, faint dark stubble tracing his jaw. He looks even younger without his uniform on, and also like he just woke up. "Ellery. Thank God. Have you been here all night?"

"Ryan, what on earth?" Nana shuts the door and folds her arms tightly across her chest. "Is this about the homecoming threats? Did something new happen?"

"Yes, but it's not . . . it's a different . . ." He runs a hand through his hair and takes a deep breath. "Brooke Bennett didn't come home last night. Her parents aren't sure where she is."

I don't even realize I've gotten to my feet until I hear a loud thud—the photo album has slipped from my hand to the floor. Ezra rises more slowly, his face pale and his eyes darting between me and Officer Rodriguez. But before either of us can say anything, Nana lets out a strangled cry. Every drop of color drains from her face, and for a second I think she might faint. "Oh, dear God." She walks unsteadily to a chair and collapses into it, clutching at the armrests. "It happened. It happened again, right in front of your faces, and you didn't do a thing to stop it!"

"We don't know what happened. We're trying to—" Officer Rodriguez starts, but Nana doesn't let him finish.

"A girl is *missing*. A girl who was threatened in front of the entire town two days ago. Just like my granddaughter." I've never seen Nana like this; it's as if every emotion she's been suppressing for the past twenty years just flooded to the surface. Her face is red, her eyes watery, and her entire body trembles as she speaks. The sight of my calm, no-nonsense grandmother this upset makes my heart pound even harder. "No one on the police force did anything of substance to protect Ellery *or* Brooke. *You let this happen.*"

Officer Rodriguez flinches, as startled as if she'd slapped him. "We didn't— Look, I know how upsetting this is. We're all concerned, that's why I'm here. But we don't know Brooke's missing. She might very well be with a friend. We have several officers looking into that. It's too early to assume the worst."

Nana folds her hands in her lap, her fingers threaded so tightly together that her knuckles are white. "Missing girls don't come home in Echo Ridge, Ryan," she says in a hollow voice. "You know that."

Neither of them are paying any attention to Ezra or me. "El," my brother says in a low voice, and I know what's coming next. *We have to tell them.* And we do, of course. From what Officer Rodriguez has said so far, it doesn't sound as though he has any idea that Brooke left Fright Farm with us. Or that Malcolm was the one who ultimately took her home. Alone.

Last night, slumped in the passenger seat as Malcolm dropped us off, Brooke had looked so tired and defeated that I couldn't help but check in with her one last time.

Are you going to be okay?

Why wouldn't I be?

Nana and Officer Rodriguez are still talking, but I can only process scraps of what they're saying. My chest shakes when

I take a breath. I know I have to speak up. I know I have to tell Officer Rodriguez and my grandmother that our friend—*Declan Kelly's brother*—was very likely the last person to see an Echo Ridge homecoming princess before she went missing.

And I know exactly how that's going to look.

CHAPTER SIXTEEN

MALCOLM
SUNDAY, SEPTEMBER 29

I don't realize it's déjà vu until I'm in the middle of it.

When I wander into the kitchen Sunday morning, it doesn't strike me as strange at first that Officer McNulty is sitting at our kitchen island. He and Peter are both on the town council, so I figure they're probably talking stoplights again. Even though it's barely eight-thirty in the morning, and even though Officer McNulty is listening with a surprising amount of interest to Katrin's long-winded description of her date with Theo last night.

My mother is fluttering around the kitchen, trying to fill cups of coffee that people haven't emptied yet. Officer McNulty lets her top his off, then asks, "So you didn't see Brooke at all last night? She didn't call you or text you at any point in the evening?"

"She texted to see if I was coming to the party. But I wasn't."

"And what time was that?"

Katrin scrunches her face up, thinking. "Around . . . ten, maybe?"

"Could I see your phone, please."

The official tone of the request makes my skin prickle. I've heard it before. "Is something going on with Brooke?" I ask.

Peter rubs a hand over his unshaven jaw. "Apparently she wasn't in her room this morning, and it looks as though her bed wasn't slept in. Her parents haven't seen her since she left for work last night, and she's not answering her phone."

My throat closes and my palms start to sweat. "She's not?"

Officer McNulty hands Katrin's phone back to her just as it buzzes. She looks down, reads the message that's popped up on her screen, and pales. "It's from Viv," she says, her voice suddenly shaky. "She says she lost track of Brooke at the party and hasn't talked to her since." Katrin bites her lower lip and shoves the phone at Officer McNulty, like maybe he can make the text say something different. "I really thought they'd be together. Brooke stays over after work sometimes because Viv's house is closer."

Dread starts inching up my spine. *No. This can't be happening.*

Mom sets down the coffeepot and turns toward me. "Malcolm, you didn't happen to see Brooke when you picked the twins up, did you?"

Officer McNulty looks up. "You were at Fright Farm last night, Malcolm?"

Shit. Shit. Shit.

"Just to give the Corcoran twins a ride home," Mom says quickly. But not as though she's really worried that I'm going to get into trouble.

146

My stomach twists. She has *no* idea.

Officer McNulty rests his forearms on the kitchen island's shiny, swirling black marble. "Did you happen to see Brooke while you were there?" His tone is interested, but not intense like it was when he interrogated Declan.

Not yet.

Five years ago we were in a different kitchen: our tiny ranch, two miles from here. My dad glowered in a corner and my mother twisted her hands together while Declan sat at the table across from Officer McNulty and repeated the same things over and over again. *I hadn't seen Lacey in two days. I don't know what she was doing that night. I was out driving.*

Driving where?

Just driving. I do that sometimes.

Was anybody with you?

No.

Did you call anybody? Text anybody?

No.

So you just drove by yourself for—what? Two, three hours?

Yeah.

Lacey was dead by then. Not just missing. Workers found her body in the park before her parents even knew she hadn't come home. I sat in the living room while Officer McNulty fired questions at Declan, my eyes glued to a television program I wasn't watching. I never went into the kitchen. Never said a word. Because none of it involved me, not really, except for the part where it became this slowly burning fuse that eventually blew my family apart.

"I . . ." I'm taking too long to answer. I scan the faces around me like they'll give me some clue how to respond, but all I can see are the same expressions they always wear whenever I start to talk: Mom looks attentive, Katrin exasperated, and Peter is all patient forbearance marred only by a slight nostril flare. Officer McNulty scratches a note on the pad in front of him, then flicks his eyes toward me in a cursory, almost lazy way. Until he sees something in my face that makes him tense, like he's a cat batting at a toy that suddenly came to life. He leans forward, his blue-gray eyes locked on mine.

"Do you have something to tell us, Malcolm?" he asks.

CHAPTER SEVENTEEN

ELLERY
SUNDAY, SEPTEMBER 29

This time, unlike after the hit-and-run with Mr. Bowman, I'm a good witness. I remember everything.

I remember taking the paper clip from Brooke's hand, and picking up a second one from the floor. "Paper clips?" Officer Rodriguez asks. He went directly into questioning mode as soon as Ezra told him we'd left Fright Farm with Brooke. We moved into the kitchen, and Nana made cocoa for everyone. I grasp the still-warm mug gratefully as I explain what happened before Ezra joined Malcolm and me.

"Yeah. They were pulled apart, you know, so they were almost straight. People do that kind of thing sometimes, like a nervous habit?" I do, anyway. I've never met a paper clip I didn't immediately twist out of its preexisting shape.

I remember Brooke being sort of goofy and funny and

rambling at first. "She made a *that's what she said* joke," I tell Officer Rodriguez.

His face is a total blank. "That's what she said?"

"Yeah, you know, from *The Office*? The TV show?" I tilt my head at him, waiting for it to click, but his brow stays knit in confusion. How can anyone in his twenties not get that reference? "It's something the lead character used to say as, like, a punch line after a double entendre. Like when someone says something is hard, they could be referring to a difficult situation or, you know. To a penis."

Ezra spits out his cocoa as Officer Rodriguez turns bright red. "For heaven's sake, Ellery," Nana snaps. "That's hardly pertinent to the conversation at hand."

"I thought it was," I say, shrugging. It's never *not* interesting observing Officer Rodriguez's reactions to things he doesn't expect.

He clears his throat and avoids my eyes. "And what happened after the . . . joke?"

"She drank some water. I asked her what she was doing in the basement. Then she started seeming more upset." I remember Brooke's words like she'd just spoken them five minutes ago: *I shouldn't have. I have to show them. It's not right, it's not okay. What happened? Wouldn't you like to know?*

My stomach squeezes. Those are the sort of things that seem like nonsense when a drunk girl is babbling at a party, but ominous when she's missing. Brooke is *missing*. I don't think that's really sunk in yet. I keep thinking Officer Rodriguez is going to get a call any second telling him she met up with friends after she got home. "She got a little teary when she said all that," I say. "I asked her if it was about the pep rally, but she said no."

"Did you press her?" Officer Rodriguez asks.

"No. She said she wanted to go home. I offered to get Kyle and she said they'd broken up. And that he wasn't there anyway. So Malcolm offered her a ride home, and she said okay. That's when I left to get Ezra. Driving Brooke home was . . ." I pause, weighing what to say next. "It wasn't planned. At all. It just happened."

Officer Rodriguez's forehead creases in a quizzical frown. "What do you mean?"

Good question. What *do* I mean? My brain has been whirring since Officer Rodriguez said Brooke was missing. We don't know what it means yet, but I do know this: if she doesn't show up soon people will expect the worst, and they'll start pointing fingers at the most obvious suspect. Which would be the person who saw her last.

It's the cliché moment of every *Dateline* special: the friend or neighbor or colleague who says, *He's always been such a nice guy, nobody ever would have believed he could be capable of this.* I can't think everything through clearly yet, but I do know this: there was no master plan to get Brooke alone. I never got the sense that Malcolm was doing anything except trying to help her out. "I mean, it was just random chance that Malcolm ended up giving Brooke a ride," I say. "We didn't even know she was in the office at first."

"Okay," Officer Rodriguez says, his expression neutral. "So you left to find Ezra, and Malcolm was alone with Brooke for . . . how long?"

I look at Ezra, who shrugs. "Five minutes, maybe?" I say.

"Was Brooke's demeanor any different when you returned?"

"No. She was still sad."

"But you said she wasn't sad earlier. That she was joking."

"She was joking and *then* she was sad," I remind him.

"Right. So, describe the walk to the car for me, please. Both of you."

It goes on like that for another ten minutes until we finally, painstakingly get to the moment in our driveway when I asked Brooke if she was going to be okay. I gloss over the part where Malcolm asked if he could call me, which doesn't seem important right now. Ezra doesn't bring it up, either.

"She said, *Why wouldn't I be?*" Officer Rodriguez repeats.

"Yeah."

"And did you answer?"

"No." I didn't. It hits me with a sharp stab of regret, now, that I should have.

"All right." Officer Rodriguez snaps the notebook shut. "Thank you. This has been helpful. I'll let you know if I have any follow-up questions."

I unclench my hands, realizing I've been knotting them in my lap. They're covered with a thin sheen of sweat. "And if you find Brooke? Will you let us know she's all right?"

"Of course. I'm heading to the station now. Maybe she's already home, getting a talking-to from her parents. Most of the time that's—" He stops suddenly, his neck going red as he darts a glance at Nana. "That's what we hope for."

I know what he was about to say. *Most of the time that's*

how these things turn out. It's the sort of thing police officers are trained to tell worried people so they won't spiral into panic when somebody goes missing. But it's not comforting in Echo Ridge.

Because Nana's right. It's never been true.

CHAPTER EIGHTEEN

MALCOLM
SUNDAY, SEPTEMBER 29

"You're an important witness here, Malcolm. Take your time."

Officer McNulty is still resting his forearms on the kitchen island. His sleeves are rolled up, and his watch reads 9:15. Brooke has been missing for almost ten hours. It's not that much time, but it feels like forever when you start imagining all the things that could happen to a person while the rest of the world is sleeping.

I'm sitting on the stool beside him. There are only a couple of feet between us, which doesn't feel like enough. Officer McNulty's eyes are still on me, cold and flat. He said *witness,* not *suspect,* but that isn't how he's looking at me. "That's it," I say. "That's everything I remember."

"So the Corcoran twins can corroborate your story right up until you dropped them off at their house?"

Jesus. *Corroborate your story.* My stomach tightens. I should've brought Brooke home first. Everything would look a lot different if I had. "Yeah," I say.

What the hell must Ellery be thinking right now? Does she even know?

Who am I kidding? This is Echo Ridge. Officer McNulty has been at our house for more than an hour. *Everyone* knows.

"All right," Officer McNulty says. "Let's go back a little while, before last night. Did you notice anything unusual about Brooke in the past few weeks? Anything that concerned or surprised you?"

I slide my eyes toward Katrin. She's leaning against the counter, but stiffly, like she's a mannequin somebody propped there. "I don't really know Brooke," I say. "I don't see her much."

"She's here a lot though, isn't she?" Officer McNulty asks.

It feels like he's after something, but I don't know what. Officer McNulty's eyes drop from my face to my knee, and I realize it's jiggling nervously. I press a fist onto my leg to stop the movement. "Yeah, but not to hang out with me."

"She thought you were cute," Katrin says abruptly.

What the hell? My throat closes, and I couldn't answer even if I knew what to say.

Everyone turns toward Katrin. "She's been saying that for a while," she continues. Her voice is low, but every word is perfectly clear and precise. "Last weekend, when she was sleeping over, I woke up and she wasn't in the room. I waited for, like, twenty minutes before I fell asleep again, but she didn't come back. I thought maybe she was visiting *you*. Especially since she broke up with Kyle a couple of days later."

The words hit me like a punch to the gut as all the heads in the room swivel to me. Jesus Christ, why would Katrin say something like that? She has to know how it would make me look. Even more suspicious than I already do. "She wasn't," I manage to say.

"Malcolm doesn't have a girlfriend," my mother says quickly. In the space of a half hour she's aged a year: her cheeks are hollow, her hair's straggling out of its neat bun, and there's a deep line etched between her brows. I know she's been traveling down the same memory lane that I have. "He's not like . . . he's always spent more time with his friends than with girls."

He's not like Declan. That's what she was about to say.

Officer McNulty's eyes bore into mine. "If there was anything going on with you and Brooke, Malcolm, now is the time to mention it. Doesn't mean you're in trouble." His jaw twitches, betraying the lie. "Just another piece of this puzzle we're trying to figure out."

"There wasn't," I say, meeting Katrin's cool stare. She edges closer to Peter. He's been silent all this time, arms folded, an expression of deep concern on his face. "The only time I ever see Brooke is when she's with Katrin. Except . . ." A thought hits me, and I look at Officer McNulty again. He's fully alert, leaning forward. "I did see her a few days ago. I was in the car with Mia," I add hastily. "We saw Brooke downtown, talking with Vance Puckett."

Officer McNulty blinks. Frowns. Whatever he was expecting me to say, that wasn't it. "Vance Puckett?"

"Yeah. He was painting over the graffiti on Armstrong's Auto Repair, and Brooke walked up to him. They were talking sort of . . . intensely. You asked about anything unusual, and that was, um, unusual." Even as the words spill out of me, I know how they sound.

Like a guy with something to hide who's trying to deflect attention.

"Interesting." Officer McNulty nods. "Vance Puckett was in the drunk tank last night, and in fact"—he glances at his watch—"is most likely still there. Thank you for the information, though. We'll be sure to follow up with him." He sits back and crosses his arms. He's wearing a dress shirt, and nicely pressed pants. I realize he was probably getting ready for church when all this happened. "Is there anything else you think would be good for us to know?"

My phone sits heavy in my pocket. It hasn't been buzzing, which means Mia probably isn't even awake yet. The last text I have was the one Declan sent before I entered the House of Horrors to pick up the twins.

In town for a few hours. Don't freak out.

Why was he here? Why was my brother here, *again,* when a girl goes missing?

If I showed that text to Officer McNulty now, everything would change. Katrin would stop looking daggers at me. Officer McNulty wouldn't keep asking the same question a dozen different ways. His suspicion would shift away from me, and go back to where it's been ever since Lacey died. To Declan.

I swallow hard and keep my phone where it is. "No. There's nothing."

CHAPTER NINETEEN

ELLERY

SUNDAY, SEPTEMBER 29

I can't sit still.

I pace through Nana's house all afternoon, picking things up and then putting them down. The bookshelves in her living room are full of those porcelain figures she likes—Hummels, Nana calls them. Little boys and girls with blond hair and apple cheeks, climbing trees and carrying baskets and hugging one another. Nana told me, when I picked one up a couple of days ago, that Sadie had broken it when she was ten.

"Knocked that one on the ground so its head split in two," Nana said. "She glued the pieces back together. I didn't notice for weeks."

Once you know to look for it, though, it's obvious. I held the porcelain girl in my hand and stared at the jagged white line running down one side of her face. "Were you mad?" I'd asked Nana.

"Furious," she said. "Those are collector's items. The girls weren't supposed to touch them. But Sadie couldn't keep her hands off them. I knew it was her, even when Sarah told me *she'd* done it."

"Sarah did? Why?"

"She didn't want her sister to get punished," Nana said. For the first time when talking about Sarah, a spasm of grief crossed her face. "I was always a little harder on Sadie, I suppose. Because she was usually the one causing trouble."

It didn't occur to me, until just now, that some of that sadness might have been for my mother. For another cracked girl, broken and pieced clumsily back together. Still standing, but not the same.

There's only one family photo in the living room: it's of Nana and my grandfather, looking like they're in their late thirties, and Sadie and Sarah around twelve years old. I pick it up and study their faces. All I can think is: *they had no idea.*

Just like Brooke's family had no idea. Or maybe they did. Maybe they've been worried since Brooke's locker was vandalized and the bloody meat was thrown on her car, wondering if there was something they should be doing. Maybe they're sick about it now. Because it's almost one o'clock, and nobody's heard a word from her.

My phone buzzes, and I put the photo down to pull it from my pocket. My pulse jumps when I see a text from Malcolm: *Can we talk?*

I hesitate. I'd thought about texting him after Officer Rodriguez left, but I didn't know what to say. I still don't. Gray dots appear, and I forget to breathe while I watch them.

I understand if you don't want to.

The thing is, I do.

I text back, *Okay. Where?*

Wherever you want. I could come by?

That's a good idea, because there's no way Nana's letting me out of the house today. I'm surprised she even went to the basement to do laundry. *When?* I ask.

Ten minutes?

Okay.

I go upstairs and knock on Ezra's bedroom door. He doesn't answer, probably because he's blasting music with his headphones on. It's his go-to escape whenever he's worried. I twist the knob and push open the door and sure enough, he's at his desk with a pair of Bose clamped firmly over his ears, staring at his laptop. He jumps when I tap his shoulder.

"Malcolm's coming over," I say once he's pulled off the headphones.

"He is? Why?"

"Um. He didn't say, exactly. But I assume . . . you know. He wants to talk about Brooke and maybe . . ." I think about his second message. *I understand if you don't want to.* "Maybe explain what happened after he dropped us off."

"We know what happened," Ezra says. We already heard a version of it from Nana, who heard it from Melanie, who probably heard it from Peter Nilsson. Or one of those other people in Echo Ridge who seem to know everything as soon as it happens. "Malcolm dropped Brooke off and she went inside." He frowns when I don't answer. "What, do you not believe that? Ellery, come on. He's our *friend.*"

"Who we've known a month," I say. "And the first time I met

him, he was holding a can of spray paint at Lacey's fund-raiser."
Ezra's mouth opens, but I plow ahead before he can interrupt.
"Look, all I'm saying is that it's not unreasonable to question
him right now."

"*Do* you question him?" Ezra asks.

I hesitate. I don't want to. I've never seen Malcolm be anything but kind, even when he was frustrated. Not to mention,
he's spent the past five years in the shadow of *Declan Kelly—
murder suspect.* Even if he was the sort of person who wanted
to hurt Brooke, he's not an idiot. He wouldn't put himself in a
Declan-like situation before doing it.

Unless it wasn't premeditated.

God. It's exhausting, thinking this way. Ezra is lucky he hasn't
read as many true-crime books as I have. I can't shut them out.

He shakes his head at me, looking disappointed but not
particularly surprised. "This is exactly what we don't need right
now, El. Wild theories that distract people from what's really
going on."

"Which is?"

He rubs a hand over his face. "Hell if I know. But I don't
think it involves our friend just because he was in the wrong
place at the wrong time."

I twist my hands and tap my foot. I still can't stop moving.
"I'm going to wait outside. You coming?"

"Yeah," Ezra says, pulling his headphones from around his
neck and dropping them on the cluttered desk. He's done more
to personalize his room than I have, covering the walls with pictures from our last school and posters of his favorite bands. It
looks like a teenager's room, while mine still looks like a guest

room. I don't know what I'm waiting for. Some feeling like I belong here, maybe.

We go downstairs and outside to Nana's front porch, settling ourselves on the bench beside the door. We haven't been there more than a couple of minutes when Mrs. Nilsson's car pulls into our driveway. Malcolm gets out and lifts his hand in an anemic wave, then makes his way up the lawn to us. There's room for one more on our bench, but Malcolm doesn't sit there. He leans against the porch railing, facing us, and shoves his hands into his pockets. I don't know where to look, so I pick a spot over his shoulder. "Hey, guys," he says quietly.

"How are you holding up, Mal?" Ezra asks.

I steal a glance at Malcolm as the tense lines of his face briefly relax. It means the world to him, I realize, that Ezra greeted him like normal.

"Been better," he says. "I just wanted to tell you"—he's looking at me, as if he knows Ezra never had a second's doubt—"I wanted you to hear from me what I told Officer McNulty, that I saw Brooke get home safely. I watched her go inside and close the door. And then I drove home, and that's all I knew about anything until this morning."

"We know. Wrong place, wrong time," Ezra says, echoing what he said upstairs. "People can't hold that against you."

"Well." Malcolm slouches lower against the railing. "The thing is— Katrin is saying stuff." He swallows hard. "She thinks Brooke and I were hooking up."

I go rigid as Ezra inhales sharply. "What?" he asks. "Why?"

Malcolm shrugs helplessly. "I don't know. She asked me last week if I'd take Brooke to homecoming. Since she'd just broken up with Kyle and didn't have a date." He darts a glance at me, which I catch out of the corner of my eye because I'm staring over his shoulder again. "I didn't ask her, and Katrin never brought it up again. But that's the only time she's ever talked about Brooke and me. Even then, she said we'd just go as friends."

I look down and watch a ladybug crawl across one of the porch floorboards until it slips through a crack. "I thought you and Katrin got along," I say.

"I thought so, too," Malcolm says, his voice heavy. "I honestly don't know where this is coming from. I'm sick about it. I'm worried out of my mind about Brooke. But it isn't true. At all. So I wanted you to know that, too."

I finally meet his eyes full-on. They're sad and scared and, yes, kind. In that moment, I choose to believe he's not *a Kelly boy with a temper,* or *someone with opportunity and motive,* or *the quiet kind you'd never suspect.* I choose to believe he's the person he's always shown himself to be.

I choose to trust him.

"We believe you," I say, and he sags visibly with relief.

CHAPTER TWENTY

MALCOLM

MONDAY, SEPTEMBER 30

Brooke is still missing at lunchtime. And I'm getting a firsthand look at what my brother went through five years ago.

The entire Echo Ridge High student body has been staring at me all morning. Everybody's whispering behind my back, except the few who get right in my face. Like Kyle McNulty. He and his sister, Liz, were away all weekend visiting her friends at the University of Vermont, so nobody's interrogating *him*. Almost as soon as I walked into the hallway this morning, he grabbed my arm and slammed me against the locker bay. "If you did anything to Brooke, I will *end* you," he growled.

I broke away and shoved him back. "Fuck you, McNulty." He probably would've hit me then if a teacher hadn't stepped between us.

Now Mia and I are headed for the cafeteria, passing a

homecoming poster along the way. During morning announcements, Principal Slate said that while they hadn't decided whether to cancel Saturday's dance, it was being "significantly scaled back," with no homecoming court. He ended with a reminder to report anything or anyone suspicious.

Which, for most of the student body, is me.

If I weren't so sick to my stomach, I might laugh at how fiercely Mia glares at everyone we pass in the hallway. "Go ahead and try it," she mutters, as a couple of Kyle's teammates who are twice her size give me the once-over. "I hope you do."

In the cafeteria we grab trays. I pile food on mine that I know I won't be able to eat and then we make our way to our usual table. By unspoken agreement we both sit with our backs against the wall, facing the cafeteria. If anybody's coming for me, I'd rather see them do it.

Mia sends a look of pure loathing toward Katrin's table, where Viv is gesturing dramatically. "Already working on her next story, I'll bet. This is exactly the plot twist she was waiting for."

I force down a sip of water. "Jesus, Mia. They're friends."

"Stop thinking the best of people, Mal," Mia says. "Nobody's doing it for you. We should . . ." She trails off as the noise level in the cafeteria grows louder. The Corcoran twins have emerged from the food line, trays in hand. I haven't talked to them yet today, and every time I've spotted one of them they were surrounded by knots of students. The whole school knows they were the second-to-last people to see Brooke before she disappeared, and everybody wants their take on Saturday night. I don't have to be within earshot to know what kind of questions they're getting: *Have you guys heard that Brooke and Malcolm were hooking up? Did they act weird around each other? Were they fighting?*

Do you think he did something to her?

I could tell yesterday that Ezra is exactly like Mia: it never even occurred to him that I might've done anything except drop Brooke off. Ellery's mind doesn't work that way, though. She's naturally suspicious. I get it, but . . . it stung. And even though it seemed like she came around eventually, I'm not sure it's going to last when half the school is whispering in her ear.

Mia watches the two of them like she's having the exact same thought. Ezra's eyes light on us at almost the same time Katrin's hand shoots into the air. "Ellery!" Katrin calls. "Over here!" She doesn't include Ezra, and I feel pathetically grateful when he starts toward us. Even though I know it's probably just because he wasn't invited anywhere else.

Ellery hesitates, and it feels as though the entire cafeteria is watching her. Her curly hair is long and loose today, and when she looks toward Katrin it obscures half her face. My heart jack-hammers in my chest as I try to tell myself it doesn't matter what she does. It won't change anything. Brooke will still be missing, and half the town will still hate me because I'm a Kelly.

Ellery lifts her hand and waves at Katrin, then turns away from her and follows Ezra to our table. I exhale for what feels like the first time all day, relieved, but the buzz in the cafeteria only gets louder. Ezra reaches us first, pulling out two chairs with a noisy scrape and lowering himself into one of them. "Hey," he says quietly. Ellery puts her tray next to his and slips into the remaining chair, offering me a tentative smile.

Just like that, we're all outsiders together.

· · ·

It's not right, it's not okay.

That's the part of what Brooke said in the Fright Farm office that sticks with me the most. With Ellery, too. "The one time I sat with her and Katrin at lunch, she looked worn down," she says. "Something was definitely bothering her."

We're at Mia's house after school, scattered around her living room. I'm keeping a constant eye on social media, hoping for some kind of positive update on Brooke, but all I see are posts about organizing a search. The police don't want people doing anything on their own, so they're recruiting volunteers for a co-ordinated effort.

Daisy is holed up in her bedroom as usual, and Mia's parents aren't home. Thank God. I'd like to think Dr. and Mr. Kwon wouldn't treat me any different from how they always have, but I'm not ready to find out.

"Maybe that's why she was talking to Vance," Mia says. She's still seething that nobody took me seriously about that. "She could've been asking for help."

Ezra looks dubious. "I don't know. I've only met the guy once, but he didn't strike me as the helpful type."

"He was Sadie's homecoming date," Ellery says. "That means nothing, I guess, but . . . it's weird how he keeps popping up, isn't it?"

"Yeah," I agree. "But he was locked up all night."

"According to Officer McNulty," Ellery says darkly.

I blink at her. "What, you—you think he was making that up?" At least she's equal opportunity with her conspiracy theories.

"I don't think the Echo Ridge police are very competent, do

you?" she asks. "Somebody basically drew them a map that was all, *hey, hello, here's my next victim.* And she disappeared anyway."

She half swallows the last word, hunching down in the Kwons' oversized leather armchair. I blink, surprised at how lost she suddenly looks, and then I could kick myself for being so caught up in my own problems that I didn't make the connection sooner. "You're scared," I say, because *of course* she is. She was on that list too.

Ezra leans forward on the couch. "Nothing's going to happen to you, El," he says. Like he can make it true through sheer force of will. Mia nods vigorously beside him.

"I know." Ellery hugs her knees to her chest and rests her chin on them. "That's not how this works, right? It's always one girl. There's no reason to worry about me right now, or Katrin. Just Brooke."

There's no way in hell I'm going to remind her that we don't have a clue how any of this works. "We can worry about all of you. But it'll be all right, Ellery. We'll make sure of it." It's the worst reassurance ever, coming from the guy who thought he got Brooke home safely. But it's all I've got.

Light footsteps sound on the stairs, and Daisy appears on the landing. She's wearing giant sunglasses and an oversized sweater, clutching her bag like a shield. "I'm going out for a little while," she says, heading for the Kwons' front door and pulling a jacket off their coatrack. She moves so quickly, she looks as though she's gliding across the floor.

"'Kay," Mia says, scrolling through her phone like she's barely listening. But as soon as the door closes behind Daisy, Mia's head snaps up. "Let's follow her," she says in a loud whisper, springing to her feet.

Ezra and Ellery lift their brows in almost comical unison. "We already know where she goes," I object, my face getting hot as the twins exchange surprised glances. Great. Nothing like outing yourself as a stalker in front of your only friends.

"But we don't know why," Mia says, peering through the blinds of the window next to the door. "Daisy's seeing a psychologist and she never told me," she adds over her shoulder to the twins. "It's all very mysterious and I, for one, am sick of mysteries around here. At least we can do something about this one if we're quick enough. Okay, she just pulled out. Let's go."

"Mia, this is ridiculous," I protest, but to my surprise Ellery's already halfway to the door, with Ezra right behind her. Neither of them seems concerned about the fact that Mia's spying on her own sister with my help. So we pile into my mother's Volvo, and head down the same road Daisy took last Thursday. We catch up to her pretty quickly, and keep a few car lengths behind her.

"Don't lose her," Mia says, her eyes on the road. "We need answers."

"What are you going to do? Try to listen in on her session?" Ezra sounds both confused and disturbed. I'm with him; even if that wasn't a massive violation of Daisy's privacy and probably illegal, I don't see how you could do it.

"I don't know," Mia says with a shrug. Typical Mia: all action, no planning. "She's going twice in one week. That seems like a lot, doesn't it?"

"Beats me," I say, getting into the left lane in preparation for a turn that Daisy will be making at the next intersection. Except she doesn't. I swerve to stay straight and the car behind me blares its horn as I run a yellow light.

"Smooth," Ezra notes. "This is going well. Very stealthy."

Mia frowns. "*Now* where's she going?"

"Gym?" I guess, starting to feel foolish. "Shopping?"

But Daisy doesn't head downtown, or toward the highway that would take us to the nearest mall. She sticks to back roads until we pass Bukowski's Tavern and enter Solsbury, the next town over. The houses are smaller and closer together here than they are in Echo Ridge, and the lawns look like they get mowed a lot less. Daisy's blinker comes on after we pass a liquor store, and she turns in front of a sign that reads "Pine Crest Estates."

That's an optimistic name, I think. It's an apartment complex, full of the kind of cheap, boxy places you can't find in Echo Ridge but that are all over Solsbury. Mom and I checked out someplace similar right before she and Peter got together. If they hadn't, we weren't going to be able to hang on to our house for much longer. Even if it *was* the smallest, crappiest house in all of Echo Ridge.

"Is she moving out?" Mia wonders. Daisy inches through the parking lot, angling the gray Nissan in front of number 9. There's a blue car to her right, and I pull into an empty spot next to that. We all scrunch down in our seats as she gets out of the car, like that'll keep us incognito. All Daisy would have to do is turn her head to catch sight of my mother's Volvo. But she doesn't look around as she gets out, just strides forward and knocks on the door.

Once, twice, and then a third time.

Daisy pulls off her sunglasses, stuffs them into her bag, and knocks again. "Maybe we should leave before she gives up. I don't think they're ho—" I stop talking when the door to number 9 opens. Somebody wraps his arms around Daisy and swings her halfway around, kissing her so deeply that Mia lets out a gasp beside me.

"Oh my God, Daisy has a boyfriend," she says, scrambling out of her seat belt and leaning so far left that she's practically in my lap. "And here she's been so Mopey McMoperson since she moved home! I did *not* see that coming." We're all craning our necks for a better view, but it's not until Daisy breaks away that I catch sight of who she's with—along with something I haven't seen in years.

My brother grinning like his face is about to break, before he pulls Daisy inside and shuts the door behind her.

CHAPTER TWENTY-ONE

ELLERY

"So," Malcolm says, plugging tokens into one end of a foosball table. "That was interesting."

After leaving Declan's apartment, we stopped at the first place we came to that we were pretty sure he and Daisy wouldn't show up on a date. It happened to be a Chuck E. Cheese's. I haven't been to one in years, so I've forgotten what a sensory assault they are: flashing lights, beeping games, tinny music, and screaming children.

The guy letting people in at the door wasn't sure about us at first. "You're supposed to come with kids," he said, glancing behind us at the empty hallway.

"We *are* kids," Mia pointed out, extending her hand for a stamp.

Turns out, Chuck E. Cheese's is the perfect location for a clandestine debrief. Every adult in the place is too busy either chasing after or hiding from their children to pay us any attention. I feel weirdly calm after our trip to Pine Crest Estates, the dread that came over me at Mia's house almost entirely gone. There's something satisfying about unlocking another piece of the Echo Ridge puzzle, even if I'm not yet sure where it fits.

"So," Mia echoes, gripping a handle on the other end of the foosball table. Ezra is next to her, and I'm beside Malcolm. A ball pops out of one side, and Mia spins a bar furiously, missing the ball completely. "Your brother and my sister. How long do you think that's been going on?"

Malcolm maneuvers one of his players carefully before smacking the ball, and would have scored if Ezra hadn't blocked it. "Damned if I know. Since they both came back, maybe? But that still doesn't explain what they're doing here. Couldn't they hook up in New Hampshire? Or Boston?" He passes the ball to one of his own men, then backward to me, and I rocket a shot across the field into the open goal. Malcolm gives me a surprised, disarmed grin that dissolves the tense set of his jaw. "Not bad."

I want to smile back, but I can't. There's something I've been thinking ever since we pulled away from Pine Crest Estates, and I keep weighing how—or whether—to bring it up.

"I don't think they can hook up *anywhere*," Mia says. "Can you imagine if one of the reporters who've been prowling around Echo Ridge got wind of this? Lacey Kilduff's boyfriend and best friend, together five years later? While somebody's making a mockery of her death by writing bullshit all around town and another girl's just gone missing?" She shudders, managing to nick the ball with the edge of one of her men. "People would *hate* them."

"What if it's not five years later?" The words pop out of me,

173

and Malcolm goes still. The foosball rolls unchallenged down the length of the table and settles into a corner. "I mean," I add, almost apologetically, "they might've been together for a while."

Mia shakes her head. "Daisy's had other boyfriends. She almost got engaged to the guy she was dating at Princeton."

"Okay, so not all five years," I say. "But maybe . . . at some point in high school?"

Malcolm's jaw has gone tense again. He braces his forearms on the table and fastens his green eyes on me. Both are disconcerting at close range, if I'm being honest. "Like when?"

Like while Declan was still dating Lacey. It'd be the classic deadly love triangle. I have to bite the inside of my cheeks to keep from saying it out loud. What if Declan and Daisy fell in love years ago and wanted to be together, but Lacey wouldn't let him go? Or threatened to do something to Daisy in retaliation? And it infuriated Declan so much that he lost control one night and killed her? Then Daisy broke things off with him, obviously, and tried to forget him, but couldn't. I'm itching to expand on my theory, but one look at Malcolm's frozen face tells me I shouldn't. "I don't know," I hedge, dropping my eyes. "Just throwing out ideas."

It's like I told Ezra in the library: You can't spring a *your-siblings-might-be-murderers* theory onto people all at once.

Mia doesn't notice the subtext of my back-and-forth with Malcolm. She's too busy savagely jerking her rod of blue players without ever touching the ball. "It wouldn't be an issue if Daisy would just *talk* to me. Or to anyone in our family."

"Maybe you need to pull a little-sister power play," Ezra suggests.

"Such as?"

He shrugs. "She tells you what's going on, or you tell your parents what you just saw."

Mia goggles at him. "That's straight-up *evil*."

"But effective, I'll bet," Ezra says. He glances at Malcolm. "I'd suggest the same thing to you, but I just saw your brother, so."

"Oh yeah." Malcolm grimaces. "He'd kill me. Not literally," he adds hastily, with a sideways glance at me. "But also, he knows I'd never do it. Our father wouldn't care, but our mom would lose it. Especially now."

Mia's eyes gleam as she lines one of her men up for a shot. "I have no such concerns."

We play for a few minutes without speaking. My mind keeps racing along the Declan-Daisy theory that I didn't say, testing it for holes. There are a few, admittedly. But it's such a true-crime staple when girls go missing or are harmed: *it's always the boyfriend.* Or a frustrated wannabe. Because when you're seventeen, and beautiful, and you're found murdered in a place known for hookups, what could it possibly be except a crime of passion?

So that leaves Declan. The only other person I'm even remotely suspicious of is the guy Lacey never noticed—Officer Ryan Rodriguez. I can't forget his photo in the yearbook, or Sadie's description of him breaking down at Lacey's funeral. Still, Officer Rodriguez doesn't *fit* like Declan does—he makes perfect sense, especially now that we know about him and Daisy.

I don't believe for one second that they're a new thing. The only question in my mind is whether Malcolm's willing to admit it.

I steal a glance at Malcolm as he twists his handles, fully concentrating on the game. Brow furrowed, green eyes crinkling when he makes a good shot, lean arms flexing. He has absolutely no idea how attractive he is, and it's kind of a problem. He's so used to living in his brother's shadow that he doesn't believe he's the kind of guy who could've snagged the attention of a girl like Brooke. Anybody else can see it from a mile away.

He looks up and meets my eyes. *Busted.* I feel myself go red as his mouth lifts in a half smile. Then he glances down again, pulling his phone from his pocket and unlocking the screen. His face changes in an instant. Mia sees it too and stops spinning her handles. "Any news?" she asks.

"A text from my mom. Nothing about Brooke," Malcolm says, and we all relax. Because from the look on his face, it wouldn't have been good. "Except there's a search party tomorrow. During the day, so Echo Ridge students aren't supposed to go. And there's an article in the *Boston Globe.*" He sighs heavily. "My mom's freaking out. She gets traumatized any time the news mentions Lacey."

"Can I see?" I ask. He hands the phone to me, and I read the section framed within the screen:

> The small town was already on edge after a series of vandalism incidents beginning in early September. Buildings and signs were defaced with messages written as though they were from Lacey Kilduff's killer. The anonymous threats promised another attack on one of the girls elected to homecoming court—a short list that included Brooke Bennett. But those who've been following the story closely don't see any real connection.

"Even if someone was unhinged enough to get away with murder and brag about it five years later, the MO's are completely different," says Vivian Cantrell, a senior at Echo Ridge High who has covered the story for her school paper. "Strangulation is a brutal crime of passion. The threats are public, and they require planning. I don't think there's any relation at all to what happened to Lacey, or what's going on with Brooke."

I grip the phone more tightly. That's almost exactly what I said two weeks ago at lunch. Viv basically stole my entire spiel and used it to replace her original point of view. Before this, she'd been telling everybody that Lacey's death and the anonymous threats *had* to be related.

Why did Viv suddenly change her tune?

CHAPTER TWENTY-TWO

ELLERY

WEDNESDAY, OCTOBER 2

It's the first week in October, and starting to get dark earlier. But even if it weren't, Nana would insist on driving Ezra and me to our shift at Fright Farm after dinner.

I don't bother reminding her that it's only a ten-minute walk as she plucks her keys from a hook next to her wall-mounted phone. Brooke has been missing for four days, and the entire town is on edge. Search parties all day, and candlelight vigils at night. After two days of heated debate at school, homecoming is still on for Saturday—but without a court. I'm no longer techni-cally a princess. Which is fine, I guess, since I still don't have a date.

The same few theories keep circulating: that Brooke ran away, that she's the victim of the Murderland killer, that one of the Kelly boys did something to her. Everything in Echo Ridge feels like a thick, bubbling mess that's about to boil over.

Nana is silent on the ride over, clutching the steering wheel and driving fifteen miles below the speed limit until we near the entrance. Then she pulls to the side of the road and says, "The House of Horrors closes at eleven, right?"

"Right."

"I'll be outside the gates at eleven-oh-five."

That's two hours past her bedtime, but we don't argue. I told her earlier that Malcolm could give us a ride, and she insisted on picking us up anyway. I don't think she believes he's involved in Brooke's disappearance—she hasn't told us to stop hanging out with him—but she's not taking any chances, and I can't blame her. I'm a little surprised she's still letting us go to work.

Ezra and I climb out of the car and watch its taillights recede so slowly that a bicycle passes it. We're halfway through the gates when my phone rings with a familiar California number.

I hold it up to Ezra. "Sadie must've heard."

It was only a matter of time. Brooke's disappearance has become national news, and Nana's been hanging up all week on reporters angling for a "One Town, Three Missing Girls" story. Hamilton House Rehabilitation Facility allegedly bans Internet access, but since Sadie's already used her borrowed cell phone to check out Ezra's Instagram before FaceTiming us, she's obviously flouting that rule, too.

I slide to answer and press the phone to my ear. "Hi, Sadie."

"Ellery, thank God you picked up." Her agitated voice crackles across the line. "I just read about what's happening there. Are you and Ezra all right?"

"We're fine. Just worried about Brooke."

"Oh my God, of course you are. That poor girl. Her poor family." She pauses for a beat, her breath harsh in my ear. "So

179

the article . . . it said there were *threats* beforehand? Toward three girls, and that one of them was someone who . . . who was related to . . . Was it you, Ellery?"

"It was me," I confirm. Ezra gestures like he wants me to FaceTime, but I wave him off. It's too crowded here.

"Why didn't you *tell* me?"

The bitter laugh springs out of me without warning. "Why would I?"

Silence on the other end, so complete that I think she's disconnected. I'm about to pull the phone away from my ear to check when Sadie says, "Because I'm your mother and I have a right to know."

It's exactly the wrong thing to say. Resentment floods my veins, and I have to grip the phone extra tight to stop myself from hurling it to the ground. "Oh, really? You have a *right to know*? That's rich coming from somebody who's never told us anything that matters."

"What are you talking about?"

"Our father? We're not allowed to ask questions about him! Our grandmother? We barely knew her until we had to live with her! Our aunt? You had a twin sister, as close as me and Ezra are, and you never, *ever* talk about her. Now we're stuck here watching the same horrible story unfold *again* and everybody's talking about the first girl who went missing. Except us. We don't know anything about Sarah because you won't even say her name!"

I'm breathing hard, my heart pounding as I stalk through the park. I don't know whether I'm relieved or horrified to finally be saying these things to Sadie. All I know is that I can't stop.

"You're not okay, Sadie. I mean, you get that, right? You're not in rehab because of some freak accident that'll be a funny

180

story to tell at parties when you get out. You weren't taking those pills to *relax*. I've spent years waiting for something like this to happen, and I thought . . . I was afraid . . ." Tears blur my vision and slide down my face. "This whole year I've been expecting *that* phone call. The one Nana got, and Melanie got. The one that says you're never coming home."

She's been silent during my entire tirade, but this time, before I can check to see whether she's hung up on me, I hear a choked sob. "I . . . *can't*," Sadie says in a ragged voice that I'd never recognize if I didn't know it was her. "I can't talk about her. It *kills* me."

I've wandered near the games section, and I have to plug my free ear against the noise of the park. Ezra stands a short distance away, his arms folded and his face grave. "It's killing you not to," I say. She doesn't answer, and I squeeze my eyelids shut. I can't look at my brother right now. "Sadie, I *know*, okay? I know exactly how you must feel. Me and Ezra both do. It's horrible what happened to Sarah. It sucks and it's not fair and I'm so, so sorry. For you and for Nana and for her." My mother's sobs on the other end of the line pierce me like a knife to the heart. "And I'm sorry I yelled at you. I didn't mean to. It's just . . . I feel like we're going to be stuck like this forever if we can't talk about it."

I open my eyes while I wait for her to answer. It's almost dark now, and the park lights glow against the deep blue sky. Screams and catcalls fill the air and little kids chase one another with their parents a safe distance behind. All of Fright Farm's success is based on how much people love to be scared in a controlled environment. There's something deeply, fundamentally satisfying about confronting a monster and escaping unscathed.

Real monsters aren't anything like that. They don't let go.

181

"Do you know what I was doing the night Sarah disappeared?" Sadie asks in the same hoarse voice.

My reply is barely a whisper. "No."

"Losing my virginity to my homecoming date." She lets out a hysterical half laugh, half sob. "I was supposed to be with Sarah. But I blew her off. For *that*."

"Oh, Sadie." I don't even realize I've sunk to the ground until my free hand touches grass. "It's not your fault."

"Of course it's my fault! If I'd been with her she'd still be here!"

"You don't know that. You can't— You were just living your life. Being *normal*. You didn't do anything wrong. None of this is your fault."

"Would you feel that way? If something happened to Ezra when you were supposed to be with him?" I don't answer right away, and she cries harder. "I can't look at my mother. I couldn't look at my father. I didn't speak to him for almost a year before he died and then I drank my way through the entire funeral. You and your brother are the only thing I've ever done right since Sarah disappeared. And now I've ruined that too."

"You didn't ruin anything." I say it automatically to comfort her, but as soon as the words are out of my mouth, I realize they're true. Ezra and I might not have had the most stable childhood, but we never had any doubt that our mother loved us. She never put a job or a boyfriend ahead of us, and it wasn't until the pills took hold that her haphazard parenting turned into actual neglect. Sadie's made mistakes, but they're not the kind that leave you feeling like you don't matter. "We're fine and we love you and please don't do this to yourself. Don't blame yourself for something so awful that you never could've seen coming." I'm babbling now, my words tripping over themselves, and Sadie lets out a teary laugh.

"Listen to us. You wanted to talk, huh? Be careful what you wish for."

There's so much I want to say, but all I can manage is, "I'm glad we're talking."

"Me too." She takes a deep, shuddering breath. "There's more I should tell you. Not about Sarah, but about— Oh hell. I have to go, Ellery, I'm sorry. Please be careful there, and I'll call again when I can." Then she's gone. I drop the phone from my ear and get to my feet as Ezra strides toward me, looking ready to burst.

"What's going on? I heard some of it, but—"

Movement over his shoulder catches my eye, and I put a hand on his arm. "Hang on. I have a *lot* to tell you, but . . . there's somebody I want to talk to first." I wipe my eyes and glance at my phone. We're already late for work, but oh well.

An older woman is manning the shooting gallery where Brooke used to work, yawning as she makes change and pulls levers. Vance Puckett stands with a toy gun mounted on his shoulder, methodically knocking over targets. Malcolm told us at lunch that he was interrogated again last night by Officer Mc-Nulty, who said the police interviewed Vance about his conversation with Brooke downtown. According to Vance, Brooke just asked him what time it was. Malcolm was frustrated, but Mia threw up her hands in resignation. "Of course. Why should he help out? There's nothing in it for him, and he doesn't care about anybody in this town."

Maybe she's right. Or maybe he's just broken in his own way.

Vance fishes in his pockets for change to play another round. I sidle past a trio of preteens and plunk two dollars on the counter. "My treat this time," I say.

He turns and squints, tapping his forefinger to his chin. It takes a few seconds for him to recognize me. "Shooter girl. You got lucky that last game."

"Maybe," I say. "I have six bucks on me. Should we play best two out of three?" He nods, and I gesture toward the targets. "Champions first."

Vance gets off to a shaky start, only hitting eight out of twelve targets. It kills my competitive spirit to miss five when it's my turn, but all this will be pointless if he stalks off in a huff again when we're done.

"You lost your touch." Vance smirks when I lower my gun. Ezra, who's watching us with his hands on his hips, looks like he's physically biting his tongue.

"I was just warming up," I lie.

I keep it close in the next couple of rounds, losing by one each time. Vance is pumped up by the end, preening and chuckling, going so far as to slap me on the back when I miss my final shot. "Nice try, kid. You almost pulled one out."

"I guess I did get lucky last time," I say with a theatrical sigh. I don't have Sadie's talent, which is obvious from Ezra's grimace as we move to one side so the people waiting behind us can play. But I'm hoping it's good enough for a drunk guy. "My mother told me it probably wouldn't happen again."

Vance adjusts his cap over oily hair. "Your mother?"

"Sadie Corcoran," I say. "You're Vance, right? She said you

184

guys went to homecoming together and that I should introduce myself. I'm Ellery."

It's weird holding out my hand after what Sadie just told me. But he takes it, looking genuinely flummoxed.

"She said that? Wouldn't have thought she even remembers me."

She talks about you all the time, I almost say, but decide to keep things believable. "She does. It's not easy for her to talk about Echo Ridge after what happened to her sister, but— She's always spoken well of you."

It's close enough to true, I guess. And I'm feeling pretty charitable toward him myself, since he's the only person in Echo Ridge who has an alibi for both Sarah's and Brooke's disappearances. Suddenly, Vance Puckett is the most trustworthy man in town.

He spits on the ground, close to my sneakers. Somehow, I manage not to flinch. "Damn shame what happened."

"I know. She's never gotten over it. And now my friend is missing. . . ." I glance at the new woman behind the counter. "I guess you knew Brooke, huh? Since you play here all the time."

"Nice kid," he says gruffly. He shuffles his feet, looking antsy and ready to move on. Ezra taps his watch and raises his brows at me. *Get to the point.*

"The worst thing is, I know something was bothering her before she disappeared," I say. "We were supposed to get together on Sunday so she could tell me what was going on, but we never got the chance. And it's killing me." Tears spring into my eyes, still close to the surface from my conversation with Sadie, and spill down my cheeks. I'm playing a part, but Sadie's always said the best acting happens when you're emotionally connected to the scene. I'm torn up enough about what happened to Brooke to pull it off. "I just— I wish I knew what she needed."

Vance rubs his jaw. Rocks back on his heels, twists to look at the crowd over his shoulder. "I don't like getting involved," he mumbles. "Not with people in this town, and especially not with the police."

"Me either," I say quickly. "We're total outsiders here. Brooke was—*is*—one of my only friends." I fish around in my bag for a Kleenex and blow my nose.

"She asked me a strange question last week." Vance speaks quietly, in a rush, and my heart leaps into my throat. "Wanted to know how to pick a lock." A shifty expression crosses his face. "Not sure why she'd think *I'd* know. I told her to Google it, or watch a YouTube video or something. Or just use a couple of paper clips."

"Paper clips?" I ask.

Vance swats at a hovering bug. "Those work sometimes. So I'm told. Anyway . . ." He meets my gaze, and I see a glimmer of something like kindness in his bloodshot eyes. "That's a thing that was on her mind. So now you know."

"Thanks," I say, feeling a pinprick of shame for manipulating him. "You have no idea how much that helps."

"Well. You tell your mother I said hello." He tips his baseball cap and shuffles past Ezra, who brings his hands together in a slow clap once Vance is out of hearing range.

"Well played, El. Although that guy's never gonna let you live down the loss."

"I know," I sigh, digging for another Kleenex to dry my still-damp cheeks. As I watch Vance melt into the crowd, a prickle of excitement works its way up my spine. "Did you hear what he said, though? He told Brooke to pick a lock with *paper clips*."

"Yeah. So?"

"So that's what she was holding in the House of Horrors office, remember? A straightened paper clip. I took it from her. She said something like, *This is harder than he said it would be.* " My voice climbs with anticipation, and I force it back down. "She was trying to pick a lock right then and there. And we interrupted her."

"The desk, maybe?" Ezra wonders.

I shake my head. "I get stuff out of that desk all the time. It isn't locked. But—" Heat floods my face as I remember where Brooke was sitting. "But I think I know what is."

CHAPTER TWENTY-THREE

MALCOLM

THURSDAY, OCTOBER 3

By Thursday, search parties for Brooke aren't limited to school hours anymore. There's one this afternoon, covering the woods behind the Nilssons' house. Peter's a volunteer captain, and when I get home from band practice he's loading a cardboard box filled with flyers, bottled water, and flashlights into the back of his Range Rover.

"Hello, Malcolm." He doesn't look at me as I get out of Mom's Volvo. Just brushes his palms together as though they're dusty. I'm sure they aren't. Peter's car is as pristine as everything else the Nilssons own. "How was school?"

"Same." In other words: *not good.* "When are we leaving?"

Peter crosses his arms, displaying razor-sharp creases in the sleeves of his shirt. "*We* are leaving in ten minutes," he says. The emphasis is clear, but when I don't respond he adds, "I don't think it's a good idea for you to come, Malcolm."

My heart sinks. "Why?" It's a pointless question. I know why. Officer McNulty has been back twice already to ask me follow-up questions.

Peter's nostrils flare. "Emotions are running high right now. You'd be a distraction. I'm sorry. I know that's hard to hear, but it's the truth, and our first priority is finding Brooke."

My temper spikes. "I *know*. I want to help."

"The best way you can help is to stay here," Peter says, and my palms itch with an almost irresistible desire to punch the smug look off his face. I'm sure he's genuinely concerned, and he might even be right. But he gets off on being the hero, too. Always has.

He claps a hand on my shoulder, quickly, like he's killing a bug. "Why don't you go inside and see if there's any more water in the fridge? That would be helpful."

A vein above my eye starts to throb. "Sure," I say, swallowing my anger because getting into a pissing match with Peter isn't going to help Brooke.

When I get inside, I hear the staircase in the foyer creak. I'm hoping for my mother, but it's Katrin with a heap of red fabric hanging over her arm, followed by Viv. Katrin freezes when she sees me, and Viv almost bumps into her. Both of their faces harden into the mask of dislike I've been seeing everywhere since Sunday.

I make an effort to act like I normally would. "What's that?" I ask, gesturing toward Katrin's arm.

"My homecoming dress," she snaps.

I eye the dress with a feeling of mild dread. I've been trying to block out the fact that homecoming is Saturday. "It's weird they're still having that." Katrin doesn't reply, and I add, "What are you doing with your dress?"

"Your mom's going to have it pressed." She gives me a wide

berth as she makes her way into the kitchen, carefully draping the dress over the back of a chair. It's nice, I guess, that my mom does stuff like that for Katrin. Peter says Katrin's own mother hasn't responded to any of his calls all week, other than to text something about bad cell reception in the South of France. There's always some excuse.

When she's finished arranging the dress, Katrin stares at me with glacial blue eyes. "I'd better not see you there."

Somehow, Katrin doesn't make me angry like Peter does. Maybe because I know she's barely eaten or slept since Brooke went missing. Her cheeks are hollow, her lips chapped, her hair in a messy ponytail. "Katrin, come on," I say, my palms spread wide. The universal gesture of a guy who has nothing to hide. "Can we talk about this? What have I ever done to make you think I'd be capable of hurting Brooke?"

She presses her lips together, nostrils flaring slightly. For a second she looks exactly like Peter. "You were involved with her and you didn't tell anyone."

"Jesus." I rake a hand through my hair, feeling a tug in my chest. "Why do you keep *saying* that? Because you lost track of her during a sleepover? She was probably in the bathroom." Katrin and I were never friends, exactly, but I thought she knew me better than this.

"My room *has* a bathroom," Katrin points out. "She wasn't there."

"So she went for a walk."

"She's afraid of the dark."

I give up. She's latched onto this for some reason, and there's no talking her out of it. I guess whatever bond I thought we had was just in my head. Or something that amused her when she had nothing better to do. "Your dad's getting ready to leave," I say instead.

"I know. I need a phone charger. Wait here, Viv," she instructs. She stalks down the hallway leading to the study, leaving Viv and me to eye one another warily. I half expect her to follow Katrin, but she's a good minion. She stays put.

"Still writing that article?" I ask.

Viv flushes. "No. I'm much too upset about Brooke to even think about that." Her eyes are dry, though. Have been all week. "Anyway, I already told the media what I think, so . . . as far as I'm concerned, it's done."

"Good," I say. I turn away from her and open the double doors of the refrigerator. There are two six-packs of bottled water on the middle shelf, and I tuck them under my arm before heading outside.

The back of Peter's Range Rover is still open. I push aside a cardboard box and drop the water beside it. The flash of a familiar face catches my eye, and I pull out a flyer from the box. Brooke's class picture is plastered next to the word MISSING, her hair tumbling loose around her shoulders and her smile bright. It startles me, because I can't remember the last time I saw Brooke looking that happy. I scan the rest of the flyer:

Name: Brooke Adrienne Bennett
Age: 17
Eyes: Hazel
Hair: Brown
Height: 5'4"
Weight: 110 pounds
Last seen wearing: Olive blazer, white T-shirt, black jeans, leopard-print flats

Somebody else must have told them that last part; I was no help when Officer McNulty asked me to describe Brooke's clothes. *She looked nice,* I said.

"I think that's everything." Peter's voice startles me, and I drop the flyer back into the box. He opens the driver's side door and glances at his watch with a small frown. "Could you ask Katrin and Viv to come to the car, please?"

"Okay." My phone buzzes as I head back inside, and when I get into the kitchen I pull it out, to a series of texts from Mia:

Hey.

You should come over.

This just popped up online and it's already everywhere.

The last message links to a *Burlington Free Press* article titled "A Tragic Past—and a Common Thread." My stomach drops as I start to read.

Echo Ridge is reeling.

This picturesque town, nestled near the Canadian border and boasting the highest per capita income in the county, experienced its first tragic loss in 1996 when high school senior Sarah Corcoran vanished while walking home from the library. Then, five years ago, homecoming queen Lacey Kilduff was found dead in the aptly named (and since renamed) Murderland Halloween park.

Now another beautiful and popular teenager, seventeen-year-old Brooke Bennett, is missing. Though Brooke and Lacey are close in age, there seems to be little connection between the two young women, except an odd coincidence: the high school senior who dropped Bennett off at home the night she disappeared is the younger brother of Lacey Kilduff's former boyfriend, Declan Kelly.

Kelly, who was questioned repeatedly after Lacey Kilduff's death but never arrested, moved out of state four years ago and has maintained a low profile since. So it came as a surprise to many in this close-knit community that Kelly relocated to the neighboring town of Solsbury shortly before Brooke Bennett's disappearance.

Shit. Viv might not be writing any more articles, but someone else sure is. Suddenly, Peter looks like a genius. If I weren't going to cause drama during the search for Brooke before, I sure as hell would now.

Katrin enters the kitchen gripping her phone. Her cheeks are bright red, and I brace myself for another tirade. She probably just read the same article. "Peter wants you guys outside," I say, hoping to cut off whatever lecture she has planned.

She nods mechanically without speaking, looking first at Viv and then at me. Her face is weirdly immobile, like she's wearing a Katrin mask. Her hands shake as she shoves her phone into her pocket.

"He's not letting me come," I add. "He says I'll be a distraction."

I'm testing her, waiting for the expected *Well, you would be* or *Distraction doesn't cover it, asshole.* But all she says is, "Okay."

She swallows hard once, then twice. "Okay," she repeats, like she's trying to convince herself of something. She meets my eyes and looks down quickly, but not before I catch how huge her pupils are.

She doesn't look mad anymore. She looks afraid.

CHAPTER TWENTY-FOUR

MALCOLM
THURSDAY, OCTOBER 3

I get to Mia's house half an hour later and I hear shouting as soon as I step onto the driveway. It's too early for her parents to be home, and anyway, they're not yellers. Mia's the only Kwon who ever raises her voice. But it's not her making all that noise.

Nobody answers the doorbell, so I push the door open and step into the Kwons' living room. The first thing I see is Ellery, sitting cross-legged in an armchair, her eyes wide as she surveys the scene in front of us. Mia stands barefoot next to the fireplace, hands on her hips, looking defiant but tiny without the height her boots give her. Daisy is across from her, a candlestick gripped in one hand and an expression of pure rage distorting her usually serene features.

"I'm going to *kill you,*" Daisy shrieks, drawing her arm back threateningly.

"Stop being so dramatic," Mia says, but her eyes don't leave the candlestick.

"What the hell?" I ask, and they both turn toward me.

Daisy's furious expression briefly recedes, then comes roaring back like a tidal wave. "Oh, him too? You've got the entire Scooby Gang here while you lay this bullshit on me?"

I blink. I've never heard Daisy swear before. "What bullshit?"

Mia speaks before Daisy can. "I told her I know all about Declan, and I'm going to tell Mom and Dad if she doesn't explain why they're both back in Echo Ridge." She takes an involuntary step back as Daisy fastens her with a withering stare. "It's going a little worse than I expected."

"You have some nerve—" Daisy brandishes the candlestick for emphasis, but stops in slack-jawed horror when she loses her grip and sends it flying directly toward Mia's head. Mia is too startled to move out of the way, and when it clocks her in the temple she drops like a stone.

Daisy's hands fly to her mouth. "Oh my God. Oh my God, Mia. Are you all right?" She falls to her knees and scrambles toward her sister, but Ellery—who I never even saw move— is already there.

"Malcolm, can you get a wet towel?" she asks.

I stare down at Mia. Her eyes are open, her face pale, and a stream of blood runs down one side of her head. "Oh no, oh no," Daisy moans, her hands covering her face now. "I'm sorry. I'm so, so sorry." I fast-track it to the bathroom and grab a hand towel, then run it under the faucet and jam back to the living room.

Mia is sitting up now, looking dazed. I hand Ellery the towel and she gently pats up and down the side of Mia's head until the blood is cleared away. "Is she going to need stitches?" Daisy asks in a shaking voice.

Ellery presses the towel to Mia's temple for a few seconds, then pulls it away and peers at the cut. "I don't think so. I mean, I'm no expert, but it's actually tiny. Looks like one of those shallow scrapes that just happens to bleed a lot. It'll probably leave a bruise, but it should be fine with a Band-Aid."

"I'll get it," I volunteer, returning to the Kwons' bathroom. Dr. Kwon is an obstetrician and her medicine cabinet is so perfectly organized, I find what I need within seconds. When I return this time, some of the color is back in Mia's face.

"God, Daze," she says reproachfully as Ellery positions the Band-Aid on her temple and presses down. "I didn't realize you *literally* wanted to kill me."

Daisy slumps back, her legs tucked to one side. "It was an accident," she says, skimming her fingers across the hardwood floor. She looks up, her mouth half twisted in a wry grin. "I'm sorry for drawing blood. But you sort of deserved it."

Mia brushes an index finger across her bandage. "I just want to know what's going on."

"So you ambush me while your friend is here?" Daisy's voice starts to rise again, but she checks herself and lowers it. "Seriously, Mia? Not cool."

"I needed the moral support," Mia grumbles. "And the protection, apparently. But come on, Daisy. You can't keep on like this. People know where Declan lives now. Stuff is gonna come out. You need someone on your side." She gestures toward me as I lower myself onto the edge of the Kwons' stone fireplace. "We're all on Mal's side. We can be on yours too."

I glance at Ellery, who doesn't look convinced. I don't think Mia picked up on what Ellery was hinting at in Chuck E. Cheese's—that Daisy and Declan could have been involved with one another while Lacey was still alive. That kind of thing would fly right over Mia's head, because even though she complains about Daisy, she also trusts her completely. I've never been able to say the same thing about Declan.

Daisy turns toward me, her dark eyes brimming with sympathy. "Oh, Malcolm. I haven't even told you how sorry I am about what's been going on. The way people are . . . whispering. Accusing you without any proof. It all brings back so many memories."

"Daisy." Mia interrupts before I can answer. Her voice is calm and quiet, nothing like her usual strident tone. "Why did you leave your job after you'd barely started it?"

Daisy heaves a deep sigh. She lifts a hunk of shiny dark hair and spills it over her shoulder. "I had a nervous breakdown." She purses her lips as Mia's brows shoot up. "Not expecting that one?"

Mia, wisely, doesn't mention trailing Daisy to her psychologist. "What, were you, like . . . in the hospital or something?"

"Briefly." Daisy lowers her eyes. "The thing is, I never really dealt with Lacey's death, you know? It was so horrible. So twisted and awful and painful that I pushed it down and forced myself to forget about it." She gives a strangled little laugh. "Great plan, right? Totally worked. It was okay while I was at school, I guess. But when I moved to Boston and had so many new responsibilities, I couldn't function. I started having nightmares, then panic attacks. At one point I called an ambulance because I thought I was dying of a heart attack."

"You went through a horrible loss," Mia says comfortingly.

Daisy's lashes flicker. "Yes. But I wasn't just sad. I was guilty."

Out of the corner of my eye, I see Ellery tense. "About what?" Mia asks.

Daisy pauses. "Circle of trust, right? This can't leave the room. Not yet." She glances toward me, then Ellery, and bites her lip.

Mia reads her mind. "Ellery's totally trustworthy."

"I can leave," Ellery volunteers. "I understand. We don't know one another."

Daisy hesitates, then shakes her head. "It's all right. You've heard this much, you might as well hear the rest. My psychologist keeps telling me I have to stop being ashamed. It's starting to sink in, although I still feel like a terrible friend." She turns toward Mia. "I was in love with Declan all through high school. I never said a word. It was just this . . . thing I lived with. And then the summer before senior year, he started treating me differently. Like he *saw* me." She gives an embarrassed little laugh. "God, I sound like an eighth grader. But it gave me this, I don't know, *hope*, I guess, that things could be different someday. Then one night he told me he was in love with me, too."

Daisy's whole face glows, and I remember why I used to have such a crush on her. Mia is sitting as still as I've ever seen her, like she's afraid the slightest movement will end the conversation. "I told him we couldn't do anything about it," Daisy continues. "I wasn't *that* bad of a friend. He said he thought Lacey had found someone else, anyway. She was acting distant. But when he asked her, she wouldn't admit it. They started fighting. It got really messy and ugly and— I just sort of withdrew. I didn't want to be the cause of that."

Daisy's eyes get shiny as she continues. "Then Lacey died and the whole world fell apart. I couldn't *stand* myself. Couldn't deal with knowing I'd been keeping this secret that I'd never get to explain to her." Tears spill down her cheeks and she lets out a choked little sob. "And I *missed* her. I still miss her, so much."

I steal a glance at Ellery, who's wiping her own eyes. I get the feeling that she just took Daisy off her mental list of suspects in Lacey's murder. If Daisy feels guilty about anything other than liking her best friend's boyfriend, she's one hell of an actress.

Mia grabs Daisy's hand in both of her own as Daisy continues. "I told Declan we couldn't talk anymore, and I got out of Echo Ridge as soon as I could. I thought it was the right thing to do for both of us. We'd been wrong not to be open with Lacey from the start, and there wasn't a way to fix that anymore." She drops her head. "Plus, there's this whole other layer when you're one of the only minority families in town. You can't make a mistake, you know? We've always had to be so perfect."

Mia regards her sister thoughtfully. "I thought you liked being perfect," she says in a small voice.

Daisy sniffs. "It's fucking *exhausting*."

Mia lets out a surprised snort of laughter. "Well, if *you* can't handle it, there's no hope for me in this town." She's still holding Daisy's hand, and shakes it like she's trying to knock some sense into her sister. "Your psychologist is right, Daze. You didn't do anything wrong. You liked a guy. You stayed away from him, even when he liked you back. That's being a good friend."

Daisy dabs at her eyes with her free hand. "I wasn't, though. I couldn't stand to think about the investigation, and I shut down anytime I was near the police. It wasn't until years later that I started thinking about things that might actually be helpful."

"What do you mean?" I ask. Ellery leans forward like a puppet that just got its strings yanked.

"I remembered something," Daisy says. "A bracelet Lacey started wearing right before she died. It was really unusual—a bangle that almost looked like antlers twisted together." She shrugs at Mia's dubious expression. "Sounds weird, I know, but it was gorgeous. She was really coy about where she got it, too. Said it wasn't from Declan, or her parents. When I was in the hospital in Boston, trying to figure out how my life had gotten so far off track, I started wondering who'd given it to her and whether it was somebody who, well . . ." She trails off. "You know. I wondered."

"So you came back here to investigate?" Ellery looks like she approves.

"I came back here to *recover*," Daisy corrects. "But I also asked Lacey's mom if I could have the bracelet, as a keepsake. She didn't mind. I started Googling it, trying to find something similar. And I did." A note of pride creeps into her voice. "There's a local artist who makes them. I wanted to check her out, but I didn't feel quite strong enough to do it on my own." Her voice dips a little. "Declan used to text me occasionally. The first time he did after all this happened, I asked him to visit the jeweler with me."

And there you have it, I think. An actual, rational explanation for what Declan has been doing in Echo Ridge. Would've been nice if he'd ever told me any of this himself.

Mia raises her brows. "Was that the first time you'd seen him since you left for Princeton? I'll bet you two had a lot to talk about. Or, you know, *not* talk about."

Daisy's entire face goes red. "We were mostly focused on the bracelet."

"*Sure* you were." Mia smirks.

This conversation is going off the rails. "You guys have any luck?" I ask, trying to get it back on track.

Daisy sighs. "No. I thought maybe the jeweler would look through her sale records when I told her why I was there, but she wasn't at all helpful. I handed the bracelet off to the police, hoping she'd take it more seriously if they followed up with her, but I haven't heard anything since." She lets go of Mia's hand and rolls her shoulders like she just finished an exhausting workout. "And that's the whole sordid tale. Except for the part where Declan and I finally got together. I love him." She shrugs helplessly. "I always have."

Mia leans back on her haunches. "That's quite a story."

"You *cannot* tell Mom and Dad," Daisy says, and Mia mimes zipping her lips.

"I have a question," Ellery pipes up. She starts doing that twisty thing with her hair again as Daisy turns to face her. "I was just wondering who you gave the bracelet to? What police officer, I mean. Was it someone in Echo Ridge?"

Daisy nods. "Ryan Rodriguez. He graduated from Echo Ridge High the same year I did. Do you know him?"

Ellery nods. "Yeah. Were you guys friends at school?" She looks like she's back in investigative mode, which I'm starting to realize is her default setting.

"No." Daisy looks amused at the idea. "He was really quiet

back then. I barely knew him. But he was on duty when I got to the station, so . . ." She shrugs. "I gave it to him."

"Do you, um, think he was the best person to handle something like this?" Ellery asks.

Daisy crinkles her brow. "I don't know. I guess. Why not?"

"Well. I'm just wondering." Ellery leans forward, elbows on her knees. "Did it ever occur to you that *he* might've given the bracelet to Lacey?"

CHAPTER TWENTY-FIVE

ELLERY
FRIDAY, OCTOBER 4

When I knock on the cellar door, I'm not sure anyone will answer. It's four o'clock on Friday afternoon, three hours before the House of Horrors is supposed to open. I'm not working tonight, and no one's expecting me. Unless you count my grandmother, who's *expecting me* to be in my room and is going to be furious if she realizes I've left and walked through the woods on my own. Even in the middle of the afternoon.

Brooke's been missing almost a week now, and nobody in Echo Ridge is supposed to walk anywhere alone.

I knock louder. The park is noisy and crowded, a blend of music, laughter, and shrieks as a roller coaster rattles nearby. The door cracks just enough for an eye to peer out. It's deep brown and winged with expertly applied liner. I flutter my fingers. "Hi, Shauna."

"Ellery?" The Fright Farm makeup artist swings the door open with one tattooed arm. "What are you doing here?"

I step inside and look around for any sign of Murph, my boss. He's a stickler for rules. Shauna is a lot more laid-back. I can't believe my luck that she's here and he isn't, although I half expect him to come barreling through the velvet curtain with a clipboard any second. "Are you here alone?" I ask.

Shauna raises a brow at me. "That's an ominous question." She doesn't look worried, though. Shauna has at least six inches on me, and is all slender muscle and perfectly toned arms. Plus her spiky heels would make lethal weapons in a pinch.

"Heh. Sorry. But I have a favor to ask, and I didn't want to ask Murph."

Shauna leans against the doorframe. "Well, now you've got my attention. What's up?"

I channel Sadie again, twisting my hands with fake nerves. "My grandmother gave me an envelope to deposit at the bank the other day, and I can't find it. I was trying to figure out where it went, and I remembered that I tossed a bunch of stuff into the recycling bin the last time I was here." I bite my lip and look at the ground. "I'm pretty sure the envelope went with it."

"Ooh, sorry." Shauna grimaces. "Can she write another check?"

I'm ready for that objection. "It wasn't a check. It was cash." I tug at my dagger necklace, running my thumb over the sharp point at the bottom. "Almost five hundred dollars."

Shauna's eyes widen. "Who the hell carries around that much cash?"

Gah. Maybe she noticed I lifted my entire excuse from *It's a*

Wonderful Life. "My grandmother," I say as innocently as I can. "She doesn't trust checks. Or credit cards. Or ATMs."

"But she trusts you?" Shauna looks as though she'd like to give Nana a detailed explanation of why that's a terrible idea.

"She won't when she finds out. Shauna, is there any chance . . . do you think I could get the keys to the recycling bin? Do you know where they are?" She hesitates, and I put my hands together in a praying gesture. "Please? Just this once, to save me from having to hand every cent I've earned over to my grandmother? I'll owe you big-time."

Shauna chuckles. "Look, you don't have to beg. I'd open the damn thing if I had a key, but I don't. No idea where it is. You'll have to ask Murph." She gives my arm a sympathetic pat. "He'll understand. Five hundred dollars is a lot of money."

He would, probably. He'd also stand over me the entire time. "Okay," I sigh.

Shauna goes to the vanity and plucks a few makeup brushes from a can, dropping them into a half-open leather bag resting on the chair. "I have to get a move on. You caught me on the way out. The evil clowns need touching up at Bloody Big Top." She zips the bag closed and slings it over her shoulder, crossing to the door and pulling it open. "You wanna come with? Murph might be there."

"Sure." I make as if to follow her, then wince and put a hand on my belly. "Ugh. Do you mind if I use the bathroom first? I've had kind of a stomach virus all day. I thought it was better, but—"

Shauna waves me away. "Just meet me there. Make sure the door locks behind you."

"Thanks." I dash toward the tiny restroom for effect, but

she's already out the door. As soon as I hear it click, I pull two paper clips out of my pocket and head for the office.

I've never tried to pick a lock before. But I took Vance's advice, and I've watched a lot of YouTube videos in the past twenty-four hours.

"You took it *all*?" Ezra stares at me as I empty a trash bag's worth of paper onto Mia's bedroom floor.

"Well, how was I supposed to know what's important and what isn't? I couldn't sit there on the floor and sift through it. Anybody might've walked in."

Malcolm eyes the pile. "At least we know they haven't emptied it in a while."

Mia plops down cross-legged on the floor and scoops up a handful of paper. "What are we even looking for?" she mutters. "This is some kind of invoice. This looks like an envelope for an electric bill." She makes a face. "We're gonna be here for a while."

The four of us sit in a circle around the pile and start sifting through its contents. My pulse has slowed since I left the House of Horrors, but it's still jumping. I checked the office thoroughly and didn't see any security cameras, but I know they're all over the park. It's entirely possible that someone's staring at footage of me hauling a garbage bag through Fright Farm right now. Which, okay, could easily be the sort of thing an employee would do in the normal course of business. But it could also look weird, and I wasn't exactly subtle about it. I didn't even wear a baseball cap or pull my hair back.

So I hope it's worth it.

We're silent for almost fifteen minutes until Malcolm, who's sprawled next to me, clears his throat. "The police want to look at my phone."

Mia freezes, a scrap of paper dangling from her fingers. *"What?"*

We're all staring at him, but he doesn't meet anyone's eyes. "Officer McNulty said that with Brooke still missing, they need to dig a little deeper. I didn't know what to do. Peter was . . . kind of great, actually. He managed to get across the point that they shouldn't be asking for access to my personal stuff without a warrant while still sounding totally helpful. Officer McNulty ended up apologizing to *him*."

"So they didn't do it?" I ask, placing another invoice on our reject pile. That's all we've found so far: invoices for food, maintenance, supplies, and the like. I guess I shouldn't be surprised that it takes a huge amount of fake blood to keep a Halloween theme park running.

"Not yet," Malcolm says grimly. He finally looks up, and I'm struck by how dull his eyes are. "They won't find anything about Brooke if they do. Other than that text from Katrin telling me I should invite her to homecoming, which could go either way. But there are a bunch of texts between me and Declan and . . . I don't know. After that article yesterday, I'd rather not get scrutinized like that." He tosses aside a sheet of paper with a frustrated grunt. "Everything looks bad when you examine it too closely, right?"

Thursday's *Burlington Free Press* article rehashed the past five years of Declan's life, from the time Lacey died to his recent move to Solsbury, sprinkled with occasional references to the unnamed younger brother who was a key witness in

Brooke's disappearance. It was the sort of article Viv might have written—no actual news, but lots of speculation and innuendo.

Last night, I sat in my room in front of my bookshelf full of true-crime novels and made a timeline of everything I could think of related to the three missing girls and Echo Ridge:

October 1996: *Sadie & Vance are crowned homecoming queen/king*

October 1996: *Sarah disappears while Sadie is with Vance*

June 1997: *Sadie leaves Echo Ridge*

August 2001: *Sadie returns for Grandpa's funeral*

June 2014: *Lacey's junior class picnic with Declan, Daisy & Ryan*

August 2014: *Declan and Daisy get together—Lacey has a secret boyfriend?*

October 2014: *Lacey and Declan are crowned homecoming queen/king*

October 2014: *Lacey is killed at Murderland (Fright Farm)*

October 2014: *Sadie returns for Lacey's funeral*

June 2015: *Daisy & Declan graduate, leave Echo Ridge (separately?)*

July 2019: *Daisy returns to Echo Ridge*

August 2019: *Daisy gives Lacey's bracelet to Ryan Rodriguez*

August 30, 2019: *Ellery & Ezra move to Echo Ridge*

September (or August??) 2019: *Declan returns to Echo Ridge*

September 4, 2019: *Anonymous homecoming threats start*

September 28, 2019: *Brooke disappears*

Then I hung it on my wall and stared at it for over an hour, hoping I'd see some kind of pattern emerge. I didn't, but when Ezra came in, he noticed something I hadn't. "Look at this," he said, tapping a finger on *August 2001.*

"What about it?"

"Sadie came back to Echo Ridge in August 2001."

"I know. I wrote it. So?"

"So we were born in May 2002." I stared at him blankly and he added, "Nine. Months. Later," enunciating each word slowly.

I gaped at him, blindsided. Of all the mysteries in Echo Ridge, our paternity has been the last one on my mind. "*Oh* no. No, no, no," I said, leaping backward as though the timeline had caught fire. "No way. That's not what this is for, Ezra!"

He shrugged. "Sadie said she had something more to tell us, didn't she? That stuntman story has always been kind of sketchy. Maybe she looked up an old flame while she was—"

"Get out!" I yelled before he could finish. I yanked *In Cold Blood* out of the bookcase and threw it at him. "And don't come back unless you have something useful, or at least not *horrifying,* to contribute."

I've been trying to put what Ezra said out of my mind ever since. Whatever it could mean is totally separate from the missing girls, and anyway, I'm sure the timing's just a coincidence. I would've brought it up with Sadie last night at our weekly Skype call if she hadn't skipped it. Her counselor told Nana she was "exhausted."

One step forward, one step back.

"Huh." Ezra's voice brings me back to the present. "This is different." He separates a thin yellow sheet from everything else, smoothing a wrinkled corner.

I scoot closer to him. "What is it?"

"Car repair," he says. "For somebody named Amy Nelson. A place called Dailey's Auto in . . ." He squints at the sheet of paper. "Bellingham, New Hampshire."

We both turn instinctively toward Malcolm. The only thing I know about New Hampshire is that his brother lives there. *Used* to live there.

Malcolm's expression tightens. "I've never heard of it."

Ezra keeps reading. *"Front of vehicle damage due to unknown impact. Remove and replace front bumper, repair hood, repaint vehicle. Rush charges, forty-eight hours."* His brows rise. "Yikes. The bill's more than two grand. Paid in cash. For a . . ." He pauses, his eyes scanning the bill. "A 2016 BMW X6. Red."

Malcolm shifts beside me. "Can I see?" Ezra hands him the receipt, and a deep crease appears between Malcolm's brows as he studies it. "This is Katrin's car," he says finally, looking up. "It's her make and model. And her license plate."

Mia grabs the thin yellow paper out of his hand. "Really? Are you sure?"

"Positive," Malcolm says. "She drives me to school most days. And I park next to that car every time I drive my mom's."

"Who's Amy Nelson?" Ezra asks.

Malcolm shakes his head. "No idea."

"There's a phone number for her," Mia says, holding the paper in front of Malcolm. "Is that Katrin's number?"

"I don't know her number off the top of my head. Let me

check." Malcolm pulls his phone out and presses a few keys. "It's not hers. But hang on, that number's in my phone. It's . . ." He sucks in a breath and turns to Mia. "You remember how Katrin sent me that text, asking me to invite Brooke to homecoming?" Mia nods. "She sent Brooke's phone number, too. I saved it to Contacts. This is it."

"Wait, what?" Ezra asks. "Brooke's number is on a repair receipt for Katrin's car?"

While Malcolm was scrolling, I was on my phone looking up Bellingham, New Hampshire. "The repair shop is three hours away," I report.

"So Brooke . . ." Mia studies the receipt. "So Brooke helped Katrin fix her car, I guess. But they didn't take it to Armstrong's Auto—or even anyplace in Vermont. And they used a fake name. Why would they do that?"

"What did Katrin say about her car being wrecked?" I ask, looking at Malcolm.

Malcolm knits his brow. "Nothing. It wasn't." I blink at him, confused, and he adds, "It wasn't wrecked, I mean. It's fine. Maybe there's some kind of mistake. Unless . . . wait." He turns back to Mia, who's still staring at the receipt. "When was the car fixed?"

"Um . . ." Mia's eyes flick to the top of the paper. "It was brought in August thirty-first, and 'Amy' picked it up on September second. Oh, right." She looks at Malcolm. "You and your mom were on vacation then, weren't you? When did you get back?"

"September fourth," Malcolm says. "The day of Lacey's fund-raiser."

"So you wouldn't have known the car was gone," Mia says. "But wouldn't Mr. Nilsson have said something?"

"Maybe not. Katrin spent days at a time at Brooke's house over the summer." Malcolm taps an unconscious beat on his knee with one fist, his expression thoughtful. "So maybe that's why Brooke got involved. She was Katrin's cover while the car was getting fixed. Peter's always telling her she needs to drive more carefully. She was probably afraid he'd take it away if he knew."

"Okay," Ezra says. "That all makes sense, I guess. The fake name is kind of dumb—I mean, all anybody would have to do is look up the license plate number to know who the car really belongs to. But they probably figured it wouldn't come to that." He pauses, frowning. "The only thing I don't understand is, if that's what happened, why was Brooke so desperate to get the receipt back? Assuming this is what she was looking for, but"—he gestures at the pile of invoices we've already discarded—"nothing else seems relevant. If you've gone through the trouble of having an undercover car repair and disposing of the evidence, wouldn't you just leave it to be shredded? Mission accomplished, right?"

I think back to Brooke's words in the Fright Farm office. *That's the million-dollar question, isn't it? What happened? Wouldn't you like to know?* My heart rate starts rising. "Mia," I say, turning toward her. "What date was the car brought in, again?"

"August thirty-first," she says.

"August thirty-first." I repeat. My skin prickles, every nerve twitching.

Ezra tilts his head. "Why do you look like you just swallowed a grenade?"

"Because we came in from LA the night before that. August thirtieth, remember? The hailstorm. The night Mr. Bowman was killed in a hit-and-run." Nobody says anything for a second, and I tap the paper Mia is holding. *"Front of vehicle damage due to unknown impact?"*

Mia's entire body goes rigid. Ezra says "Holy shit," at the same time Malcolm says, "No." He turns toward me, his eyes pained. "Mr. Bowman? Katrin wouldn't . . ." He trails off when Mia drops the repair receipt in his lap.

"I hate to say it," she says with surprising gentleness. "But it's starting to look an awful lot like she did."

CHAPTER TWENTY-SIX

MALCOLM
SATURDAY, OCTOBER 5

"You look absolutely beautiful, Katrin."

I turn from the refrigerator at the sound of my mother's voice, grasping a too-warm seltzer and stepping closer to the foyer so I have a clear view of the staircase. Katrin's descending it like royalty in a red dress, her hair pulled back in some kind of complicated twist. She looks better than she has all week, but she still doesn't have her usual sparkle. There's something brittle about her face.

The neckline on her dress dips low, displaying a lot more cleavage than Katrin usually shows. It should be distracting, but even that doesn't derail the train of thought that's been running through my brain since yesterday afternoon.

What do you know? What did you do?

"Whoa." Katrin's boyfriend, Theo, doesn't have the same

problem. His eyes zero in on her chest until he remembers that her dad's in the room. "You look amazing."

I can't see Peter, but his voice is full of forced heartiness. "Let's get some pictures of the four of you."

That's my cue to leave. Katrin and Theo are doubling to homecoming with two of my least favorite people at Echo Ridge High: Kyle McNulty and Viv Cantrell. It's not a date, Katrin explained to my mother. Just two people who are worried about Brooke, coming together while the town tries to hang on to some kind of normal. From the glimpse I saw of Kyle when they arrived, he looks as though he got talked into it and already regrets saying yes.

All the money raised from selling homecoming tickets is going toward a reward fund for information leading to Brooke's safe return. Most of the businesses in town are giving matching donations, and Peter's law firm is doubling theirs.

I retreat into the study while everyone poses. Mia's still going with Ezra, and she was texting me until an hour ago trying to convince me to ask Ellery. Under different circumstances I probably would have. But I couldn't get Katrin's words out of my head: *I'd better not see you there.* She's backed off on treating me like a criminal, but I know that's what everyone at school is thinking. I don't care enough about a pointless dance to deal with three hours of getting whispered about and judged.

Besides, I'm not sure I can act normal around my stepsister right now.

I haven't told anyone what we found yesterday. Despite the wild theories, all it really amounts to is a receipt with questionable contact information. Still, it's been eating at me all day, making it almost impossible to look at Katrin without the words bursting out of me: *What do you know? What did you do?*

The murmur of voices in the foyer grows louder as Katrin and her friends get ready to leave for the dance. Pretty soon, only Peter and Mom will be home. Suddenly, the last thing in the world I want to do is spend a Saturday night alone with my thoughts. Before I second-guess myself too much, I fire off a text to Ellery. *Do you want to hang out tonight? Watch a movie or something?*

I don't know if she'll be up for it, or if her grandmother will even let her. But Ellery replies within a few minutes, and the vise gripping my chest loosens a little when I read her response.

Yeah, sure.

Turns out, if you invite a girl over on homecoming night, your mother *will* read into it.

Mom flutters around Ellery with zero chill after her grandmother drops her off at our house. "Do you two want popcorn? I can make some. Are you going to be in the den, or the living room? The den is more comfortable, probably, but I don't think that television has Netflix. Maybe we could set it up real quick, Peter?"

Peter puts a hand on her shoulder, like that'll stop her from spinning out. "I'm sure Malcolm will let us know if he has any pressing technological requirements." He gives Ellery the full Peter Nilsson smile experience as she unwinds a scarf from around her neck and stuffs it into her bag. "Very nice to see you again, Ellery. I didn't get a chance to tell you at Lacey's fund-raiser, but your mother was one of my favorite people in town while she was here." He gives a self-deprecating laugh. "I even took her to the movies a couple of times, although I think I bored her to tears. I hope she's doing well, and that you're enjoying your time in Echo Ridge, even though . . ." A shadow passes over his face. "We're not at our best right now."

I keep my expression neutral to hide how much I wish he'd shut up. Way to remind everyone that half the town thinks I did something to Brooke. Which I guess is the other reason I didn't ask Ellery to homecoming. I'm not sure she'd say yes.

"I know," Ellery says. "We moved here at a strange time. Everyone's been really nice, though." She smiles at me, and my bad mood lifts. Her hair is long and loose around her shoulders, the way I like it. I didn't realize till now that I had a preference, but it turns out I do.

"Can I get you something to drink?" Mom asks. "We have seltzer, or juice, or—" She looks ready to document the entire contents of our refrigerator, but Peter starts gently steering her toward the balcony staircase before Ellery can reply. Thank God.

"Malcolm knows where everything is, Alicia. Why don't we finish up the Burns documentary upstairs?" He favors me with a smile almost as warm as the one he gave Ellery. It doesn't reach his eyes, but points for trying, I guess. "Give us a shout if you need anything."

"Sorry," I say when the sound of their footsteps on the stairs has faded. "Mom's a little rusty at the meeting-new-friends thing. You want some popcorn?"

"Sure," she says, and grins. Her dimple flashes, and I'm happy I texted her.

I lead her into the kitchen, where she hops onto a stool

in front of the island. I open the cabinet next to the sink and root around until I find a box of microwave popcorn. "And don't worry, your mom's cool. Your stepfather, too." She sounds surprised as she says it, as if she wasn't expecting that from Katrin's dad.

"He's all right," I say grudgingly, extracting a bag of popcorn and tossing it into the microwave.

Ellery winds a curl around her finger. "You don't talk about your dad much. Do you see him, or . . . ?" She hesitates, like she's not one hundred percent sure he's even still alive.

The sound of popping kernels fills the air. "Not really. He lives in southern Vermont now, near Massachusetts. I spent a week there over the summer. Mostly he emails sports-related articles under the mistaken assumption that I'll find them interesting. Peter tries a little harder than that." When I say it, it surprises me to realize it's true. "He talks a lot about college, what I want to do after, stuff like that."

"What *do* you want to do?" Ellery asks.

The popping sounds slow. I pull the bag from the microwave and tear it open, releasing a cloud of buttery steam. "I don't have a clue," I admit. "What about you?"

"I'm not sure. I have this idea that I'd like to be a lawyer, but— I don't know if it's realistic. I didn't even think till this year that college was a thing that might happen. Sadie never could have sent us. But my grandmother keeps talking about it like she will."

"Same for me, with Peter," I say. "You know he's a lawyer, right? I'm sure he'd be happy to talk to you about it. Fair warning, though—ninety percent of his job sounds really boring. Although maybe that's just him."

She laughs. "Noted. I might take you up on that." My back is to her as I hunt in a cabinet for a popcorn bowl, and when she speaks again her voice is much quieter. "It's weird, but for the longest time I almost couldn't . . . *see* myself in the future," she says. "I'd think about what happened to my aunt and imagine that one of us, out of me and my brother, might not make it all the way through high school. Like only one Corcoran twin gets to move on. And Ezra's so much more like my mom than I am, so . . ." I turn to see her staring out our kitchen window into the darkness, her expression reflective. Then she shivers, and flashes me an apologetic grimace. "Sorry. That got morbid fast."

"We have screwed-up family histories," I tell her. "Morbid comes with the territory."

I lead her into the Nilssons' living room and lower myself into one corner of the sofa, the bowl of popcorn next to me. She curls up beside it and hands me my drink. "What do you want to watch?" I ask, flicking on the remote and scrolling through the channel guide.

"I don't care," Ellery says. She plucks a small handful of popcorn from the bowl between us. "I'm just glad to be out of my house for the night."

My channel-hopping lands us on the first *Defender* movie. It's past the part where Sadie appears, but I keep it there in her honor anyway. "Yeah, I get it. I keep thinking how it was almost exactly a week ago that I dropped Brooke off." I unscrew the top of my seltzer. "I've been meaning to thank you, by the way. For, you know. Believing me."

Ellery's liquid dark eyes hold mine. "It's been an awful week for you, hasn't it?"

"I saw what Declan went through, remember?" Images of a futuristic city with dark, rain-slicked streets flash across the screen in front of us. The hero is on the ground, cowering as a couple of muscle-bound, leather-clad guys loom over him. He's not half cyborg yet, so he's about to get his ass kicked. "This was better."

Ellery shifts beside me. "But he had a whole history with Lacey. It's not like you were Brooke's boyfriend, or . . ." She hesitates briefly. "Her best friend."

We managed to go almost fifteen minutes without poking the elephant in the room. Good for us, I guess.

"Do you think we should show the police what we found?" I ask.

Ellery chews her lip. "I don't know. I'm kind of worried about how I got it, to be honest. And it might look sketchy to have you involved. Plus I still don't trust Ryan Rodriguez." She frowns at the television screen. "Something's off with that guy."

"There are other police officers," I say. But Officer McNulty is the lead on this case, and the thought of talking to him again makes my stomach churn.

"The thing is . . . I've been wondering about something." Ellery picks up the remote like she's about to change the channel, but juggles it meditatively in her hand instead. "Assuming our leap of logic is right and Katrin actually"—she lowers her voice to a near whisper—"ran over Mr. Bowman. Do you think, um, that's *all* she did?"

I try to swallow a piece of popcorn, but I can't. My throat is too dry. I take a deep gulp of my drink before answering Ellery, and while I do, I think about Katrin gliding down our stairs today with that masklike expression. The way she'd thrown me under the bus when I was first questioned. The scared look in her eyes the day of Peter's search party. "What do you mean?"

"Well." Ellery says the word slowly, reluctantly, like someone's prying it out of her. "I should probably preface this by saying . . . I think about crime a lot. Like, an abnormal amount. I get that. It's sort of a problem. So you have to take what I say with a grain of salt, because I'm just this . . . naturally suspicious person, I guess."

"You suspected me, right? For a while." Ellery freezes, eyes wide. Shit, I didn't mean to come out with that. I almost apologize and change the subject. But I don't, because now that I've said it, I want to hear her response.

"I . . . I honestly hate that I'm like this, Mal." I think that might be the first time she's ever called me by my nickname, but before I can process that momentous occasion, I'm horrified to see her eyes water. "It's just— I grew up never knowing what happened to my aunt. Nobody would tell me anything, so I'd read terrible crime stories to try to understand. But all that did was make me more confused and paranoid. Now I'm at the point where I feel like I can't trust anybody who's not my literal twin." A tear slips down her cheek. She drops the remote onto the couch to swipe angrily at her cheek, leaving a red mark on her pale skin. "I don't know how to relate to people. Like, I pretty much only ever had one friend before I moved here. Then I met you and Mia, and you guys were so great, but all this happened and . . . I'm sorry. I didn't really think *that* about you, but I did . . . think about it. If that makes sense. It probably doesn't."

A knot releases in my chest. "It does. It's okay. Look, I get it." I gesture around the room. "Check out my big homecoming night. Not sure if you noticed, but I only have one friend, too. I said it in the kitchen, right? We have screwed-up family histories. It's crap most of the time, but it does mean I understand you. And I . . . like you."

I move the popcorn bowl onto the coffee table and put a tentative arm around her. She sighs and leans into me. I mean it as a friendly hug, mostly, but her hair's tumbling across one eye, so I push it back, and before I know it both my hands are cupping her cheeks. Which feels really good. Ellery's eyes are steady on mine, her lips curved in a small, questioning smile. I draw her face closer and before I can overthink it, I kiss her.

Her mouth is soft and warm and just a little bit buttery. Heat spreads through me slowly as she slides her hand up my chest and around the back of my neck. Then she nips lightly at my bottom lip, and the heat turns into an electric jolt. I wrap my arms around her and pull her half on my lap, kissing her lips and the skin between her jaw and her collarbone. She pushes me back against the pillows and molds her body to mine and, holy hell, this night is going a *lot* better than I expected.

A loud, clattering noise makes both of us freeze. Somehow we dislodged the remote and sent it flying across the floor. Ellery sits up just as my mother's voice, which is much too close for someone who's supposed to be upstairs, calls, "Malcolm? Is everything all right?"

Crap. She's in the kitchen. Ellery and I disentangle as I call, "Fine. We just dropped the remote." We put a foot between us on the couch, both of us red-faced with sheepish grins, waiting for my mother's response.

"Oh, okay. I'm making hot chocolate, do you want some?"

"No thanks," I say, as Ellery tries to get her curls under control. My hands are itching to mess them up again.

"What about you, Ellery?" Mom asks.

"I'm all set, thanks." Ellery says, biting her lip.

"All right." I wait an endless minute for my mother to go back upstairs, but before it's up Ellery has scooted all the way to the other end of the couch.

"It's probably good we were interrupted," she says, going even redder. "I feel like maybe I should tell you my theory before . . . anything."

My brain isn't working all that well right now. "Tell me your what?"

"My criminal theory."

"Your— Oh. Yeah, that." I suck in a breath for composure and adjust my position on the couch. "It's not about me, though, right?"

"Definitely not," she says. "But it *is* about Katrin. And how I think that if we're right about Mr. Bowman, maybe that was just the beginning of, um, things." She winds a strand of hair around her finger, which I'm starting to realize is never a good sign. I still can't wrap my brain around Katrin possibly running over Mr. Bowman; I'm not sure I'm ready for more *things*. But I've spent the past five years avoiding conversations about Lacey and Declan, and that never solved anything.

"What do you mean?" I ask.

"Well. If we go back to the receipt, we're pretty sure Brooke knew about the accident, right? She was either in the car when it happened, or Katrin told her after." Ellery releases her hair to start pulling on her necklace. "Katrin must've been terrified about people finding out. It's one thing to have an accident, but to leave afterward without stopping to help . . . she'd be a pariah at school, plus it'd ruin her dad's standing in town. Not to mention the criminal charges. So she decided to cover it up. And Brooke agreed to help, but I think she must have regretted that. She always looked so worried and sad. Ever since I met her, which was *right* after Mr. Bowman died. Unless she was always like that?"

"No," I say, my stomach twisting as I think of Brooke's smiling class picture on the MISSING poster. "She wasn't."

"And then in the Fright Farm office, she kept saying things like, *I shouldn't have, I have to tell them, it's not okay.* Which makes me think she felt guilty."

Pressure clamps down on my skull. "She asked me if I'd ever made a really bad mistake."

Ellery's eyes widen. "She did? When?"

"In the office. While you were looking for Ezra. She said . . ." I search my memory, but the exact words won't come. "Something about making a mistake that wasn't, like, a regular mistake. And that she wished she had different friends."

Ellery nods seriously. "That fits," she says.

I'm pretty sure I don't want to know, but I ask anyway. "With what?"

"Lots of things. Starting with the vandalism," Ellery says. I blink at her, startled. "The messages didn't appear until after Katrin repaired her car. She got it back on September second, and Lacey's fund-raiser was September fourth, right?" I nod, and Ellery continues, "I kept thinking about what it must've been like for Katrin then, with the whole town mourning Mr. Bowman and looking for answers. She was probably walking on eggshells, terrified of getting found out or giving herself away. So I thought, what if *Katrin* was the one who started the vandalism?"

"Why would she do that?" I can't keep the disbelieving edge out of my voice.

Ellery runs a fingernail along the floral pattern of the couch, refusing to look at me. "As a distraction," she says quietly. "The whole town started focusing on the threats instead of what happened to Mr. Bowman."

I feel a stab of nausea, because she's not wrong. The Homecoming Stalker made Mr. Bowman's hit-and-run fade into the background a lot faster than should have been possible for such a popular teacher. "But why pull *you* into it?" I ask. "And herself, and Brooke?"

"Well, Katrin and Brooke make sense because if they're targets, nobody would think they're involved. Me, I don't know." Ellery keeps tracing the pattern, her eyes trained on her hand like if she loses concentration for even a second, the entire couch will disappear. "Maybe I was just a way to . . . thicken the intrigue, or something. Because my family is loosely tied to tragic homecomings, too, even though Sadie was the queen and not Sarah."

"How would Katrin even do it, though? She was in the cultural center when the sign got vandalized," I point out. "And onstage with the rest of the cheerleaders when the screen started flashing all that stuff at Fright Farm."

"The screen could've been set up beforehand. But for the

rest . . . she'd have needed help, I guess. Brooke was already pulled in, and Viv and Theo would do anything Katrin says, wouldn't they? Or was there a time at the cultural center when you lost sight of her?"

"I mean . . . yeah." I think of Katrin slipping away as soon as all eyes turned toward my mother and me. *Oh, there's Theo.* How long was she gone? I rub a hand across my temple like that'll help me remember. It doesn't. The more Ellery and I talk, the more agitated I feel. "Maybe. But if I'm being honest, it's kind of a stretch, Ellery. And it still doesn't explain what happened to Brooke."

"That's what I'm worried about," Ellery says in the same low voice. "I keep thinking that while Katrin was distracting the town, Brooke was working up the courage to tell people what happened. And she wanted to get the proof back. What if Katrin knew that and . . . did something to keep her quiet?"

A chill settles over me. "Like what?"

"I don't know. And I really, really hope I'm wrong." Ellery speaks quickly, in a rush, like she hates what she's saying but needs to get it out anyway. "But Katrin had motive. She had opportunity. That's two out of the three things you need to commit a crime."

My stomach feels like lead. "What's the third?"

"You have to be the kind of person who would do something like that." Ellery finally looks up, her expression pensive.

"Katrin wouldn't." The words spring out of me without thought.

"Even if she thought she'd lose everything?" I'm not as quick to speak this time, and Ellery presses on, "It might explain why she threw out that random accusation about you and Brooke, right? Anything to deflect."

"But, Ellery . . . Christ, what are you even talking about here?" My voice drops to a tense whisper. "Kidnapping? Worse? I can get on board with the rest of it, sort of. The hit-and-run, even planting all those messages around town. That's extreme, but I can imagine someone doing it under pressure. Making Brooke actually . . . *go missing* is a whole other level."

"I know," Ellery says. "Katrin would either have to be so desperate that she lost all sense of right or wrong, or be a cold-blooded criminal." She's back to tracing patterns on the sofa again. "You've lived with her for a few months. Do you see a possibility for either of those?"

"No way. Katrin leads a charmed life." But even as I say it, I know it's not entirely true. Peter might dote on Katrin, but in the four months I've lived here I've barely heard anything about the first Mrs. Nilsson. Katrin doesn't just not talk *to* her mother, she doesn't talk *about* her. It's almost like she has only one parent. It's one of the few things we have in common. It sucks, but it doesn't mean you're warped for life. Probably.

Ellery and I are silent for a few minutes, watching the robotically enhanced Defender mow down his former nemesis. That's what made this series so popular, I think: that a regular guy who's constantly beaten down could suddenly become special and powerful. In Hollywood, no plotline is impossible. Maybe Ellery's spent too much time in that world.

Or maybe I don't know my stepsister at all.

"If any of it's true, you'd think she'd make another move with the anonymous threats, wouldn't you?" I finally ask. "They stopped when Brooke disappeared. If you wanted to distract people, now would be the time." The TV screen flickers as the Defender extinguishes all the lights on a city block. "*Right* now, actually. At homecoming."

Ellery sends me a cautious look. "You know, I was thinking that, but . . . I didn't want to say anything. I kind of feel like I've already said too much."

"I don't like hearing it," I admit. "But . . . there's a lot about Katrin lately that doesn't fit. Maybe we should pay more attention to what she's up to. And where she is."

Ellery raises her brows. "Do you think we should go to homecoming?"

"We could." I glance at the clock on the wall. "It's been going on for less than an hour. Still plenty of time for her to make a move, if she's going to."

Ellery gestures at her black shirt and jeans. "I'm not exactly dressed for it."

"Do you have anything at home that could work? We could stop there first."

"Nothing super formal, but . . . I guess so." She looks uncertain. "Are you sure, though? I feel like I kind of sprang a lot on you at once. Maybe you should let it sink in for a while."

I give her a half grin. "Are you trying to get out of going to homecoming with me?"

She flushes. "No! I just . . . it's, um . . . huh." I've never seen her at a loss for words before. It's cute. Ellery might be a walking *Forensic Files* episode, but there's still something about her that I can't stop thinking about. Lots of things.

It's not just that, though. Earlier today it seemed like a

no-brainer to stay home. All I wanted was to keep my head down and avoid conflict. Except now I'm stuck here watching a bad '90s movie like I have something to be ashamed of, while Katrin—who at the very least has been shady about her car— put on a bright-red dress and went to a party.

I'm tired of watching my life turn into Declan Part Two. And I'm tired of doing nothing while my friends try to figure out how to dig me out of trouble I shouldn't even be in.

"Then let's go," I say.

CHAPTER TWENTY-SEVEN

ELLERY

SATURDAY, OCTOBER 5

Nana is, to put it mildly, not pleased with this turn of events.

"You said you were going to watch a movie," she says from the other side of my closed bedroom door as I yank a dress over my head. It's black and sleeveless, with a flared A-line skirt that ends just above my knees. The material is casual jersey, but I put on a few long, glittering necklaces to dress it up. With my one and only pair of heels, it can pass for semiformal.

"We changed our minds," I say, reaching for a bottle of curl enhancer and squeezing a small amount into my palm. I already spent more time than I'd like to admit on my hair before leaving for Malcolm's, but the battle against frizz never ends.

"I don't like the idea of you going to this dance, Ellery. Not after everything that's happened over the past few weeks."

"You let Ezra go," I point out, slipping into my shoes.

"Ezra wasn't targeted like you were. One of the girls who was on the homecoming court with you is *missing*, for God's sake. It could be dangerous."

"But, Nana, there's not even a court anymore. Now the whole thing is more of a fund-raiser. There'll be kids and teachers everywhere. Brooke didn't disappear when she was in the middle of a crowd like that. She was at home with her parents." I run my hands through my hair, brush mascara across my lashes, and coat my lips with sheer red gloss. Done.

Nana doesn't have a good response for that. When I open my door, she's standing there with her arms folded, and she frowns as she looks me up and down. "Since when do you wear makeup?" she asks.

"It's a dance." I wait for her to move, but she doesn't.

"Is this a date?"

I get full-body butterflies as I think about kissing Malcolm on his couch, but blink at Nana like it's the first time I'd ever considered her question. "What? No! We're going as friends, like Mia and Ezra. We got bored and decided to meet up with them. That's all."

I can feel my cheeks flame. I do not, as Sadie would put it, have the appropriate emotional connection to this scene. Nana looks entirely unconvinced. We regard one another in silence for a few seconds until she sags against the doorway. "I could forbid you, I suppose, though that never worked with your mother. She'd just go behind my back. But I want you to call when you get there, and I want you to come straight home after. With your *brother*. Daisy Kwon is a chaperone. She brought him and Mia, and she can take you home, too."

"Okay, Nana." I try to sound grateful, because I know this

isn't easy for her. Plus if I'm going to be annoyed with anyone it should be me, for somehow managing to turn my first kiss with Malcolm into a stakeout. Maybe I need to work out a system with Ezra so he can text *Nobody wants to hear your murder theories* the next time I get the urge to ruin my own night.

I follow her downstairs, where my seriously cute not-date is waiting. The side benefit to me forcing us off the couch is getting to see Malcolm in a suit again. "Hi, Mrs. Corcoran," he says, and then his eyes go satisfyingly wide when he catches sight of me. "Wow. You look great."

"Thanks. So do you," I say, even though I already told him that at his house. We smile at one another in a way that's not helping the *we're just friends* argument.

"Ellery needs to be back by ten-thirty," Nana interjects, throwing out an arbitrary time that we did *not* agree to upstairs. "She'll be coming home with Ezra."

"No problem, Mrs. Corcoran," Malcolm says before I can reply. "Thanks for letting her go with me."

I'm not positive, but I think Nana's expression might soften a little as she opens the door for us. "Have a good time. And a *safe* time."

We cross the lawn to the Volvo, and Malcolm opens the passenger door for me. I tip my head back to look up at him. I'm about to make a joke—something to ease the tension caused by my grandmother's obvious nerves—but my eyes wander to his lips and the slope of his neck where it meets his crisp white shirt collar, and I forget what I was about to say.

His knuckles brush against my arm, raising goose bumps. "Do you want to get a coat? It's cold out."

"No, that's okay." I tear my eyes away from his weirdly

enticing collar and fold myself into the seat. We veer away from the heavy topics of the night while we drive, talking about a comic-book series we both like and a spin-off movie that neither of us has seen.

The school parking lot is packed, and Malcolm grabs one of the last open spots at the far end. I immediately regret my decision not to bring a coat, but when I start shivering Malcolm pulls his suit jacket off and settles it over my shoulders. It smells like him, a clean mix of shampoo and laundry detergent. I try not to inhale too obviously while we walk.

"Here goes nothing," he says, opening the front doors.

I pull out my phone and call Nana to let her know we've arrived safely, then disconnect as we turn the corner that leads to the auditorium. The first thing we see is a purple-draped table, staffed by a blond woman in a flowered dress. Her bangs are teased higher than average for the decade we're in. "Oh no," Malcolm mutters, halting his steps.

"What?" I ask, putting my phone into the pocket of my dress. I slip Malcolm's jacket off my shoulders and hand it back to him.

Malcolm takes his time putting it back on before he starts moving again. "That's Liz McNulty. Kyle's sister. She *hates* me. Looks like she's a chaperone."

"That woman?" I peer at her. "The one Declan broke up with for Lacey?" Malcolm nods. "I thought she was your brother's age."

"She is."

"She looks forty!"

I'm whispering, but he still shushes me as we approach the table. "Hi, Liz," Malcolm says in a resigned tone.

The woman glances up from her phone, and her expression immediately settles into a look of deep dislike. "Tickets," she growls without returning the greeting.

"We don't have them yet," Malcolm says. "Can I get two, please?"

Liz looks positively triumphant when she tells him, "We're not selling them at the door."

Malcolm pauses in the act of reaching for his wallet. "That's kind of a flawed system."

"You're supposed to buy them ahead of time," Liz sniffs.

"Hey, guys," a melodic voice calls behind us. I turn to see Daisy coming out of the gym, looking pretty in a formfitting blue dress and high heels. A blast of loud music accompanies her until she closes the door.

"Hi," I say, relieved to see a friendly face. "You look nice."

"Gotta dress up for chaperone duty, right, Liz?" Daisy says. Liz smooths the front of her frumpy dress, and I feel a pang of sympathy for her. Daisy flicks her eyes between Malcolm and me. "I'm surprised to see you two here. Mia said you weren't coming."

"We changed our minds. But we didn't know you needed tickets ahead of time," I add, giving Liz my most ingratiating smile.

Liz crosses her arms over her chest, ready to argue until Daisy puts a placating hand on her arm. "Oh, I'm sure it's okay now that the dance is more than half over. Right, Liz?" No response, but Daisy presses on. "Principal Slate wouldn't want to turn anyone away. Not on a night like this, when the school is trying to bring people together. And we need every penny we can get for the reward fund." She flashes the kind of sweet, winning smile that probably got her elected to student council all four years at Echo Ridge High. Liz continues to glower, but with less certainty. I guess Daisy's secret relationship with Declan is still under wraps, or Liz would probably be a lot less charitable.

"We'd really appreciate it," I say. Malcolm, wisely, keeps his mouth shut.

Liz holds out her palm with an annoyed snort. "Fine. Five dollars. *Each.*"

Malcolm hands over a ten and we walk with Daisy into the gymnasium. Loud, thumping music hits us again, and I blink as my eyes adjust to the dim lighting. Purple streamers and silver balloons are everywhere and the room is packed with dancing students. "Should we look for Mia and Ezra?" Malcolm asks, raising his voice to be heard over the thumping noise. I nod and he turns toward the center of the room, but Daisy pulls at my arm before I can follow.

"Can I ask you something?" she shouts.

I hesitate as Malcolm disappears into the crowd without realizing I'm not behind him. "Um, okay," I say, not sure what to expect.

Daisy puts her head close to mine so she doesn't have to yell. "I've been thinking about what you said. About Ryan Rodriguez and the bracelet?" I nod. We hadn't gotten much chance to discuss that on Thursday, once Mia and Daisy's parents came home and started hyperventilating over Mia's head injury. She told them she tripped headfirst into the fireplace mantel. "It's been worrying me. Why do you think he might have given it to Lacey? Do you know something?"

"No," I admit. I don't want to catalog all my vague suspicions to Daisy, especially after what she'd said that day: *There's this whole other layer when you're one of the only minority families in town.* Sometimes I forget how . . . *not* diverse Echo Ridge is. But when I look around at the crowded gym, I remember. And it feels less harmless to toss speculation around about someone whose last name is Rodriguez.

Besides, even though I crossed Daisy off my suspect list after getting to know her better, I still think Declan is sketchy. Malcolm might not talk to him much, but I'm sure Daisy does.

"It's just because he knew her," I say instead.

Daisy's brow creases. "But . . . it's not like they were friends."

"He was so devastated when she died, though."

She straightens up in surprise, her pretty eyes wide. "Says who?"

"My mother." Daisy still looks confused, so I add, "She saw him at the funeral. When he got hysterical and had to be carried out?"

"*Ryan Rodriguez* did?" Daisy's tone is incredulous, and she shakes her head decisively. "That didn't happen."

"Maybe you missed it?" I suggest.

"No. Our class was small, we were all on one side of the church. I would've noticed." Daisy's mouth curves in an indulgent smile. "Your mom was probably being dramatic. Hollywood, right?"

I pause. Daisy's response is almost exactly what Nana said when I brought it up a couple of weeks ago. *That didn't happen.* Then, I thought Nana was being dismissive. But that was before I'd fully experienced how odd Sadie can be when it comes to talking about Echo Ridge. "Yeah, I guess," I say slowly.

I don't think Daisy has any reason to lie about Ryan's behavior at Lacey's funeral. But does Sadie?

"Sorry, I separated you from your date, didn't I?" Daisy says as we spy Malcolm emerging from a crowd in the middle of the room. "I better circulate and make myself useful. Have fun." She waves and heads for the sidelines, pirouetting to avoid a couple of theater kids starting a dramatic waltz as the music slows down.

"What happened to you?" Malcolm asks when he reaches me. He looks more disheveled than he did when we got here, like someone who found himself at the edge of a mosh pit but didn't go all in: jacket unbuttoned, tie loosened, hair mussed.

"Sorry. Daisy wanted to ask me something. Did you find them?"

"No. I got intercepted by Viv." His shoulders twitch in an irritated shudder. "She's already lost Kyle and she's not happy about it. And she's mad at Theo because he brought a flask and Katrin's half drunk."

I scan the gym until I spot a bright-red dress. "Speaking of," I say, nodding toward the dance floor. Katrin and Theo are slow-dancing in the middle of the room, her arms wrapped around his neck like she's trying to keep from drowning. "There she is."

Malcolm follows my gaze. "Yep. Doesn't look much like a killer, does she?"

Something in me deflates. "You think I'm ridiculous, don't you?"

"What? No," Malcolm says quickly. "I just meant— Whatever might happen isn't happening right this second, so . . . maybe we could dance?" He slides a finger beneath his tie and tugs to loosen it further. "Since we're here and all."

My stomach starts doing that fluttering thing again. "Well. We do need to blend," I say, and accept the hand he holds out to me.

My arms circle his neck and his hands graze my waist. It's the classic awkward slow-dance position, but after a couple of offbeat sways he pulls me closer and then, suddenly, we fit. I relax against him, my head on his chest. For a few minutes I just enjoy how solid he feels, and the steady beat of his heart beneath my cheek.

Malcolm leans toward my ear. "Can I ask you something?" I lift my head, hoping he's going to ask if he can kiss me again, and almost say yes preemptively before he adds, "Are you afraid of clowns?"

Huh. That was a letdown.

I lean back and stare into his eyes, which look steely gray instead of green beneath the dim lights. "Um. What?"

"Are you afraid of clowns?" he asks patiently, like it's a perfectly normal conversation starter.

So I go with it. "No. I've never understood the whole clown phobia, to be honest." I shake my head, and a stray curl grazes my lips and sticks to the gloss. Reminding me, once again, why I don't wear makeup. Before I can figure out a graceful way to extricate it, Malcolm does it for me, tucking the curl behind my ear and letting his hand settle briefly on my neck before it returns to my waist.

A jolt of energy shoots down my spine. *Oh.* All right. Maybe lip gloss has its uses.

"Me either," he says. "I feel like clowns get kind of a bad rap, you know? They just want to entertain."

"Are you, like, their spokesperson?" I ask, and he grins.

"No. But there's this clown museum in Solsbury— Well, calling it a museum is kind of a stretch. It's this old woman's house that's crammed full of antique clown stuff. She gives anybody who shows up a giant box of popcorn and she has, like, six dogs that just hang out there in the middle of all the clown memorabilia. And sometimes she plays movies against one of the walls, but they don't always have clowns in them. Or usually, even. Last time I went the movie was *Legally Blonde*."

I laugh. "Sounds delightful."

"It's weird," Malcolm admits. "But I like it. It's funny and sort of interesting, as long as you're not afraid of clowns." His hands tighten on my waist, just a little. "I thought maybe you'd like to go sometime."

I have a lot of questions, starting with *Only me, or me and my brother plus Mia?* and *Will it be a date, or is it just a strange thing you like that nobody else will do?* and *Should we get you one hundred percent cleared of any felonies first?* But I bite them back and respond with, "I'd like that."

Because I would.

"Okay. Good," Malcolm says with a crooked smile. Suddenly, whatever rhythm we've managed to find vanishes; he steps on my foot, I clock him with my elbow, my hair sticks to my face for reasons I can't even comprehend. It's all going to hell very quickly, until he freezes and says, "Do you see Katrin?"

I look toward the center of the gym where we'd seen her last, but she's gone. "Theo's still there," I say, tilting my chin in his direction. He's doing a terrible job of trying to look casual while pouring the contents of a flask into his Solo cup. "But I don't see her."

240

The music switches to a fast song and Malcolm motions for me to follow him. We wind our way off the dance floor, weaving in and out of the crowd, and circle the perimeter of the auditorium. I catch a couple of people staring at Malcolm, and before I can think too much about it I grab hold of his hand. I spot Mia and Ezra within a bigger group, dancing frenetically. Daisy is off to the side with a couple of chaperones, standing slightly apart from them with a preoccupied expression. It makes me wonder what homecoming was like for her five years ago, watching the boy she loved and her best friend get crowned king and queen. Whether she was jealous—or unconcerned, thinking her turn would come soon enough.

And I wonder what it was like for Sadie more than twenty years ago, there without her sister, dancing with a boy she must have liked at least a little bit. A perfect night turned into a cruel memory.

"She's not here," Malcolm says, but just then, I see a flash of bright red where I wasn't expecting it to be.

The far corner of the gym has an exit next to the bleachers that's been covered with balloons and streamers in an attempt to make it look inaccessible. Katrin emerges from beneath the stands and, without checking to see whether a chaperone's in sight, pushes the door open and slips outside.

Malcolm and I exchange glances. The straight path to the door is strewn with dancing classmates and chaperones, so we stick to the edge of the gym until we come to the opposite side. We slip underneath the bleachers and make our way along the wall toward the door, encountering only one couple making out. When we emerge on the other side, we look around more carefully than Katrin did before following her out the door.

It's cool and quiet outside, the moon full and bright above us. Katrin's nowhere in sight. The football field is to our left, the front of the building to our right. By unspoken agreement, we both go right.

When we turn the corner nearest the school entrance, Katrin is standing frozen near the Echo Ridge High sign. Malcolm tugs me back into the shadows as she half turns, and I spy a clutch in her hands. My eyes strain and my breath catches as I watch her fumble with the clasp. Even though the sensible part of my brain wonders what she could possibly manage to fit in there other than keys and a tube of lip gloss, I pull out my cell phone and set it to Video.

But before Katrin can take anything out of the bag, she drops it. My phone frames her in almost cinematic moonlight as she freezes, bends at the waist, and vomits loudly into the grass.

CHAPTER TWENTY-EIGHT

ELLERY
SUNDAY, OCTOBER 8

Post-homecoming Echo Ridge seems tired on Sunday, as though the entire town is hung over. Church is emptier than usual, and we hardly see anyone while we run errands with Nana after. Even Melanie Kilduff, who usually jogs past at some point while we're doing yard work, is nowhere in sight when Ezra and I pull weeds from the side lawn.

"So how did you end things with Malcolm?" Ezra asks.

I yank on a dandelion and accidentally behead it instead of pulling it out by the roots. "I mean, you saw," I say, annoyed. The dance ended promptly at ten o'clock last night, and we all got herded out of the auditorium like cattle with a strict curfew. Daisy beat Nana's deadline by fifteen minutes. Nana stayed up unusually late, hovering around Ezra and me, and I ended up texting him an update of my night instead of describing it in person. "We said good night."

"Yeah, but you must've made plans, right?"

I extract the rest of the dandelion and toss it into the plastic bucket between us. "I think we might go to a clown museum."

Ezra frowns. "A what now?"

"A clown museum. That's kind of beside the point, though, isn't it?" I sit back on my haunches, frustrated. "I really thought something else would happen last night. With Katrin, I mean. But all we did was catch her in the dastardly act of throwing up."

Ezra shrugs. "It wasn't a bad idea. She's pretty central to everything that's been going on around here, but . . ." He trails off and wipes his brow, leaving a faint smear of dirt on his forehead. "But maybe we should let the experts handle it. Give the receipt to the police. You don't have to tell them how you got it. Malcolm could say he found it."

"But then it doesn't make any sense. The only reason the receipt is meaningful is because Brooke was trying to get it back."

"Oh. Right."

The faint roar of a car engine approaches, and I turn to see Officer Rodriguez's police cruiser pass our house and turn into his driveway a few doors down. "Too bad our local officer is so sketchy," I mutter.

"Haven't you given that up yet?" Ezra asks. "Daisy told you last night that Officer Rodriguez didn't make a scene at Lacey's funeral. Nana said the same thing. I don't know why Sadie would say he did if it wasn't true, but at the very least, whatever she thinks she saw is open to interpretation. Other than that, what has the guy done? Taken a bad yearbook photo? Maybe you should give him a chance."

I get to my feet and brush off my jeans. "Maybe you're right. Come on."

"Huh?" Ezra squints up at me. "I didn't mean *now*."

"Why not? Nana's been after us to bring over those moving boxes, right? So he can pack up his house before he tries to sell it? Let's do it now. Maybe we can feel him out about what's happening with the investigation."

We leave our yard tools where they are and head inside. Nana is upstairs dusting when we gather a couple dozen flattened cardboard boxes from the basement. When we shout up to her what we're doing, she doesn't protest.

Ezra takes the lion's share of the boxes and I grab the rest, following him outside onto the wide dirt road that leads to the Rodriguezes' house. It's a dark-brown Cape, smaller than the rest of the neighborhood homes and set back from the street. I've never seen it up close before. The front windows have bright blue flower boxes, but everything inside them looks like it's been dead for months.

Officer Rodriguez answers within a few seconds of Ezra pressing the bell. He's out of uniform in a blue T-shirt and sweatpants, and his hair looks overdue for a trim. "Oh, hey," he says, pulling the door open wide. "Nora mentioned she'd be sending those over. Great timing. I'm taking some things out of the living room now."

He didn't invite us in, exactly, but I step into the hallway anyway. "You're moving?" I ask, hoping to keep the conversation going. Now that I'm inside the Rodriguezes' house, I'm more curious about him than ever.

Officer Rodriguez takes the boxes from us and props them against the wall. "Eventually. Now that my dad's gone it's too much house for one person, you know? But there's no rush. Gotta figure out where to go first." He lifts an arm to scratch the back of his head. "You guys want something to drink? Water, maybe?"

"Do you have any coffee?" Ezra asks.

Officer Rodriguez looks doubtful. "Are you allowed to drink that?"

"We're, like, five years younger than you," Ezra points out. "And it's *coffee*. I'm not asking you for meth." I snicker, even as I realize that Ezra must have a decent comfort level with Officer Rodriguez to give him a hard time like that. He doesn't usually openly challenge authority figures, even as a joke.

Officer Rodriguez smiles sheepishly. "Well, your grandmother's kind of strict. But yeah, I just made some." He turns, and we trail him into a kitchen with mustard-colored appliances and old-fashioned flowered wallpaper. Officer Rodriguez pulls a couple of mismatched mugs out of a cabinet and roots around in a drawer for spoons.

I lean against the counter. "We were wondering, um, how things are going with the investigation about Brooke," I say, feeling a familiar tightening in my chest. Some days, like yesterday, I'm almost busy enough to forget how every passing hour makes it less and less likely that Brooke is going to come home safely. "Any news?"

"Nothing I can share," Officer Rodriguez says, his tone turning more businesslike. "I'm sorry. I know it's hard on you guys, having seen her right before she disappeared."

He looks like he means it. And right now, as he fills a snowman mug with steaming coffee and hands it to me, he seems so nice and normal and decidedly non-murder-y that I wish I'd brought the car repair receipt with me.

Except I still don't know much about him. Not really.

"How is her family doing?" Ezra asks, settling into a kitchen chair. There's a stray penny on the table in front of him, and he starts spinning it across the surface.

"About as you'd expect. They're worried sick. But they appreciate everything the town is doing," Officer Rodriguez says. He crosses to the refrigerator and opens it, pushing around the contents. "Do you guys take milk? Or half-and-half?"

"Either," Ezra says, catching the penny midspin between two fingers.

I peer into the attached living room, where an oversized picture of three little kids hangs over the mantel. "Is that you when you were little?" I ask. Since I have so few of my own, family photos are like catnip to me. I always feel like they must say a lot about the person they belong to, which is probably why Sadie hates them. She doesn't like giving anything away.

Officer Rodriguez is still looking through the refrigerator, his back toward me. "What?"

"That picture over your fireplace." I set my mug down on the counter and go out to the living room for a closer look. The top of the mantel is crowded with more pictures, and I gravitate toward a triple-frame one with what looks like graduation photos.

"You shouldn't—" Officer Rodriguez calls, and there's a crashing noise behind me. As I turn to see him tripping over an ottoman, my gaze skims past a picture of Ezra.

Wait. No. That can't be right.

My eyes lock on the framed photo of a young man in military fatigues, leaning against a helicopter and smiling into the

247

camera. Everything about him—the dark hair and eyes, the sharp planes of his face, even the slightly lopsided grin—looks exactly like my brother.

And me.

I draw in a sharp breath, my fingers closing around the frame seconds before Officer Rodriguez tries to snatch it off the mantel. I stumble backward, both hands gripping the picture as something that feels a lot like panic zips through my bloodstream. My skin is hot and my vision is clouding up. But I can still see that face with perfect clarity in my mind's eye. It could be my brother dressed up as a soldier for Halloween, but it's not.

"Who is this?" I ask. My tongue feels thick, like it's been shot through with Novocain.

Officer Rodriguez's face is beet red. He looks as though he'd rather do anything other than answer me, but he finally does. "My dad, right after he served in Desert Storm."

"Your *dad*?" The word comes out as a shriek.

"Ellery? What the hell?" Ezra's puzzled tone sounds miles away.

"Shit." Officer Rodriguez runs both hands through his hair. "This is . . . okay. This is not how I wanted things to go. I was going to, I don't know, talk to your grandmother or something. Except I had no idea what to say, so I just kept putting it off and . . . I mean, I don't even know." I meet his eyes, and he swallows hard. "It might be a coincidence."

My legs have turned into rubber bands. I drop into an armchair, still clutching the picture frame. "It's not a coincidence."

Impatience edges into Ezra's voice. "What are you talking about?"

Officer Rodriguez doesn't look anything like his father. If he did, I might've been as startled as he was the first time we met. Suddenly it all makes sense—the dropped coffee mug in Nana's kitchen, the nervous stuttering and bumbling every time he saw us. I'd taken it for ineptitude at first, then guilt about Lacey. Never, not once, did it occur to me that Ryan Rodriguez looked like a deer in perpetual headlights because he was trying to process the fact that we're probably related.

Probably? I scan the photo in my hands. I've never looked anything like Sadie except for the hair and dimple. But those near-black, upturned eyes, the sharp chin, the smile—it's what I see in the mirror every day.

Officer Rodriguez clasps his hands in front of him like he's getting ready to pray. "Maybe we should get your grandmother."

I shake my head emphatically. I don't know much right now, but I *do* know that Nana's presence wouldn't do anything except up the awkward quotient by a thousandfold. Instead, I hold the frame out to Ezra. "You need to see this."

I feel as though all seventeen years of my life flash in front of me as my brother crosses the room. My brain races at the same pace, trying to come up with some explanation for all the parts that now seem like a lie. Like, maybe Sadie really did meet up with someone named Jorge or José at a nightclub, and genuinely believed everything she'd ever told us about our father. Maybe she didn't even remember what now seems like a pretty obvious precursor to that—a fling with a married guy while she was in town for her father's funeral.

Except. I remember her expression when I'd first mentioned Officer Rodriguez's name—how something uncomfortable and almost shifty crossed her face. When I'd asked her about it, she'd told me that story about him falling apart at Lacey's funeral. Something that I'd built an entire criminal theory around until two people told me it didn't happen.

Ezra sucks in a sharp breath. "Holy shit."

I can't bring myself to look at his face, so I dart a glance at Officer Rodriguez instead. A muscle twitches in his cheek. "I'm sorry," he says. "I should have— Well, I don't know what I should've done, to be honest. We could . . . get a test or something, I guess, to make sure. . . ." He trails off and crosses his arms. "I don't think he knew. Maybe I'm wrong, but I think he would've said something if he had."

Would've. Past tense. Since his father—and ours, I guess— has been dead for three months.

It's too much to take in. Voices buzz around me, and I should probably listen because I'm sure they're saying something important and meaningful, but I can't hear the words clearly. Everything is white noise. My palms are sweating, my knees shaking. My lungs feel like they've shrunk and can only hold spoonfuls of air at a time. I'm getting so dizzy that I'm afraid I'm going to pass out in the middle of the Rodriguezes' living room.

And maybe the worst thing about it all is this: how horribly, childishly, and desperately I want my mom right now.

CHAPTER TWENTY-NINE

MALCOLM
SUNDAY, OCTOBER 6

It's one of those dreams that's really a memory.

Mia and I are on her couch, our eyes glued to her television as we watch coverage of Lacey's funeral from the day before. We'd been there, of course, but we couldn't tear ourselves away from reliving it on-screen.

Meli Dinglasa, an Echo Ridge High grad who'd been toiling in obscurity at a local news station until someone got the brilliant idea to put her in front of the camera for this story, stands on the church steps clutching a microphone. "Yesterday, this shattered New England town came together at Lacey Kilduff's funeral, mourning the loss of such a promising young woman. But amidst the sorrow, questions continue to whirl around those who knew the teen victim best."

The camera cuts to video of Declan leaving the church in

a badly fitting suit, tight-lipped and scowling. If he's trying to look the part of "Disreputable Ex with a Chip on His Shoulder," he's doing a great job.

Mia clears her throat and leans forward, clutching a pillow. "Do you think whoever did it was at the funeral yesterday?" She catches sight of my face and hastily adds, "I don't mean any of her friends. Obviously. I just mean— I wonder if it's somebody we know. Right there with us, in the middle of the crowd."

"They wouldn't show up," I say, with more certainty than I feel.

"You don't think?" Mia chews her bottom lip, eyes flicking over the screen. "They should give everybody there the killer test."

"The what?"

"I heard about it at school," Mia says. "It's a riddle about a girl. She's at her mother's funeral, and she sees some guy she doesn't know. She falls in love with him and decides he's her dream guy. A few days later, she kills her sister. Why'd she do it?"

"Nobody would do that," I scoff.

"It's a riddle. You have to answer. They say murderers always give the same answer."

"Because she . . ." I pause, trying to think of the most twisted answer possible. I feel comfortable about doing that with Mia, in a way I wouldn't with anybody else right now. She's one of the only people in Echo Ridge who's not staring accusingly at Declan—and at me, like I must be a bad seed by association. "Because the sister was the man's girlfriend and she wanted him for herself?"

"No. Because she thought the man might go to her sister's funeral, too."

I snort. "That doesn't even make sense."

"Do you have a better way to tell who's a cold-blooded killer?"

I scan the crowd on-screen, looking for an obvious sign that somebody's not right. Something twisted lurking among all the sad faces. "They're the most messed-up person in the room."

Mia curls deeper into her corner of the couch, pressing the pillow tight against her chest. "That's the problem, though, isn't it? They are, but you can't tell."

I startle awake so violently that I almost fall out of bed. My pulse is racing and my mouth is cottony dry. I haven't thought about that day in years—Mia and I sneak-watching news coverage of Lacey's funeral while I hid at her house because mine was already bubbling over with angry tension. I don't know why I'd dream about it now, except . . .

Katrin would either have to be so desperate that she lost all sense of right or wrong, or be a cold-blooded criminal. Even after catching Katrin doing nothing worse than looking for a quiet place to puke, I can't get Ellery's words out of my head.

I run a hand through sweat-dampened hair and flip over, trying to sink back into sleep. No good. My eyes keep popping open, so I roll over to check the time on my phone. Just past three a.m., so it's surprising to see a text from Ellery that's time-stamped ten minutes ago.

Sorry I didn't reply sooner. Stuff happened.

It only took her fifteen hours to get back to my *I had fun last night* text. Which was making me paranoid for a different reason.

I prop myself up on one elbow, feeling a twinge of worry. I don't like the sound of *stuff*, or the fact that Ellery's awake at three a.m. I'm about to message her back when a sound outside my door makes me pause. The light tread of footsteps is almost imperceptible, except for a tiny creak from the loose floorboard in front of my room. But now that my ears are straining, I hear someone going downstairs and opening the front door.

I push my sheets aside, climb out of bed, and cross to my window. The moon's just bright enough that I can make out a figure with a backpack walking quickly down our driveway. Not Peter-sized, and the confident stride doesn't look anything like my mother's. Which leaves Katrin.

Katrin would either have to be so desperate that she lost all sense of right or wrong, or be a cold-blooded criminal. God. Ellery's words are like my brain's very own Fright Farm Demon Rollercoaster, circling in an endless, horrifying loop. And now, watching the figure below me disappear into darkness, all I can think is that it's pretty reckless to wander around Echo Ridge at three in the morning with Brooke still missing.

Unless you know there's nothing to be afraid of.

Unless *you're* what people should be afraid of.

I root around on my floor for sneakers. Holding them in one hand, I grab my phone with the other and slip out my bedroom door into the darkened hallway. I make my way downstairs as silently as I can, although with Peter's loud snoring I probably don't need to bother. When I reach the foyer, I jam my feet into my sneakers and slowly open the front door. I don't see Katrin anywhere, and all I hear are crickets and rustling leaves.

I look both ways when I reach the end of the driveway. There are no streetlights on our stretch of road, and I can't see anything except the shadowy shapes of trees. School is toward the left, and downtown is right. *School*, I think. Where homecoming was last night. I turn left and stay at the edge of the road, walking close to the tall bushes that line our nearest neighbor's property. Our street feeds into a bigger one that's more well lit, and when I turn onto it I can make out Katrin a few blocks ahead of me.

I lift my phone and text Ellery. *I'm following Katrin.*

I don't expect a response, but she answers within seconds. *WHAT???*

Why are you up?

Long story. Why are you following Katrin?

Because she left the house at 3am & I want to know why.

Solid reason. Where's she headed?

Idk. School, maybe?

It's a good twenty-minute walk to Echo Ridge High from our house, even with both Katrin and me moving at a quick pace. My phone vibrates in my hand a couple of times as I walk, but I keep my eyes on Katrin. In the hazy moonlight there's something almost insubstantial about her, like she might disappear if I stop paying attention. I keep thinking about our parents' wedding reception last spring, when my new stepsister wore a brittle smile and a short white dress like some kind of bride in training. While Peter and Mom circled the floor for their first dance, she grabbed a couple of champagne glasses from a passing waiter's tray and handed one to me.

"We're stuck with one another now, aren't we, Mal?" she asked before downing half of hers in one gulp. She clinked her glass against mine. "Might as well get used to it. Cheers."

I liked her better than I thought I would that night. And since. So I would really fucking hate for Ellery to be right about any of this.

Katrin stops a few hundred feet short of Echo Ridge High, at a stone wall that divides the school from neighboring property. The streetlights in front of the school throw off a yellowish glow, enough for me to see her put the backpack down and crouch beside it. I kneel behind a bush, my heart beating uncomfortably fast. While I wait for Katrin to rise again, I look down at the last text I received from Ellery: *What's she up to?*

About to find out. Hang on.

I open my camera and flip it to Video, hit Zoom, and train it on Katrin as she pulls something square and white out of the backpack. She unfolds it like a map and steps toward the stone wall. I watch as she fastens one corner of what she's holding to the top of the wall with duct tape, then repeats the process until a sign with red lettering is prominently displayed.

NOW PLAYING

MURDERLAND, PART 2

TOLD YOU SO

My heart skips a beat and I almost drop my phone. Katrin puts the duct tape back in her backpack and zips it up, then slings it over her shoulder, turning and striding back the way she came. She's wearing a hoodie with her hair tucked up beneath it, but when she passes within a few feet of me I get a clear shot of her face.

When I can't hear her footsteps any longer, I move forward so

I can record the sign up close. The bright-red letters are splashed against the white background, but there's nothing else—no dolls, no pictures, none of the creepy gleefulness of her previous work. I text the video to Ellery and write, *This is what she's up to.* Then I wait, but not for long.

Oh my God.

My fingers feel numb as I type. *You called it.*

We have to give this to the police, Ellery replies. *The receipt, too. I shouldn't have hung on to it for this long.*

My stomach rolls. Jesus, what's my mother going to think? Will part of her be relieved that it takes the focus off Declan and me, or is it just the same shit show, different channel? And Peter—my brain seizes trying to imagine how he'll react to Katrin being mixed up in something like this. Especially if I'm the one bringing it to light.

But I have to. There's too much piling up, and all of it points to my stepsister.

I start walking and texting at the same time. *I know. I'm going to make sure she's headed home & not someplace else. Should we go to the station tomorrow morning?*

I'd rather show Officer Rodriguez first. Do you want to come by my house around six & we can go together?

I blink at the screen. Ellery has spent weeks telling anyone who'd listen—which, granted, is mostly Ezra, Mia, and me—that she thinks Officer Rodriguez is sketchy. Now she wants to go to his house at the crack of dawn, handing over stuff we're not supposed to have? I glance away from my phone and see that I'm gaining a little too quickly on Katrin; if I keep up my pace I'll walk right past her. I slow down and text, *Why him?*

It takes a few minutes for Ellery's message to appear. She's either writing a novel, or taking her time figuring out what to say. When her text finally comes through, it's not what I was expecting.

Let's just say he owes me one.

"So you got this receipt how, again?"

Officer Rodriguez hands me a cup of coffee in his kitchen. Early-morning sun streams through the window over the sink, striping the table with gold. I'm so tired that the effect reminds me of a pillow, and all I want to do is lay my head down and shut my eyes. I left a note for Mom and Peter saying I was going to the gym, which is only slightly more believable than what I'm actually doing.

"The recycling bin was unlocked," Ellery says, twisting a curl around her finger.

"Unlocked?" Officer Rodriguez's eyes are ringed with dark circles. Considering what Ellery told me on the way over about the picture of his father, I doubt he slept much last night either.

"Yeah."

"But everything was still inside?"

She meets his gaze without blinking. "Yeah."

"Okay." He rubs a hand over his face. "Let's go with that. Regardless of whether the bin was locked or unlocked, its contents weren't your property to take."

"I didn't think discarded items were anyone's property," Ellery says. She sounds like she really, really hopes she's right.

Officer Rodriguez leans back in his chair and regards her

in silence for a few seconds. He and Ellery don't resemble one another much. But now that I know there's a chance they're related, the stubborn set of their jaws looks exactly the same. "I'm going to treat this as an anonymous tip," he finally says, and Ellery visibly exhales. "I'll look into the car situation. Given Brooke's state of mind when you saw her at Fright Farm, it's an interesting thread to follow."

Ellery crosses her legs and jiggles one foot. She's been full of nervous energy since she got here, constantly shifting and fidgeting. Unlike Officer Rodriguez and me, she seems wide awake. "Are you going to arrest Katrin?"

Officer Rodriguez holds up a palm. "Whoa. Not so fast. There's no evidence that she's committed a crime."

She blinks, startled. "What about the video?"

"It's of interest, sure. But there's no destruction of property involved. Trespassing, maybe. Depends on who owns the wall."

"But what about all the other times?" I ask.

He shrugs. "We don't know she was involved with those. All we know is what you saw this morning."

I grip my mug. The coffee is already cold, but I drink it anyway. "So everything we gave you is useless."

"*Nothing* is useless when someone goes missing," Officer Rodriguez says. "All I'm saying is that it's premature to draw conclusions based on what you've shared. That's my job, okay? Not yours." He leans forward and raps his knuckles on the table for emphasis. "Listen up. I appreciate you guys coming to me, I really do. But you need to stay out of this from now on. Not only for your safety, but because if you *are* circling around someone who played a role in Brooke's disappearance, you don't want to tip them off. Okay?" We both nod, and he crosses his arms. "I'm going to need a verbal confirmation."

"You're better at this than I thought," Ellery says under her breath.

Officer Rodriguez frowns. "What?"

She raises her voice. "I said, okay."

He juts his chin toward me, and I nod. "Yeah, all right."

"And please keep this between us." Officer Rodriguez levels his gaze at Ellery. "I know you're close to your brother, but I'd prefer you not share what we've discussed outside this room."

I doubt she's planning to honor that request, but she nods. "Okay."

Officer Rodriguez glances at the clock on his microwave. It's almost six-thirty. "Does your grandmother know you're here?"

"No," Ellery says. "She doesn't know *anything*." Officer Rodriguez's eyes flick toward me at the emphasis, and I keep my face carefully blank. It's a little surprising, maybe, that nobody in Echo Ridge made the connection between his father and the twins before now. But Mr. Rodriguez was one of those private family guys that nobody saw much of. Even when you did, he didn't resemble the photo Ellery showed me on her phone. He'd been wearing thick glasses as long as I could remember, and had gotten a lot heavier. And balder. Ezra better enjoy his hair while he can.

"You should get home, then. She'll worry if she wakes up and you're not there. You too, Malcolm."

"Okay," Ellery says, but she doesn't move. She jiggles her foot again and adds, "I was wondering something. About you and Lacey."

Officer Rodriguez cocks his head. "What about me and Lacey?"

"I asked you once if you were friends, and you wouldn't answer me."

"I wouldn't?" His mouth twists in a wry smile. "Probably because it's none of your business."

"Did you . . ." She pauses. "Did you ever want to, you know, ask her out or anything?"

He huffs out a small laugh. "Sure. Me and most of the guys in our class. Lacey was beautiful, but . . . she wasn't just that. She cared about people. Even if you were nobody at school, she made you feel like you mattered." His expression darkens. "It still tears me up, what happened to her. I think that's half the reason I became a cop."

Ellery's eyes search his, and whatever she sees there relaxes the tense set of her shoulders. "Are you still looking into her murder?"

Officer Rodriguez shoots her an amused glance as his phone buzzes. "Give it a rest, Ellery. And go home." He glances at the screen, and all the color drains from his face. He pushes his chair back with a loud scrape and gets to his feet.

"What?" Ellery and I ask at the same time.

He reaches for a set of keys on the counter. "Go home," he says again, but this time not like it's a joke. "And stay there."

CHAPTER THIRTY

ELLERY
MONDAY, OCTOBER 7

I'm sitting on Nana's front steps, phone in hand. Malcolm left a few minutes ago, and Officer Rodriguez is long gone. Or maybe I should start calling him Ryan. I don't know the protocol for addressing probable half brothers who, until recently, were on your short list of cold-case murder suspects.

Anyway, I'm alone. Something's obviously going on with *Ryan,* but I have no idea what. All I know is that I'm sick to death of watching lies pile up on top of one another like the world's worst Jenga game. I pull up the photo I snapped of Mr. Rodriguez's army picture, studying the familiar lines of his face. When Ezra noticed the August 2001 date on my timeline I was afraid that maybe—*maybe*—we were dealing with a potential Vance Puckett paternity situation. I never imagined this.

I can't call Sadie. I don't know whose phone she's been using, and anyway, it's the middle of the night in California. Instead, I send the photo to her Gmail with the subject line *We need to talk.* Maybe she'll read her email when she borrows the aide's phone again.

I check the time; it's barely six-thirty. Nana won't be up for another half hour. I'm antsy and don't feel like going back inside, so I head for the woods behind the house instead. Now that pieces are falling into place about Katrin's involvement in Brooke's disappearance, I'm not scared about walking through the woods on my own. I follow the familiar path to Fright Farm, trying to empty my brain of thought and just enjoy the crisp fall air.

I emerge from the woods across the street from Fright Farm, and pause. I'd never noticed how different the gaping mouth of the entrance looks when the park is closed: less kitschy and more forbidding. I suck in a breath and let it out, then cross the deserted street, my eyes on the still, silent Ferris wheel cutting into the pale-blue sky.

When I reach the entrance, I put my hand on the mottled paint of the wooden mouth, trying to imagine what Lacey was feeling when she snuck into the park after hours five years ago. Was she excited? Upset? Scared? And who was she with, or who was she meeting? Without Daisy or Ryan on my list of suspects, it's back to who it's always been—Declan Kelly. Unless I'm missing someone.

"Do you have a reason for being here?"

The voice sends my heart into my throat. I whirl around to see an older man in a police uniform, one hand on the radio at his hip. It takes me a few seconds to recognize him—Officer

McNulty, the one who's been interrogating Malcolm all week. Liz and Kyle's father. He and Kyle look alike, both tall and broad with light hair, square jaws, and eyes that are just a little too close together. "I . . . was, um, taking a walk." An unexpected rush of nerves makes my voice wobble.

I don't know why I'm spooked, suddenly, by a middle-aged police officer. Maybe it's those flat, blue-gray eyes that remind me too much of his asshole son's. There's something cold and almost methodical about how thoroughly Kyle hates Malcolm. It was a stroke of good luck that we didn't run into him at home-coming the other night.

Officer McNulty eyes me carefully. "We don't recommend kids walking alone in town just now." He rubs his chin and squints. "Does your grandmother know you're here?"

"Yeah," I lie, wiping my damp palms on my pants. His radio crackles with static, and I think of how Ryan rushed out of his house this morning. I flop a hand toward the radio. "Is, um, something going on? With Brooke, or . . ."

I trail off as Officer McNulty's face hardens. "Excuse me?" he asks tersely.

"Sorry." Five weeks of Ryan's superhuman patience made me forget that most cops don't like getting pestered with questions from teenagers. "I'm just worried."

"Worry at home," he says, in the most *conversation-closed* voice I've ever heard.

I take the hint and mumble a good-bye, hightailing it across the street and back into the woods. I've never appreciated Ryan more—or at all, I guess, if I'm being truthful—and I feel sorry for Malcolm having to answer Officer McNulty's questions day after day.

The damp of the early-morning dew is seeping through my sneakers as the leaves on the ground get thicker. The discomfort increases my annoyance with Officer McNulty. No wonder his kids are sour enough to hold a five-years-long grudge about a bad breakup. I realize I don't know the whole story, and maybe Declan was a jerk to Liz. But she should leave Malcolm out of it, and Kyle should just mind his own business entirely. He's obviously not the kind of guy who knows how to let things go. He'd probably even hate Lacey if she were still around, for being the girl Declan chose over his sister. And Brooke for breaking up with him, and . . .

I slow down as it hits me, and blood rushes to my head so quickly that I grab a nearby branch for support. It never occurred to me, until right now, that the only person in Echo Ridge with a grudge against every single person involved in Lacey's death, and Brooke's disappearance, is Kyle McNulty.

But that doesn't make sense. Kyle was only twelve when Lacey died. And he has an alibi for the night Brooke disappeared: he was out of town with Liz.

The sister Declan had dumped for Lacey.

My heart squeezes in my chest as I start connecting dots. I've always thought that Lacey died because of *someone's* jealous passion. I just never considered that person might be Liz McNulty. Declan broke up with Liz, and Lacey died. Five years later, Brooke breaks up with Kyle, who's friends with Katrin, and . . . *God.* What if they teamed up to take care of a mutual problem?

I barely register that I'm in Nana's backyard as I yank my phone out of my pocket with shaking hands. Ryan gave me his phone number yesterday, after the photo fiasco in his house.

I need to call him, right now. Then movement catches my eye, and I see Nana racing toward me in her plaid bathrobe and slippers, her gray hair wild. "Hi, Nana—" I start, but she doesn't let me finish.

"What in God's name are you doing out here?" she shouts, her face stricken. "Your bed wasn't slept in last night! Your brother had no idea where you were! I thought you had *disappeared.*" Her voice cracks on the last word, sending a stab of guilt through me. I hadn't even considered that she might wake up and find me gone—and what that would be like for her.

She's still barreling my way, and then suddenly she's hugging me for the first time ever. Very tightly, and somewhat painfully.

"I'm sorry," I manage. It's a little hard to breathe.

"What were you thinking? How could you? I was about to call the police!"

"Nana, I can't . . . you're kind of crushing me."

She drops her arms, and I almost stumble. "Don't you *ever* do that again. I was worried sick. Especially . . ." She swallows visibly. "Especially now."

The back of my neck prickles. "Why now?"

"Come inside and I'll tell you." She turns and waits for me to follow, but I'm rooted to the spot. For the first time since I've been outside all morning, I realize my hands are numb with cold. I pull the sleeves of my sweater over them and wrap my arms around my body.

"Just tell me now. Please."

Nana's eyes are red around the rims. "There's a rumor going around that the police found a body in the woods near the Canadian border. And that it's Brooke's."

266

CHAPTER THIRTY-ONE

MALCOLM
MONDAY, OCTOBER 7

Somehow, we're supposed to still go to school.

"There's nothing you can do," Mom keeps repeating on Monday morning. She puts an overfull bowl of Cheerios in front of me on the kitchen island, even though I never eat cereal. "Nothing is confirmed about Brooke. We have to think positive and act normally."

The message might go over better if she didn't pour coffee into my Cheerios while she's saying it. She doesn't notice, and when she turns I grab milk off the island and top off the bowl. It's not the worst thing I've ever eaten. Plus I got back from Officer Rodriguez's an hour ago and didn't bother trying to sleep. I could use the caffeine.

"I'm not going," Katrin says flatly.

Mom eyes her nervously. Peter's gone, already left for work, and she's never been good at standing up to Katrin. "Your father would—"

"Understand," Katrin says in the same monotone. She's in the hoodie and athletic pants she wore last night, her hair pulled back into a low, messy ponytail. There's a plate of strawberries in front of her, and she keeps cutting one into smaller and smaller pieces without putting any of it into her mouth. "Anyway, I'm sick. I threw up this morning."

"Oh, well, if you're *sick*." My mother looks relieved at the excuse, and turns toward me with more confidence. "You, on the other hand, need to go."

"Fine by me." I'm good with being anywhere Katrin's not. If she hadn't played sick, I would have. There's no way I can sit in a car with her this morning. Especially not *her* car. More and more, it's sinking in that if Katrin did half the things we think she might have, chances are good she ran down Mr. Bowman and left him to die in the street. And that's just for starters. I grip my cereal spoon more tightly as I watch her methodically start cutting up a second strawberry, and it's all I can do not to reach out and smash everything on her plate into a pulp.

All this waiting is a nightmare. Especially when you know you're going to hate whatever answer comes.

Mom smooths a hand over her bathrobe. "I'm going to take a shower, unless either of you need anything?"

"Can I take your car?" I ask.

She smiles distractedly on her way to the stairs. "Yes, of course." And then she's gone, leaving Katrin and me alone in the kitchen. There's no sound except the clink of my spoon against the bowl and the loud ticking of the wall clock.

I can't handle it for even five minutes. "I'm leaving early," I say, getting up and dumping my half-finished coffee cereal in the garbage disposal. When I turn, Katrin is staring straight at me, and I'm struck silent by the cold blankness in her eyes.

"Why don't you just walk to school?" she asks. "You like walking, don't you?"

Fuck. She knows I followed her last night. I got too close on the way home.

"Who doesn't," I say tersely. I reach for Mom's keys on the kitchen island, but before I can pick them up Katrin lays a hand over them. She regards me with the same cool stare.

"You're not as smart as you think you are."

"And you're not sick." *To your stomach, anyway.* I pull the keys from beneath her hand and grab my backpack off the floor. I don't want her to see how rattled I am, so I look away, even though I'd like one last chance to read her expression.

What do you know? What did you do?

I drive to school in a haze, almost missing the entrance. It's so early that I have my pick of spots in the parking lot. I cut the engine but keep the radio on, searching for a news station. NPR is talking politics and all the local shows are breaking down the Patriots' come-from-behind win yesterday, so I pull out my phone and search the *Burlington Free Press* site. There's a blurb at the bottom of the Metro section: *Police investigate human remains found on an abandoned property in upper Huntsburg.*

Human remains. My stomach turns, and for a second I'm positive I'll puke up every single coffee-soaked Cheerio that I was stupid enough to eat this morning. But it passes, and I recline my seat and close my eyes. I just want to rest for a few minutes, but the lack of sleep catches up with me and I'm dozing when a loud rap on my window startles me awake. I look groggily at the car clock—it's two minutes past the final bell—then out the window.

Kyle and Theo are standing there, and they don't look like they're about to give me a friendly warning about being late. Viv is a few yards behind them, her arms crossed, a look of smug anticipation on her face. Like a kid at a birthday party who's about to get that pony she's always wanted.

I could drive away, I guess, but I don't want to give them the satisfaction of chasing me off. So I get out of the car.

"You're gonna be la—" is all I get out before Kyle drives his fist into my stomach. I fold in half, and my vision goes white from the pain. He follows up with another punch, to my jaw, that sends me reeling against the car. My mouth fills with the coppery taste of blood as Kyle leans forward, his face inches from mine.

"You're going down for this, Kelly," he spits, and pulls back for another punch.

Somehow I manage to duck and land a blow to Kyle's face before Theo steps in and pins my arms behind my back. I stomp on Theo's foot, but I'm off balance and he only lets out a slight grunt before tightening his grip. Sharp pain shoots through my ribs, and the entire left side of my face feels like it's on fire. Kyle wipes a trickle of blood from his mouth with a grim smile. "I should have done this years ago," he says, and hauls his fist back for a punch that'll break my face.

It doesn't come, though. A bigger fist closes over his and yanks him backward. For a few seconds I don't know what the hell is going on, until Declan steps forward and looms over

Theo. "Let him go," he says in a low, threatening tone. When Theo doesn't, Declan wrenches one of his arms so hard that Theo squeals in pain and backs off, hands up. Once I'm released I see Kyle sprawled on the ground a few feet away, motionless.

"Is he gonna get up?" I ask, rubbing my aching jaw.

"Eventually," Declan says. Theo doesn't even check on Kyle, just sprints past him on his way to the back entrance. Viv is nowhere in sight. "Fucking cowards, going two on one." Declan reaches for the Volvo's door and pulls it open. "Come on, let's get out of here. No point in you going to school today. I'll drive."

I slump in the passenger seat, nauseated and dizzy. I haven't been punched since ninth grade, and it wasn't anywhere near that hard. "Why are you here?" I ask.

Declan turns the keys I left in the ignition. "I was waiting for you."

"Why?"

His jaw sets in a hard line. "I remember the first day of school after . . . news like this."

I suck in a breath and wince. I wonder if my ribs are cracked. "What, you knew something like this was gonna happen?"

"It happened to me," he says.

"I didn't know that." I didn't know much back then, I guess. Too busy trying to pretend none of it was going on.

We drive in silence for a minute until we near a corner store, and Declan suddenly swerves into the parking lot. "Hang on a sec," he says, before shifting into park and disappearing inside. When he comes out a couple of minutes later, he's holding something square and white in one hand. He tosses it to me as he opens the door. "Put those on your face."

Frozen peas. I do as he says, almost groaning in relief as the cool seeps into my burning skin. "Thanks. For these and . . . you know. Saving my ass."

Out of the corner of my eye, I see him shake his head. "Can't believe you got out of the car. Amateur."

I'd laugh, but it hurts too much. I sit still, with the peas on my face as we leave Echo Ridge for Solsbury, tracing the path I took to his apartment last week. Declan must be thinking the same thing, because he says, "You're a little bitch for following Daisy." He looks like he's seriously considering turning the car around and leaving me in the parking lot with Kyle.

"I tried asking you what you were doing in town," I remind him. "Didn't work." He doesn't answer, just sort of grunts, which I decide means *point taken*. "When did you move here?"

"Last month," he says. "Daisy needs to be around her parents. And me. So . . . here I am."

"You could've told me about her, you know."

Declan snorts. "Really, little brother?" He turns into Pine Crest Estates and pulls into the parking spot in front of number 9. "You couldn't wait to get me out of Echo Ridge. The last thing you'd want to hear is that I'd moved one town over. No, wait, that's the second-last. The *last* thing is me being with Lacey's best friend. I mean, hell, what would the Nilssons say, right?"

"I hate the Nilssons." It slips out without thinking.

Declan raises his brows as he opens his door. "Trouble in paradise?"

I hesitate, trying to figure out how to explain, when my stomach seizes. I barely make it out of the car before I bend in half and vomit my breakfast all over the asphalt. Thank God it's quick, because the movement makes my ribs feel like someone just ripped them out. My eyes water as I clutch the side of the car for support, gasping.

"Delayed reaction," Declan says, reaching into the car for the discarded peas. "Happens sometimes." He lets me limp to the apartment on my own, unlocks the door, and points me toward the couch. "Lie down. I'll find an ice pack for your hand."

Declan's apartment is the most cliché bachelor pad ever. There's nothing in it except a couch and two armchairs, a giant television, and a bunch of milk crates for shelves. The couch is comfortable, though, and I sink into it while Declan roots around in his freezer. Something plastic digs into my back, and I pull out a remote. I aim it at the television and press the power button. A golf green with the ESPN logo in one corner fills the screen, and I click away, scrolling mindlessly through channels until the word *Huntsburg* catches my eye. I stop surfing as a man in a police uniform standing in front of a lectern says, ". . . have been able to make a positive identification."

"Declan." My throat hurts and my voice cracks, but when he doesn't answer, I rasp louder. *"Declan."*

His head emerges from the kitchen. "What? I can't find the—" He stops at the sight of my face, and comes into the living room just as the officer on-screen takes a deep breath.

"The body is that of a young woman who's been missing from Echo Ridge since last Saturday: seventeen-year-old Brooke Bennett. The Huntsburg police department would like to extend our condolences to Miss Bennett's family and friends, and our support to her hometown police department. At this time, the investigation into cause of death is ongoing and no further details will be released."

273

CHAPTER THIRTY-TWO

ELLERY

MONDAY, OCTOBER 7

I know the script. I've read it in countless books, and seen it play out dozens of times on television. All week, in the back of my mind, I knew how it would probably end.

What I didn't understand was how mind-numbingly awful it would feel.

At least I'm not alone. Ezra and Malcolm are in the living room with me Monday afternoon, six hours after the Huntsburg police found Brooke. None of us went to school today, although Malcolm's day was more eventful than ours. He showed up an hour ago, bruised and battered, and Nana has been handing him fresh ice packs every fifteen minutes.

We're arranged stiffly on her uncomfortable furniture, watching Channel 5 news coverage scroll across the screen. Meli Dinglasa is standing on Echo Ridge Common, her dark hair whipping across her face as the leafy branches behind her sway in the wind.

She's been talking nonstop since we turned the TV on, but only a few phrases sink in: . . . *dead for more than a week . . . foul play suspected but not confirmed . . . yet another taunting message found this morning near Echo Ridge High School . . .*

"Great timing, Katrin," Ezra mutters.

Malcolm's sitting next to me on the couch. One side of his jaw is bruised and swollen, the knuckles on his right hand are scraped raw, and he winces every time he moves. "Someone needs to pay this time," he says in a low, angry voice. I reach for his uninjured hand. His skin is warm, and his fingers wrap around mine without hesitation. For a couple of seconds I feel better, until I remember that Brooke is dead and everything is horrible.

Every time I close my eyes, I see her. Working the shooting range at Fright Farm, trying to stand up to Vance. Wandering the halls at Echo Ridge High looking sad and worried. Swaying and rambling her way out of the Fright Farm office on the night she disappeared. I should have pushed her harder to tell us what was wrong. I had a chance to change the course of that night, and I blew it.

When my phone rings with the familiar California number, I almost don't answer it. Then I figure, what the hell. The day can't possibly get any worse.

"Hi, Sadie," I say tonelessly.

"Oh, Ellery. I saw the news. I'm so, so sorry about your friend. And I saw—" She pauses, her voice wavering. "I saw your email. I wasn't sure what I was looking at until I zoomed in on the uniform and saw . . . his name."

275

"Did you think it was Ezra at first? Because I sure did." I'm surprised to find that beneath the heavy misery of Brooke's death, I can still manage to spare an undercurrent of anger for my mother. "How could you not tell us? How could you let us live a lie for seventeen years and think our father was *José the freaking stuntman*?" I don't bother keeping my voice down. It's not like anyone in the room doesn't know what's going on.

"It wasn't a total lie," Sadie says. "I wasn't *sure,* Ellery. The stuntman happened. And, well . . . Gabriel Rodriguez also happened, a little while afterward." Her voice drops. "Sleeping with a married man was a huge mistake. I never should have gone there."

"Yeah, well, he shouldn't have either." I don't have any empathy to spare for the man in that photograph. He doesn't feel like my father. He doesn't feel like anything. Besides, keeping the marital vows was *his* job. "But why did you?"

"I wasn't thinking straight. My father was gone, memories of Sarah were everywhere, and I just— I made a bad choice. Then the timing of the pregnancy fit better with the, um . . . other situation, and I wanted that to be true, and so . . . I convinced myself that it was."

"How?" I look at Ezra, who's staring at the floor with no indication that he's hearing any of this. "How did you convince yourself of that when—what was his name again? *Gabriel?*— looked exactly like Ezra?"

"I didn't remember what he looked like," Sadie says, and I snort out a disbelieving laugh. "I'm not kidding. I told you before, I drank my way through the entire funeral."

"Okay. But you remembered enough that you knew he was

a possibility, right? That's why you were so shifty the first time I mentioned Officer Rodriguez."

"I— Well, yes. It rattled me," she admits.

"So you lied to cover it up. You made up a story about Officer Rodriguez at Lacey's funeral, and you made me suspicious of him."

"What?" Sadie sounds bewildered. "Why would that make you suspicious of him? Suspicious about what?"

"That's not the point!" I snap. "The point is it *did*, and then I didn't ask him for help when I could have, and now Brooke is dead and maybe—" I stop, all the anger suddenly drained out of me, remembering how I hadn't told anyone what we'd found in the Fright Farm recycling bin for an entire weekend. Keeping secrets that weren't mine to hold. Like mother, like daughter. "Maybe I made everything worse."

"Made what worse? Ellery, I'm sure you didn't do anything wrong. You can't blame yourself for—"

"Ellery." Nana sticks her head into the living room. "Officer Rodriguez is here. He says you called him?" Her eyes fasten on the phone at my ear. "Who are you talking to?"

"Just someone from school," I answer Nana, then turn back to the phone. "I have to go," I tell Sadie, but before I can disconnect, Ezra extends his hand.

"Let me talk," he says, and his voice holds the same dull fury that mine did. It takes a lot to make the two of us mad, especially at Sadie. But she managed.

I hand Ezra the phone and tug Malcolm to his feet. We head for the hallway as Nana returns to the kitchen. Ryan is standing in front of the front door, his face sad and haggard. I don't know how I ever thought he looked young for his age. "Hey, guys," he says. "I was just heading home when I got your message. What's so urgent?" He catches sight of Malcolm's swollen jaw, and his eyes widen. "What happened to you?"

"Kyle McNulty," Malcolm says shortly.

"You want to press charges?" Ryan asks.

Malcolm grimaces. "No."

"Maybe you can convince him to change his mind," I say. "In the meantime, I have this kind of . . . theory about Kyle. That's why I called you." I lick my lips, trying to get my thoughts in order. "I ran into Officer McNulty this morning, and—"

Ryan frowns. "Where did you run into Officer McNulty?"

I wave my hand dismissively. "That part's not important." I don't want to get sidetracked with a lecture about not going home when Ryan told me to. "But it got me thinking about Kyle, and how connected he is to everything that's been happening around here. Declan broke up with his sister, Liz, and that was a whole big thing while you guys were in school, right?" Ryan nods warily, like he has no idea where I'm headed and isn't sure he wants to find out. Malcolm looks the same. I haven't shared any of this with him yet. I wasn't sure I'd have the energy to do it more than once.

"Then Lacey dies and Declan's basically run out of town," I continue. "And now, five years later, Brooke breaks up with Kyle. And Brooke disappears. And Kyle and Katrin are friends, and we already know Katrin is involved in the homecoming threats, so . . ." I steal a glance at Ryan to see how he's taking all this. He doesn't look as impressed as I'd hoped. "Basically, I think they're all in it together. Liz, Kyle, and Katrin."

"That's your new theory?" Ryan asks. I don't appreciate the somewhat sardonic emphasis he puts on the word *new*. Malcolm just sags against the wall, like he's too exhausted to get into any of this right now.

"Yes," I say.

Ryan folds his arms. "It doesn't concern you that Liz and Kyle have alibis?"

"They're each other's alibi!" I say. It only makes me more sure I'm on to something.

"So you think . . . what? We just took their word for it?"

"Well. No." A trickle of doubt seeps in. "Did somebody else see them?"

Ryan rakes a hand through his hair. "I shouldn't tell you this, it's not your business. But maybe it'll get you to stop trying to do my job and trust me. For once." He lowers his voice. "An entire *fraternity* saw them. There are pictures. And video. Time-stamped and posted on social media."

"Oh," I say in a small voice, embarrassment warming my cheeks.

He makes a frustrated noise in his throat. "Will you knock it off now? Please? I appreciate you coming to me this morning, but like I told you, at this point, you're more likely to hurt the investigation than help if you keep talking about it. In fact . . ." He shoves his hands into his pockets and slides his eyes toward Malcolm. "I was just telling your mother, Malcolm, that it might not be a bad idea to stay with friends for a day or two."

Malcolm goes stiff. "Why? Is something happening with Katrin? Was it the video, or—"

"I'm not talking about anything specific. But tensions are

279

running high, and I . . ." Ryan pauses, like he's searching for exactly the right words. "I wouldn't want you to accidentally say something to her that could . . . interfere."

"Interfere how?" Malcolm asks.

"It's just a suggestion. Tell your mother to consider it, all right?"

"Should I be worried about Katrin?" Malcolm asks. "Doing something, I mean?" Ryan doesn't answer, and Malcolm glowers. "It's bullshit that she's just walking around like nothing happened. You have proof she's shady and you're not doing anything with it."

"You have no idea what we're doing." Ryan's face doesn't change, but his tone gets steely. "I'm asking you to lie low. That's it. All right?" We nod, and he clears his throat. "How is, ah, everything else, Ellery? With your mom and . . . you know?"

"Horrible," I say. "But who really cares, right?"

He heaves a sigh that sounds as bone-deep exhausted as I feel. "Right."

CHAPTER THIRTY-THREE

MALCOLM
THURSDAY, OCTOBER 10

Turns out I didn't need to leave the house. Katrin did.

Her aunt swooped in two days after Brooke's body was found. She wanted to take Katrin to New York, but the Echo Ridge police asked her not to leave the state while the investigation is pending. So they're at some five-star hotel in Topnotch, instead. Which pisses me off every time I think about it. Of all the possible scenarios I thought might happen once I turned over that video of Katrin, her taking a spa vacation wasn't one of them.

"So much for keeping the key witnesses nearby," Declan snorts when I tell him. "We were all told we had to stay in Echo Ridge after Lacey died. Money talks, I guess."

I'm at his apartment, having dinner with him and Daisy. It's weird for a few reasons. One, I've never seen my brother cook before. Two, he's surprisingly good at it. And three, I can't get used to seeing him with Daisy. My brain keeps wanting to replace her with Lacey, and it's kind of unnerving.

He doesn't know about the car repair receipt, or the video I took of Katrin. I'm keeping my promise to Officer Rodriguez to stay quiet. It's not hard with Declan. We might be getting along better than usual, but he still talks a lot more than he listens.

"Peter didn't want her to go," I say, shifting in my chair and wincing at the pain in my ribs. Turns out they're only bruised, not cracked, but they still hurt like hell. "Katrin's aunt insisted."

"Getting away isn't a bad idea, though," Daisy says. She and Declan are washing dishes while I sit at the kitchen table, and she keeps brushing against him even though there's plenty of room for two in front of the double sink. "It's so horrible, those first few days after. All you can think about is what you could have done differently. At least a new environment is a distraction." She sighs and flips the towel she's holding over her shoulder, leaning into Declan. "I feel for Katrin, honestly. This brings back such awful memories of Lacey."

Declan kisses the top of her head, and the next thing I know they're whispering, nuzzling, and about ten seconds away from a full-on make-out session. It's uncomfortable, not to mention crap timing after what we've just been talking about. I realize they've been suppressing their big forbidden love for years, but I could've used another half hour. Minimum.

When the doorbell rings, I'm relieved at the interruption. "I'll get it," I volunteer, springing up as fast as my bruised ribs will let me.

Too fast, as it turns out. Even though Declan's front door is only steps away from the kitchen, I'm still wincing when I open it. Officer Ryan Rodriguez is standing on Declan's stoop, wearing his full police uniform. He blinks in surprise when he sees me. "Oh, hey, Malcolm. I wasn't expecting to see you here."

"Um. Same," I say. "Are you . . ." I try to think of a reason why he might be here, and can't come up with one. "What's up?"

"Is your brother around?"

"Yeah, come on in," I say, and he steps through the door.

Declan and Daisy have managed to separate by the time we enter the kitchen. "Hey, Declan," Officer Rodriguez says, folding his arms in front of him like a shield. I know that stance; it's the one I get around Kyle McNulty. I don't remember much about Ryan from when he was in high school, since he and Declan didn't hang out, but I do know this: if you weren't part of Declan's crew, chances are he would've treated you like shit at some point. Not slamming you into lockers, necessarily, but acting like your existence annoyed him. Or pretending you didn't exist at all.

"And . . . Daisy," Officer Rodriguez adds.

Crap. I swallow nervously and look at Declan. I forgot nobody's supposed to know those two are together. My brother doesn't acknowledge me, but I can see the muscles in his jaw tighten as he steps slightly in front of Daisy.

At least they aren't shoving their tongues down one another's throats anymore.

"Ryan, hi!" Daisy says, with the kind of forced cheerfulness I've noticed she uses whenever she's stressed. Unlike Mia, who just glares extra hard. "Nice to see you again."

Declan, on the other hand, cuts to the chase. "What are you doing here?"

Officer Rodriguez clears his throat. "I have a few questions for you."

Everybody goes still. We've heard that before.

"Sure," Declan says, a little too casually. We're all still standing in his cramped little kitchen, and he gestures to the table. "Have a seat."

Officer Rodriguez hesitates, his eyes flicking toward me. "I could, or . . . do you want to step outside for a minute? Not sure if you want Daisy and your brother here, or—" He rocks back and forth on his heels, and suddenly I can see all the nervous bumbling Ellery was talking about. It's like the guy is regressing by the minute in Declan's and Daisy's presence.

"No," Declan says shortly. "This is fine."

Officer Rodriguez shrugs and lowers himself into the nearest chair, folding his hands on the table while he waits for Declan to sit across from him. Daisy drops beside Declan, and since I can't think of anything else to do and nobody's asked me to leave, I take the last chair. Once we're all seated, Officer Rodriguez focuses his gaze on Declan and says, "Could you tell me your whereabouts the Saturday before last? September twenty-eighth?"

I feel almost exactly like I did the morning that Brooke disappeared, when I realized I'd have to tell Officer McNulty that I was the last person to see her. *This can't be happening.*

Shit. Shit. Shit.

Declan doesn't answer right away, and Officer Rodriguez clarifies, "The night Brooke Bennett disappeared."

Panic starts worming its way into my chest as Declan's voice rises. "Are you fucking kidding me?" he asks. Daisy puts a hand on his arm.

284

Officer Rodriguez's voice is mild, but firm. "No. I am not kidding you."

"You want to know where I was the night a girl disappeared. Why?"

"Are you refusing to answer the question?"

"*Should* I?"

"He was with me," Daisy says quickly.

I study her, trying to get a read on whether she's telling the truth. Her pretty face is suddenly all hard lines and angles, so maybe she's lying. Or maybe she's just scared.

Some emotion flits across Officer Rodriguez's face, but it's gone before I can figure out what it is. "Okay. And may I ask where you two were?"

"No," Declan says, at the same time Daisy replies, "Here."

I still can't tell if she's lying.

It goes on like that for a few minutes. Daisy smiles like her teeth hurt the whole time. A dull red flush creeps up Declan's neck, but Officer Rodriguez seems to be getting progressively at ease.

"All right," he says finally. "If I could switch gears for a minute. Have you ever been to Huntsburg?"

Daisy's eyes widen as Declan goes rigid. "Huntsburg," he repeats. This time he doesn't state the obvious: *You're asking me if I've ever been to the town where Brooke's body was discovered?*

"Right," Officer Rodriguez says.

"No," Declan growls.

"Never?"

"Never."

"Okay. One last thing." Officer Rodriguez digs into his pocket and pulls out something in a sealed plastic bag that glints

285

under the cheap track lighting in Declan's kitchen. "This was found in Huntsburg, in the same general area as Brooke's body. Does it look familiar to you?"

My blood turns to ice. It does to me.

The ring is big and gold with the words "Echo Ridge High" etched around a square purple stone. The number 13 is on one side, and the initials "DK" on another. Declan's class ring, although he never wore it. He gave it to Lacey junior year, and she kept it on a chain around her neck. I haven't seen it in years. Not since before she died.

It never occurred to me, until just now, to wonder where it went.

Daisy pales. Declan pushes back from the table, his face expressionless. "I think we're done talking," he says.

It's not enough to make an arrest, I guess, because Officer Rodriguez leaves after Declan stops answering his questions. Then Declan, Daisy, and I sit silently in the kitchen for the longest minute of my life. My thoughts blur together, and I can't look at either of them.

When Declan finally speaks up, his voice is stilted. "I haven't seen that ring since before Lacey died. We argued about it. We'd been fighting all week. All I wanted to do was break things off, but . . . I didn't have the guts to come right out and say it. So I asked her for my ring back. She wouldn't give it to me. That was the last time I ever saw it. Or her." His hands are clenched into tight fists. "I have no clue how it ended up in Huntsburg."

Daisy's chair is angled toward him. Her hand is on his arm again. "I know," she murmurs.

Damn it all to hell, I *still* can't tell if she's lying. I can't tell if anyone's lying.

Declan hasn't ever told that story before. Maybe he didn't remember the ring till just now, either. Maybe he didn't want to remind anyone of how much he and Lacey had been fighting before she died.

Or maybe it didn't happen.

It's been creeping up on me for weeks now how little I know my brother. When I was really young he was like a superhero to me. Later, he was more like a bully. After Lacey died, he turned into a ghost. He's helped me out since Brooke's body was discovered—but until then, all he'd done was lie and sneak around.

And now I can't shut off that corner of my brain that keeps asking, *What if?*

"Fuck you, Mal." Declan's voice makes me jump. His neck is still brick red, his expression thunderous. "You think I can't tell what's running through your head right now? It's written all over your face. You think I did it, don't you? You always have." I open my mouth to protest, but no words come. His face darkens even further. "Get the hell out of here. Just leave."

So I do. Because the answer isn't *yes,* but it's not *no,* either.

CHAPTER THIRTY-FOUR

ELLERY
THURSDAY, OCTOBER 10

"But none of it makes any sense."

I'm at Malcolm's house, curled up on his couch like on homecoming night. He has the *Defender* movie on again, but neither of us are watching it. He texted me half an hour ago: *I need your true-crime brain.*

I'm not sure why he trusts me after my Kyle-Liz theory imploded so spectacularly. But here I am. I don't think I'm helping, though. Declan being Lacey's killer has always made sense to me. But being Brooke's? Never even crossed my mind.

"What connection is there between Declan and Brooke?" I ask.

Malcolm's eyes flash. "None that I know of. Except that he was in town the night she disappeared. If the police had ever looked at my phone, they'd have seen his text." He takes out his phone and unlocks it, then swipes for a minute. He holds the phone out to me and I'm looking at a message. *In town for a few hours. Don't freak out.*

I read it twice, and when I look back up at Malcolm, his face is the picture of misery. "I thought that . . . I was trying to help Declan out by not, you know. Telling the police," he says haltingly. "I thought it was just bad timing. But what if . . . Christ, Ellery." He slumps back against the couch, rubbing a hand so hard across his bruised face that it has to hurt. "What if it was more than that?"

I study Declan's text again, wondering why I don't find it more disturbing. After all, I've had him at the top of my suspect list for weeks, and this puts him at the scene of the crime. Problem is, it's not the *right* crime. "Okay, but . . . Declan was in the process of moving then, right? Or he had moved? So he had a perfectly good reason for being here," I say, handing the phone back to Malcolm. "And why would he send you that text if he was planning something? You'd think he'd be more subtle."

"Subtle isn't how Declan rolls. I get what you're saying, though." Malcolm brightens a little, then jiggles his phone as though he's weighing it. "I should let my mother know what's up. But she's having dinner with a friend, and she's hardly done that kind of thing since she and Peter got married. I feel like I should let her have a few hours of peace before everything goes to hell again."

I think back to my one lunch at Echo Ridge High with Brooke, when she'd said that Malcolm was cute but couldn't compare to Declan. "Do you think— Could Declan and Brooke have been secretly dating or something?"

"What, while he was *also* secretly dating Daisy?"

"I'm just trying to figure out how the ring could've gotten there. Would he have given it to Brooke?"

Malcolm's voice is ragged. "Maybe? I mean, you'd think somebody would've noticed him sneaking around with a high school girl, but maybe not." He runs a hand through his hair. "I shouldn't have left Declan's place. Me and him—I don't know. It's always been complicated. We're not close. Sometimes I've almost hated him. But he's not a . . . serial killer." He almost chokes on the words.

"Do you think Daisy knows more than she's saying?"

"Do *you*?" Malcolm asks.

I'd had Daisy in mind as a potential accomplice right up to the day she clocked Mia in the head with a candlestick, then spilled her guts after. She'd seemed so sincere and heartbroken that I couldn't picture it anymore. "No," I say slowly. "I mean, why would she go through the trouble of looking for Lacey's bracelet if she were? The case was ice cold at that point. If she were involved, the last thing she'd want to do is get the police thinking about it again. And Declan helped her, didn't he? Although . . . well, I guess he's not the one who gave the bracelet to Lacey, right? Daisy said as much. So maybe he figured it didn't matter."

Malcolm rubs his temple and sighs, deep and weary. "I want to believe him. So much."

I'm a little surprised to realize that I do too. "I have to say . . . look, I guess you know I've always had questions about your brother." I rest my chin in my hand, thinking. "But a dropped ring at a murder site is a little too convenient, isn't it? And none of it fits with Katrin's anonymous messages, or what we think might've happened with Brooke and her car."

"Too many puzzle pieces," Malcolm says moodily.

We lapse into silence for a few minutes, watching *The Defender* until a light knock on the doorframe startles us both. It's Peter Nilsson, looking casually handsome in a polo shirt and khakis. He has a crystal tumbler in one hand, filled with ice and amber liquid. "You two all right? Need anything?"

Malcolm is silent, so I speak up. "No, thank you. We're fine." Mr. Nilsson doesn't leave immediately, so I feel like I should make more conversation. Plus, I'm curious. "How is Katrin doing, Mr. Nilsson? We miss her at school."

"Ah. Well." He leans against the door with a sigh. "She's devastated, of course. It's good for her to have some time away with her aunt."

"Is that her mother's sister, or yours?" I ask.

"Mine," Peter says. "Eleanor and her husband live in Brooklyn. We don't see them as often as we'd like, but she and Katrin had a nice visit last month."

Malcolm stirs beside me on the couch. "They did?"

"Sure. Katrin went to New York, did some shopping." Peter's brow creases slightly. "That was my interpretation, anyway, by the number of bags she brought home."

"I don't remember that," Malcolm says.

"You and your mother were on vacation," Peter says. "It was a last-minute thing. Eleanor's husband was out of town for business so she flew Katrin down for the weekend. Although she almost didn't make it. That was the night of that hailstorm, remember? The plane was delayed for hours." He chuckles and sips his drink. "Katrin kept texting me complaints from the runway. She has no patience."

I'm sitting close enough to Malcolm that our arms are brushing, and I can feel him tense at the same time I do. My entire body goes numb and my pulse starts to race, but I manage to speak. "Oh, that's so frustrating. I'm glad she made it there eventually."

Mr. Nilsson's eyes wander to the screen. "*The Defender,* huh? That's your mother's movie, isn't it?"

"Yeah. She only had one line, though." I don't know how I'm still talking normally when a million thoughts are zipping through my head. "'That does not compute.'"

"At least it's a memorable one. Well, I won't keep you from it. You sure I can't get you anything?"

Malcolm mutely shakes his head, and Mr. Nilsson turns and retreats back into the dark hallway. We sit in silence, my heart hammering so loudly that I can hear it in my ears. I'm sure Malcolm's is doing the same. "Fuck," he finally breathes.

I keep my voice to the lowest whisper possible. "Katrin wasn't here on Labor Day weekend. You and your mom weren't here. There's only one person in your house who could've driven Katrin's car that night."

"Fuck," Malcolm says again. "But he—he wasn't here either. He was in Burlington."

"Are you sure?"

Malcolm gets to his feet wordlessly and motions for me to follow. He leads me upstairs to his bedroom and shuts the door behind us, then pulls his phone out of his pocket. "He said he had dinner with a guy who used to live here. Mr. Coates. He was my Scout troop leader. I've got his number in here somewhere." He scrolls for a few minutes and presses the screen. I'm standing close enough to him that I can hear a faint ringing sound, then a man's voice. "Hey, Mr. Coates. This is, um, Malcolm Kelly." He laughs self-consciously. "Sorry about the blast from the past, but I had a question for you."

I can't hear what Mr. Coates is saying, but his tone is welcoming. "Yeah, so," Malcolm continues, swallowing hard. "I was just talking to my brother, you know, Declan? Right, of course you do. He's majoring in political science and he's interested in doing, like, an internship or something. I'm probably not supposed to be doing this, but Peter mentioned he had dinner with you last month and there was a chance you might have some kind of opening in your new firm." He pauses and waits for Mr. Coates to speak, his cheeks staining a deep red. "You didn't? On Labor Day weekend?" Another pause. "Oh, sorry. I must've heard wrong. I was just, you know, trying to help my brother out."

Mr. Coates talks for a minute. Malcolm nods mechanically, like Mr. Coates can see him. "Yeah, okay. Thanks a lot. I'll have him call you. It really— That'll be really helpful. Thanks again." He lowers the phone and meets my eyes. "You hear that?"

"Enough."

"Peter wasn't there," Malcolm says. "He lied."

Neither of us says anything for a beat. When I raise a hand to tug at my necklace, it's trembling so hard that my fingers knock against my chest.

"Let's think about this," I say, in a voice I have to fight to keep steady. "It sounds like Peter was probably here, driving

Katrin's car the night of the hailstorm. But if Katrin wasn't in the car when it hit something—or *someone*—why would Brooke be involved? Why would she help get the car fixed if she . . . *Oh.*" I grab hold of Malcolm's arm. The pieces are falling into place, and this time I might actually be right. "Oh my God, Mal. Katrin said Brooke took off during a sleepover once, remember? She thought Brooke was slipping out to hook up with you. What if she was with *Peter*?"

"That's impossible," Malcolm says, with no conviction whatsoever. His eyes are like glass.

"Think about it, though. If Brooke and your stepfather were having an affair—which, *ew,* but I guess that's the least of our problems right now—we've been looking at everything wrong. It's not just about the hit-and-run. It's about keeping *everything* quiet." I pull my own phone out of my pocket. "We need to tell Ryan about this. He'll know what do to."

I've just opened a new text window when the door flies open. It's like watching some alt-version of my life to see Peter standing there with a gun pointed straight at us. "Your poker face needs work, Malcolm," he says calmly. His pale hair glints silvery gold in the dim lighting, and he smiles so normally that I almost smile back. "Anyone ever tell you that?"

CHAPTER THIRTY-FIVE

MALCOLM
THURSDAY, OCTOBER 10

All these weeks of wondering what the hell was happening around town, it somehow never occurred to me that the guy I trust least of anyone might be involved.

I'm an idiot. And Ellery sucks at solving true crime. But none of that matters right now.

"I'm going to need your phones," Peter says. He's still in his polo and khakis, but he's slipped on a pair of gloves, too. Somehow that's more chilling than the gun. "This isn't a drill, kids. Put them on the side table next to the bed. One at a time, please. You first, Ellery." We both comply, and Peter waves the gun toward the hallway. "Thank you. Now come with me."

"Where?" I ask, glancing over at Ellery. She's frozen in place, her eyes trained on Peter's right hand.

His nostrils flare. "You're not really in a position to ask questions, Malcolm."

Jesus. This is bad, colossally bad. I'm only just starting to grasp how much shit we're in, but I know this much: Peter would never let any of this unfold if he planned on leaving us alive to talk about it. "Wait," I say. "You can't— Look, it's too late, all right? We found the receipt from Dailey's Auto and gave it to the police. They know something sketchy is going on with Katrin's car and they'll figure out you're involved."

Peter's expression flickers with a second's worth of doubt, then relaxes again. "There's nothing on that receipt that points toward me."

"There's the fact that you're the only family member who was at home to drive," I say.

Peter raises his shoulders in a careless shrug. "Brooke borrowed the car and had an accident. Simple enough."

I keep talking. "I just spoke to Mr. Coates. I asked him about meeting up with you that weekend and he said you never did. He knows you lied."

"I listened to every word you said, Malcolm. You told him you must have heard wrong."

"Mom was there when we talked about it," I say, hating the desperate edge that's crept into my voice. "She'll remember. She'll know something is fishy."

"Your mother will remember whatever I tell her. She's a remarkably compliant woman. It's her greatest asset."

I want to kill him then, and I think he knows it. He takes a step back and lifts the gun so it's pointed directly at my chest. I strain to keep my expression neutral as my brain cycles through every possible reason why it's too late for Peter to get away with another murder. "Officer McNulty was there when Katrin said

Brooke snuck out during a sleepover to meet up with somebody in this house. If she wasn't coming to me, it had to be you."

"If you're not here, there's no reason for anyone to think it wasn't you," Peter points out.

Shit. I wish Ellery would snap out of whatever trance she's in. I could use another brain working right now. "People are going to question another murder. Another couple of murders. Especially if your stepson is involved. First your daughter's best friend, and now me? This is going to come back on you, Peter, and it'll be ten times worse when it does."

"I agree," Peter says. He looks completely relaxed, like we're chatting about baseball scores or the latest Netflix series. Not that we've ever done either of these things. "Now is absolutely not the time for anything even remotely resembling a homicide. I have to insist you come along, though. Downstairs. You first, Ellery."

Hope pulses through me, even though the coldness in Peter's eyes tells me it shouldn't. I contemplate lunging for him, but Ellery's already moving toward the hallway and he has the gun trained on her back. I can't see any choice except to follow, so I do.

"All the way to the basement," Peter says.

He keeps his distance as we troop down two sets of stairs. The Nilssons' basement is huge, and Peter tersely directs us through the laundry room and the finished space my mother uses to exercise. The past week flashes in front of my eyes as I walk, torturing me with everything we missed. There's so much to regret that I scarcely notice where we're headed until the biggest revelation of all hits me. When it does, I halt in my tracks.

"I didn't tell you to stop, Malcolm," Peter says. Beside me, Ellery pauses. I turn slowly, and she does too.

Cold sweat coats my face. "Declan's class ring," I say. "You had it. You dropped it near Brooke's body in Huntsburg."

"And?" Peter asks.

"Declan never got the ring back from Lacey. She still had it when she died. She hadn't stopped wearing it. You took it from her. Because you—" I hesitate, waiting for some sort of signal that he's affected by what I'm about to say. But there's nothing on his face except polite attentiveness. "You killed Lacey, too."

Ellery draws in a sharp, shocked breath, but Peter just shrugs. "Your brother is a useful fall guy, Malcolm. Always has been."

"Did you . . ." Ellery's eyes are locked on Peter's face. She tugs at the silver pendant around her neck, so hard I think she might break it. "Did you do something to my aunt, too?"

Peter's calm expression doesn't change. He leans forward and whispers something in her ear, so faint I can't catch it. When she lifts her head to look at him, her hair tumbles across her face, and all I can see is curls. Then Peter raises the gun again so it's pointed directly at her heart.

"Is this a thing with you, Peter?" I'm so desperate to get his attention off Ellery that my voice bounces off the basement walls. "You hook up with girls your daughter's age, and kill them when there's a chance they might expose you? What did Lacey do, huh? Was she going to tell?" A sudden thought strikes me. "Was she pregnant?"

Peter snorts. "This isn't a soap opera, Malcolm. It's not your business what happened between Lacey and me. She overstepped. Let's leave it at that." The gun swings toward me. "Move a few steps backward, please. Both of you."

I do it automatically, my thoughts tumbling and swirling so much that I barely notice we're standing inside a room. It's in the farthest corner of the Nilssons' basement, piled high with sealed cardboard boxes.

"This is the only room in the house that locks from the outside," Peter says, one hand gripping the edge of the door. "Convenient." He slams the door shut before I can react, plunging the room into darkness.

I'm at the door seconds later, first twisting the doorknob, then pounding so hard that my bruised ribs flare with sharp pain. "You can't just leave us!" I yell against the thick wood. "People know Ellery is here. Her grandmother dropped her off!"

"I'm aware," Peter says. There's a sound of something heavy being dragged across the floor, and I stop pounding so I can hear better. "Are you familiar with how a portable electric generator works, Malcolm?" I don't answer, and he continues, "It should never be turned on inside a house on account of the carbon monoxide it emits. It kills quickly in a concentrated area like this. I'm not sure how this got switched on, but oh well. Maybe you and Ellery knocked against it accidentally while you were down here doing who knows what. We may never know."

My heart plummets to my feet as I twist the knob again. "You locked us in here, Peter! They'll know it was you!"

"I'll be back in a little bit to open the door," Peter says casually. "I'm afraid I won't be able to stay long, though. Wouldn't want to meet the same fate. Plus, I need to head to the grocery store. We ran out of popcorn." A humming noise starts outside the door, and Peter raises his voice. "I'd say it was nice knowing you, Malcolm, but quite honestly you've been a nuisance from the start. All things considered, this has worked out fairly well. So long."

His footsteps recede quickly as I stand at the door, my head reeling and my heart pounding. How did I let it get to this point? Declan wouldn't have gone into the basement like a lemming. He would have tackled Peter in the bedroom, or—

Light blazes behind me. I turn to see Ellery standing by the far wall with her hand on a switch, blinking like she just woke up. She goes back to the center of the room and kneels down in front of a box, ripping a thick strand of tape from its top. She turns the box upside down and dumps its contents on the floor. "There has to be something in here I can use to pick the lock."

"Right," I say, relief flooding through me. I join her in tearing through the boxes. The first few are full of books, stuffed animals, and wrapping paper. "I'm sorry, Ellery," I say as we tear open more boxes. "I'm sorry I invited you over here, and that I let this happen. I wasn't quick enough."

"Don't talk," she says shortly. "Save your breath."

"Right." My head is starting to pound and my stomach rolls, but I don't know whether that's stress or deadly gas. How long has Peter been gone? How much time do we have?

"Ah-ha!" Ellery says triumphantly, seizing a box of Christmas ornaments. "Hooks." She yanks a couple free and heads for the door. "I just need to straighten it and . . ." She's silent for a few seconds, then lets out a grunt of frustration. "These aren't strong enough. They just bend up. We need something else. Do you see any paper clips?"

"Not yet." I open more boxes and root through their contents, but my head is pounding in earnest now and I'm so dizzy that my vision is starting to fuzz around the edges. I struggle to stand up, and look around the room. There are no windows to break, nothing heavy enough to use as a battering ram against

300

the door. I upend more boxes, scattering their contents across the floor. At least we can make a mess, I think hazily. If nothing else, people might question what the hell happened in here.

But my movements are sluggish, and slowing by the second. All I want to do is lie down and go to sleep.

I can't believe I'm thinking that already.

I can't believe I finally learned what happened to Lacey and Brooke, too late to give any kind of closure to their parents.

I can't believe I won't get a chance to apologize to my brother.

My eyes are drooping, so heavy that I nearly miss it glinting on the floor. One small, solitary paper clip. I dive for it with a strangled cry of triumph, but it's almost impossible to pick up. My hands feel rubbery and unwieldy, like I'm wearing giant Mickey Mouse gloves. When I finally get hold of it, I turn toward Ellery and the door.

She's slumped in front of it, motionless.

"Ellery!" I grab her by the shoulders and pull her into a sitting position, cupping her cheeks in my hands until I see her release a breath. I shake her as hard as I dare, until her hair spills across her face. "Ellery, come on. Wake up. Please." She doesn't respond. I lay her carefully on the floor and turn my attention to the paper clip.

I can do this without her. I just need to unfold the clip and get to work. If only my hands hadn't turned into inflatable gloves, it would be a lot easier.

If only my brain wasn't about to pound out of my head.

If only I didn't have to stop to throw up.

If only I could see.

If only.

CHAPTER THIRTY-SIX

ELLERY
FRIDAY, OCTOBER 11

I want to open my eyes, but the light is too bright and painful. It's quiet except for a soft beeping sound, and the air smells faintly of bleach. I try to raise one hand to the agony that's my head, but it won't move properly. Something's stuck in it, or to it.

"Can you hear me?" asks a low voice. A cool, dry hand presses against my cheek. "Ellery? Can you hear me?"

I try to say yes, but it comes out more like a groan. My throat hurts almost as much as my head.

"I'm sorry. Don't talk." The hand leaves my face and curls around mine. "Squeeze if you understand me." I do, weakly, and something wet drips on my arm. "Thank God. You'll be all right. They've used hyperbaric oxygen on you and— Well, I guess the details don't matter right now, but things look good. You look good. Oh, my poor girl."

My arm is getting wetter. I crack my eyes open a slit and see the faint outline of a room. Walls and a ceiling, blending into one another with clean white lines, lit by the pale-blue glow of fluorescent lighting. A gray head is bent in front of me, framed by shaking shoulders. "How?" I ask, but it doesn't sound like a word. My throat is as dry and rough as sandpaper. I try to swallow, but it's impossible without saliva. "How?" I rasp again. It's still unintelligible, even to my own ears, but my grandmother seems to understand.

"Your brother saved you," she says.

I feel like Sadie's robot character in *The Defender. That does not compute.* How did Ezra wind up in the Nilssons' basement? But before I can ask another question, everything fades again.

The next time I wake, pale sunlight is streaming into the room. I try to sit up, until a figure in scrubs covered with sailboats gently forces me back down. "Not yet," a familiar voice says.

I blink until Melanie Kilduff's face comes into focus. I want to talk to her, but my throat is on fire. "I'm thirsty," I croak.

"I'll bet," she says sympathetically. "Just a few sips of water for now though, okay?" She raises my head and puts a plastic cup to my lips. I drink greedily until she pulls it away. "Let's see how you do with that before you have any more."

I'd protest, but my stomach is already rolling. At least it's a little easier to talk now, though. "Malcolm?" I manage.

She places a comforting hand on my arm. "In a room down the hall. He'll be all right. And your mother is on her way."

"Sadie? But she's not supposed to leave Hamilton House."

"Oh, honey. Nobody cares about that right now."

Everything about me feels as dry as dust, so it's surprising when tears start rolling down my cheeks. Melanie perches on the side of my bed and snakes her arms around me, folding me into a hug. My fingers curl onto her scrubs and clutch tight, pulling her closer. "I'm sorry," I rasp. "I'm so sorry about everything. Is Mr. Nilsson . . ." I trail off as my stomach lurches and I gag.

Melanie raises me into more of a sitting position. "Throw up if you need to," she says soothingly. "Right here is fine." But the moment passes, leaving me exhausted and coated in clammy sweat. I don't say anything else for a long while, concentrating on getting my breathing under control.

When I finally do, I ask again. "Where is he?"

Melanie's voice is pure ice. "Peter's in jail, where he belongs."

It's such an enormous relief that I don't even mind when I feel myself slipping into unconsciousness again.

By the time Ryan visits, I almost feel like myself again. I've been awake for more than thirty minutes, anyway, and I've managed to keep down an entire cupful of water.

"You just missed Ezra," I tell him. "Nana made him leave. He'd been here for seven hours straight."

Ryan lowers himself into the chair beside my bed. "I believe it," he says. He's not in uniform but wearing faded jeans and a flannel shirt instead. He gives me a nervous, lopsided smile that reminds me of Ezra's and I wish, for one irrational second, that he'd hug me like Melanie did.

Your brother saved you, Nana had said.

She was right. I just didn't realize which one.

"Thank you," I say. "Nana told me you came looking for us at the Nilssons'. But nobody told me why." I search his open, friendly face, wondering how I ever could have imagined that it harbored dark secrets. My Spidey sense is officially crap, which I'm sure Malcolm will tell me as soon as I'm allowed to see him.

"I don't want to tire you out," Ryan starts tentatively, but I cut him off.

"No, please. You won't, I promise. I need to know what happened."

"Well." He hunches his shoulders and leans forward. "I can't get into everything, but I'll tell you as much as I can. It's hard to know where to start, but it was probably with the bracelet Daisy gave me. She says she told you about that."

"The bracelet? Really?" I sit up so fast that I wince from the headache that suddenly hits me, and Ryan shoots me a worried look. I settle back into the pillows with pretend nonchalance. "I mean, okay. Sure. How so?"

He regards me in silence for a few seconds, and I press my lips together so I won't accidentally vomit. "I didn't think much of it at the time," he finally says. "I followed up with the jeweler and she had no paper trail. She'd sold a bunch of bracelets around the same time and kept lousy records. Dead end, I thought. But I asked her to contact me if any similar sales took place, and last month, she did. A guy bought the exact same bracelet and paid cash. When I asked her to describe him, he fit Peter to a T. Not that I realized it at the time. I didn't start connecting dots until you guys brought me that repair receipt. That made me question the whole Nilsson family. Then I asked Brooke's parents if I could look through her jewelry box."

I have to make myself remember how to breathe. "And?"

"She had a bracelet exactly like Lacey's. Her mother didn't know when she'd gotten it, or from whom. But we had our own theories. Obviously."

"Right, right," I say sagely. Like that had ever occurred to me, even once.

"At the same time, we were scouring Brooke's house for clues. Her phone had gone missing when she did, but we were able to seize her computer. There was a diary on it, buried among a bunch of school files and password protected. It took us a while to get it open, but once we did we had most of the story. Brooke's side, anyway. She was cagey about names and details, but we knew she'd had an affair with someone older, that she'd been with him the night something terrible happened, and that she wanted to make things right. We had the car repair receipt, so we were starting to piece things together. But it was all still circumstantial. Then the Huntsburg police found Declan's ring at the crime scene."

Ryan grimaces, burrowing his neck into his shoulders. "I screwed up there, when I questioned Declan. I was trying to rule him out while confirming that the ring was his, because at that point I was pretty sure he was getting framed. But . . . I don't know. Declan and I have never had a great dynamic. I pushed too hard, and raised doubts in Malcolm's head that didn't need to be there. If I could take anything back, it would be that."

The machine next to me beeps quietly. "Okay," I say. "But . . . how did you show up in the nick of time? *Why* did you show up?"

"Your text," Ryan says. I stare blankly at him, and his brows rise. "You didn't know? You managed to get one letter off before

306

Peter took your phone. All it said was 'P.' I texted back a few times, but you didn't answer. I got worried with everything going on, so I checked in with your grandmother. When she said you were hanging out with Malcolm at the Nilssons' house, I freaked. I'd done my best to get Mrs. Nilsson to leave the house with Malcolm while we were investigating, but she wouldn't leave. And then *you* show up there? I know how you are—always asking questions people don't want to answer. I headed over, thinking I'd make up some excuse to bring you back to Nora's. And I found . . ." He trails off, swallowing visibly. "I found you."

"Where was Peter?"

Ryan's expression darkens. "Heading out of the house just as I was heading in. I guess he'd gone back to the basement to drag you guys into the hallway so we wouldn't know you'd ever been locked in. He didn't say a word when he saw me, just got into his car and took off. Which was enough to make me start tearing through the house. Thank God I heard the hum of the generator when I got into the kitchen, because you were nearly out of time." His mouth sets in a grim line. "Peter almost made it to Canada before someone caught up with him. I can't talk about what we found in his car, but it was enough to tie him to Brooke's murder."

"So this is just . . . a thing with him? Sleeping with teenage girls and killing them when they get in his way?" Malcolm had said that in the Nilssons' house, while I stood silently beside him. Frozen and useless, like I hadn't spent nearly half my life preparing for the moment when I'd be lured into a killer's basement.

"Looks like it. Mind you, he hasn't confessed to anything,

and we don't have hard evidence when it comes to Lacey. Not yet. We don't know what the tipping point was with her. Profilers are analyzing Peter now, and they suspect that she likely wanted to take their affair public. That she threatened to tell his wife or something."

"His second wife, right?"

"Yeah. She doesn't live in Echo Ridge anymore, but she lost her husband and son in a car accident before she married Peter. I think that's his particular brand of evil—acting like some kind of hero figure to vulnerable women while preying on young girls behind their backs." Ryan's face twists with disgust. "I don't know how else to explain why he'd marry the mother of Lacey's boyfriend. It's like he wanted to stay involved with Lacey, or something."

I shudder, thinking back to Peter and Malcolm's mom in their kitchen the first time I'd gone to Malcolm's house. How charming he'd been, but also—now that I have the benefit of hindsight—how controlling. Not letting his wife talk and maneuvering her out of the room, but doing it all with a smile. He'd fooled me as much as anyone. "What a twisted creep. The only thing that would've been worse is if Melanie's husband wasn't around and he'd tried to hook up with *her*."

"Agreed," Ryan says. "Although Melanie never would've gone for it. She's tough. Alicia—not so much."

My heart aches for Malcolm, and what this is going to mean for his family. Declan is finally in the clear, at least, and maybe once people realize Lacey was under Peter's influence, they won't judge him and Daisy too harshly. On the other hand—his *mom*. I can't even begin to imagine how she must feel, and how she's going to pick up the pieces from being married to somebody like Peter.

Ryan inches forward in his chair, his elbows on his knees and his hands clasped together. "There's something I wanted to check in with you about. When I spoke to Malcolm, he said you asked Peter if he'd done anything to Sarah, and that Peter whispered something he couldn't hear. What did Peter say?"

My fingers find the worn edge of my blanket and pluck its loose threads. "I don't know. I couldn't hear him either."

His face falls. "Ah, okay. He's not answering any of our questions, including the ones about Sarah, but don't worry. We'll keep at it."

"What about Katrin?" I ask abruptly. "Why was she doing all that anonymous threat stuff? Was she trying to point people away from her dad or something?"

"No. That's another long story," Ryan says. I lift my brows, and he adds, "Katrin wasn't involved in the threats, at first. It was Vivian Cantrell who started them."

"*Viv?* Why? What does she have to do with Peter? Were they having an affair too?" I almost gag at the thought.

Ryan huffs out a humorless laugh. "No. It was completely unrelated. She's applying to journalism programs this fall, and I guess some high-profile alumni told her that her portfolio wasn't strong enough to stand out. So she decided to manufacture a story she could report on."

I'm not sure I've heard him correctly. I *almost* have my head wrapped around Mr. Nilsson's warped psyche, but Viv's calculated plotting shocks me. "You have *got* to be kidding. She did all that crap—freaked people out, brought up horrible memories, and totally traumatized Lacey's parents—so she could *write* about it?"

"Yep," Ryan says grimly. "And that's why you got dragged into it. Viv fixed the homecoming court election. She thought it'd be more newsworthy to have Sarah Corcoran's niece involved."

"Newsworthy?" The word tastes bitter in my mouth. "Wow. She's a special kind of horrible, isn't she?"

Ryan looks like he fully agrees, but all he says is, "We traced the pep rally stunt back to her, and were about to talk with her parents when Brooke disappeared. Then we couldn't give the situation as much attention as we wanted, although we did let her know she was busted. She was terrified, and swore up and down that she'd stop immediately. So I was surprised as hell when Malcolm turned up with that video."

"Why would Katrin get involved, though?"

Ryan hesitates. "I'm sorry, but I can't tell you that. We're in discussions with Katrin's lawyer about what kind of role she's going to play in the investigation. Her reasons are part of those discussions, and they're confidential."

"Did she know what her father was doing?" I press. Ryan folds his arms across his chest without answering. "Blink once for yes."

He snorts, but more in a fond sort of way than in annoyance. I think. "New subject."

I twist the blanket between my hands. "So you had the whole thing figured out, and all this time I've just been getting in your way. Does that about sum it up?"

"Not entirely. The repair receipt was genuinely useful, especially knowing how much Brooke wanted to find it. When we added it to the bracelet and her diary, we knew who we were dealing with." He gives me a half smile. "Plus, you almost getting killed gave us probable cause to search Peter's car, so . . . thanks for that."

"Any time." My eyelids are getting heavy, and I have to blink fast to keep them from drooping. Ryan notices and gets to his feet.

"I should go. Let you get some rest."

"Will you come by again?"

He looks flattered at the hopeful tone in my voice. "Yeah, sure. If you want me to."

"I do." I let my eyes close for a second, then force them open again as he stands. "Thanks again. For everything."

"You're welcome," he says, shoving his hands in his pockets awkwardly. For that moment he reminds me of the old Officer Rodriguez—the skittish, subpar cop, instead of the crack investigator he turned out to be. "Hey, so, this is maybe not the time or the place," he adds, hesitantly, "but . . . if you're feeling well enough, my sister's having a fall open house in a couple of weeks. She does it every year. She wants to meet you and Ezra. If you're up for it."

"She does?" I ask, surprised. I'd almost forgotten that Ryan has siblings.

"Yeah, but no pressure or anything. Just think about it. You can let me know later if you're interested." He smiles warmly and lifts one hand in a wave. Then he turns, disappearing into the hallway.

I sink back onto the thin pillow, my haze of tiredness suspended. I've almost gotten used to Ryan, but I'm not sure how to feel about even more strangers that I'm related to. Going from a family of three—four, with Nana—to this sudden influx of half siblings, their spouses, and their kids seems like a lot.

I kind of like the idea of a sister, though. Maybe a half one wouldn't be bad.

There's a rustling sound at the door, and the scent of jasmine. I half twist on the bed, and spy a cloud of dark curls framed in the doorway.

"Ellery," Sadie breathes, her blue eyes sparkling with tears. Before I can remember that I'm mad at her, I'm returning her hug with every ounce of strength I have left.

CHAPTER THIRTY-SEVEN

MALCOLM
SATURDAY, OCTOBER 26

"This kid hates me," Declan says.

I don't think he's wrong. The six-month-old baby he's holding is sitting stiff as a board on his knee, red-faced and screaming. Everybody at this party feels sorry for the kid, except Daisy. She's beaming like she's never seen anything so adorable.

"I can practically see her ovaries exploding," Mia murmurs beside me.

"You're holding him wrong," Ezra says. He scoops the baby up in one deft motion, cradling him in the crook of his arm. "Just relax. They can tell when you're nervous." The kid stops crying and gives Ezra a giant, toothless grin. Ezra tickles his stomach before holding him out toward Declan. "Try again."

"No thanks," Declan mutters, getting to his feet. "I need a drink."

A pretty, dark-haired woman climbs the porch stairs, squeezing Ezra's arm as she passes. "You're so good with him!" She's the baby's mother, Ryan Rodriguez's sister, and we're all hanging out at her house two weeks after Peter Nilsson's murder attempt like everything's back to normal.

I don't know. Maybe it is, or maybe we're finally figuring out that we haven't been normal for years and it's time to redefine the word.

Declan heads for a cooler in the backyard, and Mia nudges my arm. "No time like the present," she says.

I glare at my brother's back. "Why is it even my responsibility? He's older. He should extend the olive branch first."

Mia adjusts her cat's-eye sunglasses. "You thought he was guilty of murder."

"Yeah, well, Ellery suspected me at one point. I got over it."

"Ellery had known you for less than a month then. She wasn't your *brother*."

"He didn't even visit me in the hospital!"

She enunciates every word carefully. "You. Thought. He. Was. Guilty. Of. *Murder*."

"I almost *got* murdered."

"You could do this all day, *or* you could be the bigger person." Mia waits a beat, then punches me in the arm. "At least he showed up."

"All right, fine," I grumble, and take off after Declan.

I wasn't sure he'd be here. We've only spoken a couple of times since I was released from the hospital, mostly to sort stuff out related to Mom. That's a mess; all of Peter's assets are frozen, so she's got nothing to her name except a bank account that won't cover

314

more than a couple months' worth of expenses. We'll be moving to Solsbury soon, and while I can't get out of the Nilssons' house fast enough, I don't know what happens after that. Mom hasn't worked in over a year, and my dad's harder to reach than ever.

We got a semilucrative offer to tell our side of the story to a tabloid, but we're not desperate enough to take it. Yet.

Declan's at the far corner of the yard, pulling a frosted brown bottle from a blue cooler. He twists the cap off and takes a long sip, then catches sight of me and lowers the bottle. I'm a few feet away when I notice how white his knuckles are. "What's up, little brother?"

"Can I have one?" I ask.

He snorts. "You don't drink."

"I might need to start."

Declan reopens the cooler and plunges his hand into its depths, extracting a bottle identical to the one he's holding. He hands it to me, expressionless, and I manage to get the top off without wincing when the sharp edges cut into my palm. I take a tentative sip, waiting for bitterness to explode in my mouth, but it's not half bad. Smooth and almost honey flavored. I'm nervous and thirsty, and a quarter of the bottle is gone before Declan grabs my arm.

"Slow down."

I meet his eyes, and force out the words I've been practicing for two weeks. "I'm sorry."

Seconds pass that feel like minutes. I'm ready for just about any response; for him to yell at me, to walk away without saying anything, even to sock me in the jaw. The bruises from Kyle's attack are almost gone, just in time for some new ones.

But Declan doesn't do any of those things. He sips his beer, then clinks his bottle against mine. "Me too," he says.

The bottle almost slips out of my hand. "What?"

"You heard me."

"So you're not . . ." I trail off. *You're not mad* still seems impossible.

Declan looks back at the porch we left, squinting in the bright sun. It's one of those incredible late-October days we get sometimes in Vermont, upper seventies with an almost cloudless blue sky, the trees around us exploding with color. Daisy is holding the baby now, talking earnestly with Ryan's sister. Mia and Ezra are sitting side by side on the wooden railing, legs dangling and their heads bent close together. The sliding door to the house opens and a girl steps outside, dark curls bouncing around her shoulders.

I've been waiting for her to show up, but I guess I can wait to talk a little longer.

"I've been a shit brother to you, Mal," Declan says finally. "For years. I just— I'm not gonna lie, I didn't give a crap about you when we were kids. Too caught up in my own stuff. And you weren't . . . I don't know. Enough like me for me to pay attention." A muscle in his cheek jumps, his eyes still on the porch. "Then everything went to hell and I took off. I didn't think about you then, either. Not for years. So I'm not sure why I expected you to be on my side when somebody found my class ring at a murder site."

My throat's uncomfortably dry, but I don't want any more beer. "I should've realized you didn't have anything to do with that."

Declan shrugs. "Why? We barely know each other. And I'm

316

the adult, or so they tell me. So that's on me." He opens the cooler again and pulls out a ginger ale, holding it out to me. I hesitate, and he takes the beer from my hand, setting it down on a nearby table. "Come on, Mal. That's not you."

I take the ginger ale. "I don't know what's going to happen with Mom."

"I don't either. That shit's not great. We'll figure it out, though. You guys can get a place near Daisy and me. Solsbury's all right." He grins and takes a sip of beer. "The regulars at Bukowski's Tavern aren't half bad when you get to know them."

The tightness in my chest loosens. "Good to know."

A wisp of a cloud passes over the sun, briefly shading Declan's face. "You talk to Katrin?" he asks.

"No," I say. She ended up cooperating fully with the DA's office, handing off one final piece of evidence: Brooke's cell phone case. Katrin had found it the day Peter organized the search party, after she'd gone digging through his office looking for a phone charger. Apparently Peter destroyed Brooke's phone but kept the case—as though it were some kind of sick trophy. Just like he had with Lacey's ring.

It wasn't something you'd find in a store—Brooke had made it herself with a clear case, dried flowers, and nail polish. It was one of a kind, and when Katrin saw it tucked away like that, she knew her father was involved. Instead of turning him in, she'd re-created one of Viv's anonymous threats to try to deflect attention.

Katrin's lawyer painted as sympathetic a picture of her as he could. He claimed Peter had methodically estranged Katrin from her mother for years so he could control and manipulate her, to the point where she was totally dependent on him and unable to distinguish right from wrong. A different type of victim from Lacey and Brooke—but still a victim.

And maybe she was. Is. I don't know, because I haven't answered the one text she sent me since she was released into her aunt's custody. Katrin isn't allowed out of the country, and her mother's not willing to move here.

He's all I have.

I didn't answer. Not only because it wasn't true—she'd had me and my mom, at the very least, plus her aunt and even Theo and Viv—but because I can't think about my stepsister without remembering the last time I saw Brooke in her driveway, glancing back at me over her shoulder before she went inside. Soon after, according to police, she slipped out again to meet up with Peter.

I don't think I can ever accept the fact that Katrin knew Peter was involved in her best friend's disappearance, and stood by him anyway. Maybe one of these days, when everything is less raw, I can try to understand what it was like to grow up with that toxic sewer for a father. But two weeks after he tried to kill me isn't that time.

"Probably a good thing. That whole family's rotten to the core," Declan says, taking another long pull at his bottle. "Anyway, you and Mom should come over for dinner this week. Daisy and I bought a grill."

I start laughing. "Holy hell. You bought a *grill*. You're holding *babies*. What's next, suburban dad? You gonna start talking about your lawn?"

Declan narrows his eyes, and for a second I think I've gone too far. Then he grins. "There are worse fates, little brother. Much worse fates." He turns toward the porch again, shading his eyes against the sun. Ellery has her hands clasped stiffly in front of her as she talks to Ryan's sister. "Why are you still over here yapping at me? Go get your girl."

"She's not my—" I start, and Declan shoves me. Only a little too hard.

"Don't be such a wuss, Mal," he instructs, pulling the ginger ale from my hand. But he smiles when he says it.

So I leave him, crossing the yard toward the porch. Ellery spots me when I'm about halfway there and waves. She says something to her half sister, then bounds down the stairs with an energy that sets my nerves jumping. I've seen her only a couple of times since we left the hospital, always with some combination of Ezra, Mia, or her grandmother around. I even saw Sadie briefly before she went back to rehab. Ellery and I aren't alone here either, but for a few seconds in the middle of the backyard, everybody else fades away and it feels like it.

"Hey," she says, stopping within a foot of me. "I was hoping you'd be here." Her eyes flick over my shoulder to Declan. "How'd that go?"

"Better than expected. How are things with your new half siblings?"

"Same," she says. "Better than expected. They're nice. I'm not as comfortable with the other two as I am with Ryan, though. Ezra's fitting in more easily than I am. As usual." She brushes a stray curl off her temple. "How are you feeling?"

"Other than the headaches? Not too bad. No permanent effects. That's what the doctors say, anyway."

"Me too." She hesitates. "I mean . . . I guess the nightmares will go away eventually."

"I hope so." I wait a beat, then add, "Listen, I'm really sorry you didn't get any closure about your aunt. I know that would have meant a lot to your family. If it's any consolation . . . even if you didn't hear him say it, I'm pretty sure we *know*. You know?"

"I know. I just wish—" Her eyes get bright with tears, and before I can think too much about what I'm doing I pull her into my arms. She leans her head on my chest and I bury my face in her hair. For a few seconds I feel something I haven't experienced since I was a little kid, before my parents started fighting and my brother either ignored or taunted me. Hope.

"It'll be all right," I say into her hair.

Her voice is muffled against my shirt. "How? How are we supposed to get past something like this?"

I look over her head at the porch, where Declan's rejoined Daisy and they're talking with Ryan and Mrs. Corcoran. Ezra's gotten off the porch railing to hold the baby again, and Mia's making faces at it. The Kilduffs arrived at some point, and even though my mother's not here, I can almost picture her venturing into something like this one day. Forgiving herself for believing a monster's lies. We all have to figure out a way to do that. "Just living, I guess," I finally say.

Ellery pulls away from me with a small smile, swiping the back of her palm against her wet cheeks. Her dark lashes are spiky with tears. "Seriously? That's it? That's all you've got?"

"No. I have an ace in the hole I've been saving to cheer you up." Her brows rise, and I pause for dramatic effect. "Would you like to visit a clown museum with me?"

She starts to laugh. "What, now? In the middle of a party?"

"Can you think of a better time?"

"*After* the party?" Ellery suggests.

"It's right down the street. We could be there and back in half an hour. Forty-five minutes, tops. There's free popcorn, and dogs. And clowns, obviously."

"It does sound tempting."

"Then let's go." I link my fingers through hers and we start for the driveway. "Good thing it's walking distance. I've had almost half a bottle of beer."

"You rebel." She smiles at me. "But you did say *living*, after all."

I squeeze her hand and bend my head toward hers. "I'm working on it."

CHAPTER THIRTY-EIGHT

ELLERY

SATURDAY, OCTOBER 26

Malcolm's hand feels warm and solid in mine. Leaves swirl around us like oversized confetti, and the sky is a bright, brilliant blue. It's a beautiful day, the kind that makes you think maybe everything will be okay after all.

Despite all the trauma of the past two weeks, good things have happened, too. While Sadie was in town, she and Nana talked—*really* talked. They still don't understand one another much, but it finally felt like they both want to try. Since she's been back at Hamilton House, Sadie hasn't made a single random phone call.

It's only been eight days, but still. Baby steps.

Nana and Sadie agreed that Ezra and I should finish our senior year at Echo Ridge High, even if Sadie gets a clean bill of health in January. Which is all right by me. I'm making my bedroom a little homier; I bought some framed prints at an art fair last weekend, and put up pictures of Ezra and me with Mia and Malcolm. Plus I have the SATs to take, colleges to visit, half siblings to get to know, and, maybe, more dates with Malcolm.

I almost told him, just now. I wanted to.

But once I say it, I can't take it back. And even though I spent almost six weeks trying to unravel the lies in Echo Ridge, all I've been able to think about since that day in the Nilssons' basement is that some secrets shouldn't be told.

It nearly killed Sadie to believe she'd abandoned her twin on the night Sarah disappeared. There's no way she'd be able to handle this. It's hard enough for me, with no regrets or guilt weighing me down, to watch my brother smile and joke at a party and to know the truth.

We're not supposed to be here.

I grip Malcolm's hand tighter to ward off the chill that runs down my spine every time I remember Peter's voice hissing in my ear, so faint I almost missed it. I wish I had, because I'll spend the rest of my life hoping he never repeats the words he thought I'd take to my grave.

I thought she was your mother.

ACKNOWLEDGMENTS

If writing a first book is an act of faith—that someday, somebody other than your family and friends might want to read your words—writing a second book is an act of will. And boy, does it take a village. I won the literary lottery with the team I got to work with on my debut *One of Us Is Lying*, and their incredible talent and dedication are the reason that *Two Can Keep a Secret* exists.

I'll never be able to thank my agent, Rosemary Stimola, enough. Not only are you the reason I get to do what I love for a living, but you're a tireless champion, a wise counselor, and the calm in every storm. I'm deeply grateful to Allison Remcheck for your unflinching honesty, your faith in me, and the fact that you woke up in the middle of the night thinking about these characters almost as much as I did.

To my editor extraordinaire, Krista Marino: I'm in awe of your uncanny ability to see directly into the heart of a book and know exactly what it needs. You've made every step of this process a pleasure, and thanks to your insight this story is, finally, the one I wanted to tell all along.

To my publisher, Beverly Horowitz, and to Barbara Marcus and Judith Haut, thank you for welcoming me to Delacorte Press and for your guidance and support through both of my books. Thank you to Monica Jean for your endless patience and keen insight, to Alison Impey for the incredible cover design, to Heather Hughes and Colleen Fellingham for your eagle eyes, and to Aisha Cloud for the stellar promotion (and for answering my emails and texts at all hours). As a former marketer, I'm awed by the sales and marketing team that I'm fortunate enough to work with at Random House Children's Books, including Felicia Frazier, John Adamo, Jules Kelly, Kelly McGauley, Kate Keating, Elizabeth Ward, and Cayla Rasi.

Thank you to Penguin Random House UK, including managing director Francesca Dow, publishing director Amanda Punter, editorial director Holly Harris, and the marketing, publicity, and sales dream team of Gemma Rostill, Harriet Venn, and Kat Baker for taking such meticulous care of my books in the United Kingdom. Thank you also to Clementine Gaisman and Alice Natali of ILA for helping my characters travel the globe.

I couldn't have made it through my debut year or second book without my writing buddies Erin Hahn and Meredith Ireland. Thank you for your friendship, for celebrating all the ups and commiserating with all the downs, and for reading countless drafts of this book until I got it right. Thanks also to Kit Frick for your insight and thoughtful commentary at a critical juncture in the book's development.

I'm grateful to the Boston kidlit group for our community, and for all the contemporary and thriller writers I've gotten to know who inspire me, motivate me, and make this often solitary career more fun, including Kathleen Glasgow, Kristen Orlando, Tiffany D. Jackson, Caleb Roehrig, Sandhya Menon, Phil Stamper, and Kara Thomas.

A profound thank-you to my family (both Medailleu and McManus) for supporting this surprising turn my life took and telling everyone you've ever met to buy my books. A special debt of gratitude to Mom and Dad for helping out when travel calls, to Lynne for being my rock, and to Jack, who inspires me to keep dreaming big.

Finally, thanks always to my readers for caring about stories, and for choosing to spend your time with mine.

ABOUT THE AUTHOR

Karen M. McManus earned her BA in English from the College of the Holy Cross and her MA in journalism from Northeastern University. When she isn't working or writing in Cambridge, Massachusetts, McManus loves to travel with her son. She is the author of the *New York Times* bestseller *One of Us Is Lying* and *Two Can Keep a Secret*. To learn more about her, visit karenmcmanus.com or follow @writerkmc on Twitter or Instagram.